HEDGE

Praise for

HEDGE

"Reading *Hedge* is like spending time with your best friend: the daring, smart, compassionate one whose wisdom opens your eyes even as her secrets stun you. Part love story, part thriller, this novel kept me entranced until the very last page. A warm, glorious, and exciting read!"
—Jean Kwok, author of *Searching for Sylvie Lee*

"A beautiful exploration of the fragility of family life and the inherent tension between motherhood and desire. I simply could not put it down. Transfixing and utterly rewarding."
—Fiona Davis, author of *The Spectacular*

"The magnificent Delury explores the complexities of marriage, parenthood, and art in *Hedge*. Maud is an everywoman, relatable and strong, who . . . finds herself at a crossroads. . . . An unforgettable character in a story of arresting beauty and truth."
—Adriana Trigiani, author of *The Good Left Undone*

"Jane Delury has done the impossible: written a seemingly quiet novel about a woman trapped in a bad marriage that builds and builds and builds until suddenly you realize you're reading a page-turner. I could not stop turning the pages. *Hedge* is a wonderful book."
—Marcy Dermansky, author of *Hurricane Girl*

"It's impossible to turn away from Delury's newest novel, *Hedge*. I fell deeply and intensely into this story of love, loss, marriage, and parenthood. These are characters, this is a book, you will never forget."

—Jessica Anya Blau, author of *Mary Jane*

"*Hedge* begins as a contemporary love story, but grows into a complex and suspenseful narrative about family. All the big themes—love, life, loss—bind together in this page-turner, with writing that is clear and riveting throughout. A gem of a book from start to finish."

—Catie Marron, author of *Becoming a Gardener: What Reading and Digging Taught Me About Living*

"*Hedge* immediately pulls the reader in with its engaging storytelling and its exploration of themes like marital and maternal love and betrayal. I loved this novel and will recommend it widely."

—Liz Moore, author of *Long Bright River*

"Delury's immersive novel is about family and lovers, passion and responsibility, and it's filled with such gorgeous writing, compassion, and stunning surprises that I couldn't bear to tear myself from the page."

—Caroline Leavitt, author of *With or Without You*

"With language as lush as the setting, Delury pulls readers into a thicket of lust, responsibility, and betrayal that they won't want to escape."

—*Oprah Daily*

ALSO BY JANE DELURY

The Balcony

HEDGE

A NOVEL

JANE DELURY

ZIBBY BOOKS
NEW YORK

Juana Briones's petition for separation quoted from *The Archaeology of Ethnogenesis, Race and Sexuality in Colonial San Francisco* by Barbara L. Voss. Reprinted with Permission of University of Florida Press.

Library of Congress Control Number: 2022942945

ISBN: 978-1-958506-04-2
eBook ISBN: 979-8-9862418-7-6

Cover design by Emily Mahon
Book design by Neuwirth & Associates, Inc.
www.zibbybooks.com

Printed in the United States of America

10 9 8 7 6 5 4 3 2 1

For Margot and Rose

The flower bloomed and faded. The sun rose and sank.
The lover loved and went.

—Virginia Woolf, *Orlando: A Biography*

MONTGOMERY PLACE

2012

1

Maud had been at Montgomery Place for two weeks, and she still hadn't found half of the garden beds that once bloomed from the mansion to the conservatory. Sprawled on the steps of the empty glass building, Gabriel calculated measurements, a notepad balanced on his knee and a pencil clenched between his teeth. With his muddy boots, untucked shirt, and unruly hair, he resembled a boy in his mid-forties. At his feet, archaeological flags traced the rectangles and circles of the beds they'd discovered. He was thinking hard—Maud could tell by the way he tapped the fingers of his free hand against the air as if playing a piano. She continued to walk the lawn, trying to imagine flowers, statuary, and marble benches where there was now an enormous tombstone of green.

"We'll figure it out," Gabriel said. He dropped the chewed-up pencil back into his T-shirt pocket. They both liked to handwrite, thought better that way.

"We will?" Maud squinted in the May sunlight as he walked toward her, ripping the paper from the notepad.

"We have to." He folded the paper into her hand. "Actually, *you* have to. I'm officially stumped."

"Go to your dig," Maud said. "I'll sit in the archives for another hour, banging my head against the desk."

"Don't give yourself a concussion." Gabriel scooped up a bag of soil samples, the magnifying glass around his neck swinging on its leather cord. "See you at seven?" he said. "I'll bring the food and the new lab results."

"I'll bring the wine," Maud said.

As Gabriel walked away toward the woods, she headed to the mansion. Where the lawn ended in a horseshoe of gravel, the building rose three stories, painted the color of milky tea and frosted with cornices and floral festoons. A century ago, Montgomery Place had been one of the finest estates in New York's Hudson Valley, its grounds spreading for hundreds of acres through forest and field. This September, the gates would reopen with the mansion and grounds restored. Maud had been hired to turn back the clock to 1860 on the lawn she now crossed, once a labyrinthine formal garden. She planned to reseed the flowerbeds, remake the paths, and return the statues and urns to their positions. By mid-June, as the roots settled into the warming soil, she'd fill the conservatory with tropical plants.

That was the plan, but only if she could figure out the location of those missing beds. Maud mounted the steps of the mansion, feeling deflated. She wanted to resurrect the original garden, not some inauthentic, shrunken version. And she knew from her fifteen years of experience as a landscape historian in England that sometimes you failed. Sometimes you never found the documents listing the original plants. Sometimes the soil didn't turn up seeds or chemical traces and the stone wall you were sure had run through a sea of ivy turned out to be an errant mark on a faulty map. Garden archaeology was notoriously difficult. Despite Gabriel's encouragement, she knew that he was losing hope too.

At the side door to the house, she stopped under a portico to take in the view, a balm to her nerves. A skirt of lawn swept to a marble balustrade that crowned a slope of thistle and goldenrod. Fields rolled into grizzled oak forest, and then the land dove into the river. On the opposite shore, the Catskill Mountains cut smooth shadows out of the sky. Taking a long breath of the perfumed air, Maud squared her shoulders and went inside.

The archives were on the top floor and to reach them she needed to get by Harriet Tagley, the director of Montgomery Place, whom she'd seen at a window several times that morning, watching her and Gabriel. She could hear Harriet now in the library, listening to jazz as she sorted books. Quietly, Maud coaxed off her boots and put on the velvet slippers used to protect the fragile floors, then passed through the foyer under the spun-sugar chandelier. The restoration of the house's lower floor was already done. The dining room table was set for an eighteenth-century dinner: a plaster roast, ringed by plastic grapes, throned in a cornucopia of silver and crystal. Behind gilded mirrors, the wallpaper bloomed with poppies and dripped with ivy. Upstairs, however, the floors were still carpeted and the rooms furnished for the 1960s. At the end of an avocado-green hallway, a spool of plastic sheeting and a heap of power tools waited for the upcoming demolition. A sign on the door to the archives read, "No Food, Drink, Smoking, Chewing Gum. Wear gloves! Return all documents to their rightful place!!!"

From the metal shelves, Maud retrieved the box marked "MP Formal Garden" and sat at the Formica desk. Since she'd arrived at Montgomery Place from her home in California, this room with its smell of decaying cellulose, ink, and formaldehyde had become her lair. Hands in gloves, she extracted documents from their plastic sleeves: a map of the grounds drawn by a visitor in 1870; a jaundiced newspaper article from *The New York Times*; a watercolor of the formal garden by a forgotten Hudson School painter. She placed the paper with Gabriel's measurements at the center of the arrangement and waited for an epiphany.

Instead, the door swung open. Harriet had found her once again. "Any luck?" she said, then looked pityingly when Maud shook her head. In her early sixties, Harriet had hooded eyes behind rimless glasses, and a wide, sensuous mouth lacquered in magenta lipstick. Her spindly body was clad in a zigzag-patterned dress that stopped above her wrinkled knees. She tapped the back of her wrist as if she were wearing a watch instead of a fitness tracker. "Down to the wire."

"I could probably buy myself a couple more days if I work late when I start planting," Maud said.

She needed to get the plants into the ground before the blithe spring sun turned summer-hostile. And her contract at Montgomery Place was for one summer: this summer. Harriet had already let her know that it would be difficult for Maud to return next summer if she wanted to bring her children again, since the arrangement was already "experimental and potentially problematic." Maud's daughters, Ella and Louise, were back home in Marin with their father, Peter, finishing school. They'd arrive next Monday and stay with

Maud on the grounds for two months until August, attending a day camp down the road.

"I'll tell you what," Harriet said, her smile both generous
and victorious. "If you find all the beds, I'll lend you Chris
to help cut them. Gabriel has so much to do down at his
site. And he's too qualified for manual labor." Chris was the
groundskeeper's son, with whom Maud hadn't spoken since
their awkward introduction the day she arrived. "I'm bringing our charming archaeologist a lemonade once I'm done
sorting books," Harriet said with a flight of her hand. "He
forgets to hydrate. Would you like one? I can leave it for you
in the butler's pantry."

Maud politely declined, and Harriet clicked the door
shut. The last time she had offered Maud a lemonade, she
seemed to have omitted the sugar. Maud wasn't sure why
Harriet disliked her, exactly, but she supposed it had to do
with her friendship with Gabriel. He was indeed charming,
the kind of man who warmed the air when he spoke to you,
and until Maud arrived, that warmth had been all for Harriet.
Gabriel had been at Montgomery Place for a month, opening his own dig—an ancient campsite—in the forest. Once
Maud got there, he volunteered to help her locate that first
swath of beds, which had been easy to identify from the
indentations of their terra-cotta edging tiles. Then they'd
followed the trail of gravel that had once lined the paths
and dug test pits all the way to the mansion, looking for soil
rich with the nitrates of decay that proved a concentration
of former life.

After another ten minutes, measured by the *tsk-tsk* of a
grandfather clock wedged between the bookcases, Maud
abandoned the desk for the window. She gazed out at the

front lawn. In their most contentious days, Peter used to say that she was too optimistic—that was why she was bad at being married, her optimism a negative trait, like her chaoticness and distractedness and inability to correctly load the dishwasher. She could feel that stubborn optimism now. Gabriel saw it in her too, but for him it was a strength, not a flaw. These past two weeks, it had been such a relief to spend time with someone who leaned forward, elbows on knees, and listened as she described her work. Someone who understood what it meant that she was a garden historian, with her odd mix of botany, archaeology, history, and practical gardening skills. Someone who found it as interesting as she did that pea gravel had been used in nineteenth-century gardens instead of brick because it forced visitors to slow their pace and contemplate, a trick that she and Gabriel had discussed over dinner the previous night.

She leaned her forehead against the windowpane, scrutinizing the view. Honey-colored light filled the conservatory and bounced off the grass. The beds were right there; they had to be. She could see them, swimming their way past the black locust trees that sentried the lawn, blooming and tufting, whooping with color. Women in silk dresses shaped like calla lilies and mustached men in top hats strolling the paths, sipping sherry from crystal glasses. In the conservatory, a harpist playing under the dripping eaves of banana fronds. And once the guests had gone, the garden still, the chirping of robins replaced by the hooting of owls, Alexander Gilson, the estate's head gardener, would sit alone on the steps to watch night fall. He was the person Maud most wished she could talk to. He would know everything she needed to know. He could point out each bed and tell her its secrets.

As the sun dissolved and the moon appeared, she'd walk behind him in the gloaming, taking notes, asking questions, and writing down plant names.

And with that thought, an idea flashed. A trick used somewhere—where had that been? The Lost Gardens of Heligan, where she'd worked one summer during graduate school in England: a two-hundred-acre estate much like this one, left to bramble and ivy when the laborers sailed for the French front in 1914 and didn't return. The depressions of garden beds, invisible in daylight, could be seen in shadow at night. The archaeology team used spotlights at Heligan, but here she could try the headlight beams of her rental car. It might not work. But it might. To know, she'd need the grass cut shorter so she could make out the topography of the ground.

She rushed down the stairs, past Harriet, who was in the kitchen squeezing lemons into a plastic pitcher on a table covered with cheese knives, grape scissors, treacle spoons, and porcelain pie birds. Hurrying out the back doors of the mansion, she whipped off a text to Gabriel (*Idea! Will tell you at dinner*), then followed the high-pitched whine of a weedwacker that would lead her to the groundskeeper. She rounded a pond fringed by pussy willows and passed through a gateway of rhododendrons that opened into a cave of ferny shade. She only realized as the brick under her feet became gravel that she was still wearing the velvet slippers.

Frazer was exactly where she thought he'd be, trimming an enormous boxwood hedge—a scraggly anachronism, added in the twentieth century, which separated the estate's formal grounds from the forest. An atoll of gray hair ringed his otherwise bald head and his unruly eyebrows peaked like meringues. His son, Chris, a squat, thirtyish man with a baseball cap pulled low on his forehead, was plowing the ivy that throttled a hydrangea.

"I have an idea about how to find the missing beds," Maud said breathlessly. "Could the two of you mow the grass from the conservatory to the mansion as low as possible?"

"Sure thing. We'll do it now." Frazer laid down the hedge trimmer with a wheezy grunt. "What do you think, Chris? Set the blade to a quarter-inch, maybe?"

"Half an inch," Chris said between swipes of the weed-wacker. When Maud had first met him and held out her hand, he didn't take it. He looked back at her with a gaze that was more of a stare, focused too low, perhaps on her mouth. She'd assumed he was introverted, but Gabriel thought that he might be on the spectrum. That conversation—while they were having a drink on her first night—relaxed Maud with Gabriel, despite his intimidating archaeological background. He was kind about Chris and also kind to Harriet when she stopped by with a box of lightbulbs for his cottage and lingered for fifteen minutes to talk to him about their mutual love of John Coltrane. Since then, Maud and Gabriel had eaten dinner together every evening, taking turns fetching take-out food in the nearby town of Red Hook.

She thanked Frazer and Chris and walked back to the mansion as the two men headed to the coach house, which stored the mower and gardening tools, along with the original statues and urns from the formal garden. Maud smiled as she passed the pond again. Neither Frazer nor Chris had said anything about the slippers. She was back with her people. You didn't have to be sociable in gardening. You didn't have to think about how you dressed or whether you were being clever. You didn't have to do what she had been doing for the past two years in Marin, chatting with the wives of Peter's partners at cocktail parties as she tried to balance in heels. Even grouchy Harriet, who now stood on the porch with the pitcher of lemonade and an aggrieved look on her face—she must have seen how Maud left the archives—was a relief.

The farmhouse where Maud was staying perched on a hill near the front gates, close to a complex of warehouses and barns that had been repurposed for storage and as administrative offices. Across the drive, an abandoned cherry and plum orchard stretched its leafy branches from a ragweed bed. Down the hill, Saw Kill Creek raged in a foamy streak into the woods, where it filled a swimming lake before succumbing to the Hudson. Gabriel lived in a cottage on the bank, a jumble of stones under a patchy roof that had once housed workers for a woolen mill.

Inside the farmhouse a couch bulged with sateen throw pillows, and the curtains frothed with lace. Stink bugs littered the windowsills, adding their burnt-rubber smell to the odor of gas from an antiquarian stove. Dust furred the wainscoting in the dining room, and the bathroom faucets plinked. When Harriet had first opened the door for Maud ("We gave you the larger accommodation because of your children," she'd said, saying the word as if it were "lepers"), Maud had fallen in love with the moldering rooms. She was reminded of Monk's House, Virginia and Leonard Woolf's home in Sussex, England, where she'd kept the gardens during the three happiest years of her life.

Back then, Peter stayed in London during the week for his job as an investment banker, joining the family on weekends. As Maud used to joke to her friends, their marriage worked beautifully when they lived apart. But two years ago, Peter—who was British—abruptly took a job in San Francisco and the family relocated to Marin. Maud had gone from days brimming with research and gardening and freedom to no work and the relentless disappointment of her marriage. Despite having grown up in California, she was a specialist in the history of the British garden. She knew little about the state's native plants, and there was a dearth of major restorations in the listings she prowled. She had sent out her résumé, then sent it out again, her frustration climbing in tandem with her resentment of Peter. But that was all behind her now, she thought, as she stripped off her sweaty clothes and added them to a pile growing by the washing machine. She was here. She had made it. She had a garden to restore, even if it ended up being smaller than the original. And this house belonged to her for the summer— to her and the girls.

After a long shower with water as hot as the water heater could manage, she flopped on the couch in her bra and underwear and called her daughters, who would have arrived home by now, having walked up the hill from the bus stop. Ella answered her phone on the fifth ring.

"All okay?" Maud said.

"We survived again," Ella said. "Here's Louise."

"Did you guys stay on the sidewalk?" Maud asked.

"Mom," Louise said, "if we're gonna get hit by a car, it won't make a difference if you're watching us from the deck when it happens."

"I know, I know. Sorry."

Maud heard the familiar sounds of backpacks thudding to the floor and chairs scraping tile, which made her miss the girls more. She wasn't particularly concerned about the journey from the bus stop, although Louise did tend to swerve off course in pursuit of butterflies. The growing tension in her stomach came from the elephant in the room, visible only to Peter and her, but which trumpeted and stomped when she spoke to her daughters. She and Peter had separated for the summer, both geographically and maritally, and Ella and Louise didn't know. Now, listening to Louise tell her about her day in a barrage of second-grade enthusiasm, Maud reassured herself that her girls were fine. They were used to being with only one parent. Usually, though, she was that parent.

"What's your homework?" she asked Louise.

"Something," Louise said, as foil ripped from a package. Milk glugged into a glass. Before leaving for the Hudson Valley, Maud had stocked the kitchen cupboards with familiar English treats, jamming the shelves with Bakewell tarts, Nik Naks, and Jaffa Cakes. She'd left Peter a calendar of activities with notes about who would take the girls where and when during the afternoons. She'd hired a woman to come over at five and make dinner on weekdays.

"More specifically?" she said.

"Something about math. Guess who's getting a puppy?"

"Not us?"

Louise giggled. And then, through bites of cookie, she launched into a story about her friend who had a puppy, and her mother had brought it to school pickup and it was the most adorable thing in the world, and why couldn't they, anyway?

Eventually Maud asked if she could put Ella back on the line.

"She left for her room. With all the Nik Naks. She said to tell you she doesn't feel like talking."

"Is something going on at school? She didn't want to talk last night either."

"I dunna. Dad said she was acting like a statue at breakfast."

Peter had texted Maud that morning that Ella was being impossible. Maud knew how those mornings went: small, freckled Louise spouted about her plans for the day, as her tall, stoic sister stared into her plate with her long hair draped like blinders. For the past six months, Maud had found herself poised ridiculously in front of Ella's bedroom door, deciding whether or not to knock. There was no magic to the age of thirteen, any more than there was magic to the age of forty, but those numbers had changed them both. Maud's arms, no longer busy with gardening, softened, as Ella's shoulders broadened. Maud's period staggered, grew heavy, then light, as Ella's period began. And just as Maud yearned to break back into the world by working again, Ella retreated, doubled up on herself, locked herself away in her room, ready to snap at the sound of a knock.

"Take the phone to her room, please," Maud told Louise.

"She won't let me in."

"Knock on the door and tell her I said you had to. Put me on speaker and leave the phone on the bed."

After asking Louise to get out, Ella responded curtly to Maud's "How are you?" with a beleaguered "Fine."

"What's wrong, sweetheart?" Maud said.

"Nothing."

"I know there's something."

Usually, if she waited long enough, Ella would buckle, and soon enough, she did. Her friends had a sleepover the previous weekend and didn't invite her. "And they all lied about it to my face when I asked," Ella said, her voice trembling. One of the girls had posted a photo in her feed, then had taken it down, but not before Ella had seen a group of them on a couch in pajamas. "Why does everyone hate me?"

"Everyone doesn't hate you," Maud said. "But maybe it's time to find nicer friends."

Since starting middle school, Ella had yearned to be popular—American popular—with the right clothes and brand of backpack and without her British accent, which she worked to lose. The desire had landed her in a group of smooth-haired girls with straight teeth and expensive boots who cloaked their pimples under concealer and cultivated an aura of clannish aloofness.

"You don't just find friends, Mom," she said. "It's not like back home. They've known each other since kindergarten."

The word "home" snagged. Of the four of them, Maud and Ella most missed their former life in England.

"I'm sorry I'm not there to give you a hug," Maud said.

"It wouldn't change anything."

After hanging up, Maud called Peter at his office. "I got it out of her. It's those girls again. Maybe we should think about her switching schools if this keeps up."

"To private? Do you know how much that costs?"

"I mean to a different public school."

She had been thinking that, after they made their separation official in the fall, she could rent an apartment in another school district, maybe in San Francisco, somewhere close enough for Peter to see the girls when he wanted to, which she supposed would be every other weekend and a night or two for dinner.

"I don't know why she wastes her time with them," Peter said, ignoring Maud's innuendo.

He'd been bullied in boarding school in Oxford, a misfit from the Yorkshire countryside with a mended, hand-me-down uniform and an absent father. Boys used to toss his underwear and socks out the window of the dormitory and put slugs in his bed. On the other side of the world in Burlingame, a suburb of San Francisco, Maud too had been a loner. She'd wanted to be different from her parents, who read only the weekly church bulletin, different from the girls at her parochial school who watched *Guiding Light* and plotted to find boyfriends from the boys' school down the street. She'd sought out friends who also wanted to be different. But Ella was like a moth bumping against the outside of a window, trying to reach the light.

"It would be easier if she weren't so pretty," she said.

"I could get her a bad haircut," Peter said. "Buy her some ugly clothes."

Maud laughed, but Peter hadn't once taken Ella clothes shopping. He rarely went to the grocery store, and if he did, he used a basket, not a cart.

"Louise needs a field-trip slip signed," she said. "You'd better get it out of her backpack tonight or she'll forget."

"I'm doing amazingly well, wouldn't you say?"

Although he said it lightly, Maud heard the supplication in his voice. He'd understood what she meant about changing schools.

"You're doing great," she said.

He still thinks there's hope, she thought, after they'd hung up. She had told Peter clearly that she didn't see this summer as a trial or a test—she saw it as a transition. But Peter had his own stubborn optimism. He believed that he was proving to her that he could change, that he would pitch in more around the house and be more present with the girls when she returned. And yet, he was also proving that he could take care of Ella and Louise on his own.

At seven, having read an article about the origins of the gravel she and Gabriel had found in the garden, she dropped a sundress over her head and brushed out her hair, letting it fall on her shoulders instead of its usual loose ponytail.

Chopsticks or fork? Gabriel texted.

Chopsticks! she texted back.

I'm dying to know your idea for the beds.

I'll give you a clue: Light.

That doesn't help. Pls run.

Coming!

She fetched a bottle of wine from the refrigerator and the chipped coffee mugs they used as glasses. Outside, Gabriel was already at their meeting place—a wrought-iron table near the orchard—with a manila folder, two plates, and a bag of Chinese food.

"Finally," he said when she sat down across from him in one of the four rusty chairs flanking the table.

"That was two minutes. Patience is not your virtue."

He held up the folder. "I won't show you these lab results until you tell me."

"Fine," she said. As she uncorked the bottle of wine, she explained her idea about the headlights.

"That works?" Gabriel said.

"I saw it work once. Could you help with your truck?"

"Are you kidding? You think I'd miss that?"

She filled their mugs with wine. Over Gabriel's shoulder, swifts swam through the orchard, rustling glossy plum leaves. Plum blossoms in Chinese poetry. The nineteenth-century crossbreeding experimentations that resulted in the plum-cot. The cyanide in the stone. Maud's mind had awakened, new facts and anecdotes always cropping up. And so had her body, she thought, as she and Gabriel clinked mugs. In his presence, each gesture—as small as taking the manila folder he pushed across the table—felt heightened, unconsciously orchestrated. And she gathered his gestures too, like clues: the way he threw back his head as he laughed at her description of forgetting her shoes earlier, the way he caught his lower lip in his teeth as the two of them looked over the laboratory results.

"High carbon," she said.

"The conservatory fire?"

"Probably."

They were talking about work, but another conversation ran under the surface. She'd had workplace crushes before, most recently on a literary historian in Sussex whom she'd met at a pub for passionate discussions about the flowers in William Wordsworth's poems until he put his hand on her knee under the table and she realized that she'd gone too far. It was a delicate game, she thought, as she and Gabriel ate, feeding your sensuality, remembering that you had a sense of humor and a clitoris while continuing to follow the rules of marriage. Those rules were out the window now that she and Peter had separated. But she felt more at ease with Gabriel pretending they were still there, so she'd given him no indication that her marriage was in trouble.

"Twenty more minutes and we go," she said, as the moon appeared like an open parenthesis. "If I still prayed, I'd be praying right now."

"When did you stop?" Gabriel was eating chow mein out of a carton. They'd decided to skip the plates and were handing the cartons back and forth.

"April 1986."

"You seriously remember? That was a rhetorical question."

"Yes, because I had a bike accident later that month and I thought God was punishing me."

She'd been fourteen, and her liturgy class was reading Thomas Aquinas. Her doubts about the contradictions of Catholicism had been multiplying for some time, but when she realized Aquinas condoned early abortion, her faith crumbled. Now she turned in her shoulder to show Gabriel the fish-shaped scar. "I literally slammed into a brick wall."

"Did you go back to praying after your punishment?" Gabriel said.

"No. I figured it was too late. I just moved my lips during Mass. But I have arthritis now in that shoulder, so I'm still being punished."

Once stars had joined the moon in a cobalt sky, they left for the mansion. Gabriel drove behind Maud along the grand drive that led from the farmhouse into a swamp of obscurity, the lines between trunk, branch, sky, and roof indistinct. They parked parallel on the lawn by the conservatory and turned on the high beams. Gabriel stood off to the side while Maud walked past the flagged beds, crouched down, stood up, squinted in the dark. And there, faint as an Etch A Sketch drawing, she made out a vague circle. A figure eight. The suggestion of a square.

"I see them," she called to Gabriel.

"No way," he said, coming closer to look. "You were right."

"It was even bigger than I thought," Maud said. She almost dropped into one of Louise's lopsided cartwheels.

"There are plenty of flags in the back of my truck," Gabriel said. "I can help, but I'm assuming you'd like to do this alone."

"Is that okay?" Maud said. She both wanted him to stay and wanted this moment for herself.

"I know how it is," he said with a smile. "Your find. You flag. Just turn off the truck and leave the keys in the flower-pot by my door. I'll move it early in the morning so Harriet doesn't ticket me."

An hour later, having marked all the beds, Maud sat on the steps of the conservatory, filled with joyful relief. Tomorrow she and Gabriel would take soil samples from those phantom shapes to mail to the lab for analysis. Then, with Chris's help, she'd start to cut the beds, peeling away the lawn to discover the soil, which was most likely made of rich and feathery loam. She'd keep digging in the archives to find as many of the original plants plus some well-calculated guesses and get every last root into the ground by early June. Then she'd move to the conservatory with its potted lemon and acacia trees, its hibiscus and palms. The garden would start to look like itself again: luscious beds flowing in circles and squares, cast-iron urns cascading with vines, the diamond of the conservatory transformed into an emerald. Already she wanted to come back to see it with the girls next spring as a single mother. A divorcée. Finally released.

2

Three days later, Maud was back at the desk in the archives as workmen pulled up the carpeting in the hall. She'd started to design the garden in earnest, reading through documents and scribbling plant names on a notepad. She tried to keep her hands calm as she peeled open the manila folders lined up in the archival boxes and teased out papers, dyed by time to the same mushroom-brown. Streaked with sealing wax, most of the documents were letters and invoices from Andrew Jackson Downing, the American landscape designer and nursery owner who'd helped to redesign the Montgomery Place estate. His barbed, flowery handwriting was hard to read, even with a magnifying glass. Maud squinted at three words on an invoice. *Large scotch roses.* She'd use them as a nucleus for one of the round beds. Honeysuckle, clematis, lilac, silver bell—she added the names to her list.

Unlike the ancient history that Gabriel was exploring, the history of Montgomery Place was compact and well recorded. In 1802, Janet Montgomery, the blunt-faced Revolutionary War widow who watched over the library from a rococo frame, had commissioned a Federal-style mansion and opened a farm and plant nursery. She left the estate to her brother. After his death, his wife and daughter—with Andrew Jackson Downing's help—spent thirty-five years transforming the property into a "pleasure ground" in the spirit of the great European estates. Nature was subdued into prettiness here, and left to rage into dramatic wildness there. Winding paths led to transcendent vistas; pagodas and benches appeared around each bend.

In front of the mansion, now embellished with porches and arches, a rambling lawn where cows once grazed became a formal garden with a Gothic conservatory of tropical plants. Alexander Gilson, who worked at Montgomery Place for fifty years, many of them as head gardener, had probably lived in a room attached to the building. No record existed of his birth, but he had almost certainly spent the first years of his life in slavery, which New York State abolished in 1827. A photograph from 1861 showed a figure who might be him: a middle-aged man with thin shoulders sitting on the conservatory steps. Self-educated in the science of plants, he created two species of begonia: *Begonia* Gilsonii and *Iresine herbstii* Gilsoni. In the letter Maud was reading now, his talents were lauded by Downing as they were by other contemporary horticulturists. And yet, Maud thought, what racism he must have endured.

She slid the letter back into its sleeve. In England, she had butted against ugly reminders of racism, classism, and sexism, but at Montgomery Place she felt her own implication more acutely, because this was her country and, thus, her history. The garden she was restoring might not have relied on enslaved workers, but Janet Montgomery had listed twelve human beings as property of the estate in the 1820 census.

Maud described her unease to Gabriel later as they ate the burritos she'd fetched in town. "I didn't think much about the ethics of garden restoration in England," she said. "Someone has to do the labor in a garden, and historically, most of those people were disenfranchised. I guess I let myself off the hook. That's harder to do here."

"I know the feeling," Gabriel said. "On most of my digs, I'm the white guy who can't speak the language. I'm helping, yes, but I know I don't belong there. It's easy to forget all that when you get carried away by the work." He pointed at four quartz crystals lined up on the table. "You should have seen me at the site earlier when I found those. You'd have thought I was high."

He'd discovered the crystals in a firepit and thought they might have been ceremonial pieces. Maud looked at the luminous, rugged surfaces, last touched by a human being thousands of years ago. She knew what Gabriel meant about getting carried away. Montgomery Place was gorgeous beauty and also gross excess. Alexander Gilson had been admired and also oppressed. The simpler stories were appealing, but they were incomplete and often wrong.

Once again, as they ate, their conversation drifted from work to their personal lives. Gabriel had spent his childhood moving between cities in Asia, Africa, and Europe—his father had been a diplomat. Although he was based at Ithaca College now, he was rarely in the States. At the end of the summer, he'd return to a dig in Hasankeyf, Turkey, for the academic year.

"Days with a pickaxe, nights in a tent," he said, as he doused his burrito with hot sauce.

"A nomad who studies settlements."

"Yes, yes," Gabriel said. "That's been pointed out before."

His longest romantic relationship had lasted a year. The night before, when Maud asked, he'd run through one girl-friend after another: a photojournalist in Cairo, a fellow archaeologist in Peru, a college girlfriend who reemerged at the end of his thirties for a passionate fling in Paris before she went back to her wife.

"Why didn't you end up with any of them?" Maud asked.

Gabriel laughed. "No one's ever asked me that so directly."

"Sorry," Maud said. "It seems like an obvious question."

"Intimacy issues, according to a therapist I saw in Ithaca after my last breakup. We never quite got to the bottom of it before I had to leave again for Jordan."

"Well, if you bothered to go to therapy, there's hope," Maud said.

She had seen a psychologist herself in London for a few years after Ella was born, but Peter had never been to a ther-apist. He didn't believe in therapy or in marriage counseling. Maud was starting to think that she might have to convince him that Ella could use a session with someone. Earlier, on the phone, she'd been upset about her friends again.

"Being single didn't seem like a problem in my thirties," Gabriel said. "But now I can see fifty around the corner. And having my parents die in the same year . . . We weren't close, but, you know." He balled up his burrito wrapper and tossed it into the take-out bag. "The way I'm going, I'll end up get-ting old in a tent with only my artifacts to keep me warm at night."

"You have plenty of time," Maud said. "You could have a kid at seventy if you wanted to. Although it might kill you."

"First I have to stop falling for women like me. When both people in a relationship won't jump, you end up standing on the edge of a building for a long time."

"Whereas I dove right off the building at twenty-four," Maud said.

During graduate school at the University of London, she used to watch out the window as her neighbor, a tall man with slightly hunched shoulders, folded the right leg of his pants and rode off with a satchel slung over his shoulder. One morning, purposefully, she came down the stairs with a bag of garbage as he was getting on his bike and asked him if the building recycled. "You must be the American," he said. He invited her to dinner a few days later, and a year after that, they were engaged. In Maud's Irish-American family— four grandparents who had fled poverty and persecution in Ireland; great-uncles who were soldiers of the Irish Republican Brotherhood; the 1916 Easter Proclamation hanging in the bathroom—moving to England had been bad enough. Marrying an Englishman had been an official declaration of rebellion.

"It must be nice, though," Gabriel said now, "only knowing the one relationship. Nothing to compare it to. You date a lot, you get confused."

"Confusion's always possible if you think too much," Maud said.

Gabriel was studying her, doing that tapping thing with his fingers. "Fifteen years married and still happy," he said, the intonation somewhere between a statement and a question. "That's a good score."

"I got lucky with Peter," Maud said distantly.

Her nerves buzzed as Gabriel looked at her, his eyes still

blue in the dusk. He must be aware of his effect on people, especially women. He wasn't arrogant, but he had the confidence of someone unused to rejection. Maud assumed he'd been the one to end most of those relationships he'd listed. She felt protective of herself.

"I'm glad you got lucky," Gabriel said.

"Are you?" she said and toasted herself with her beer bottle.

Back in the farmhouse, as she brushed her teeth, she examined her face in the bathroom mirror and saw a residual flush in her cheeks and a playful lift to her eyes. When she'd first met Peter, her face had also bloomed, but in the heat of difference rather than of connection. Their contradictions had been exciting: his interest in numbers, her interest in words; her small, pale body, his large, hairy one. Peter's acidic sense of humor seemed like a sign of intelligence and a distance from the world that she'd never been able to find. As they curled naked in bed, whispering their pasts to each other, his every admission of vulnerability and hurt— the bullying at school, his parents' fighting, his father's philandering—felt like a gift. She'd married him thinking that he operated with a secret code that she'd eventually crack. But she could never decipher the symbols, and once Ella arrived, she stopped trying. Now she turned off the faucet and went down the hall to the sound of its dripping, which continued as she lay awake in bed. Her marriage, she thought, trying to sleep, had died of chronic illness, although the simple story was that Peter had killed it.

The evidence had been easy to find. Maud was a researcher, trained to look for clues. She'd suspected Peter of cheating when they lived apart in England, but she'd let the question drift away. It seemed impossible to leave the marriage until the girls were grown, so what good was it to know? With Peter in London and her in Sussex at Monk's House, willful blindness was surprisingly easy. Once they moved to California, though—Peter home every night, Maud without work—she had more time to reflect on the mess of her marriage. What she noticed before bothered her more: Peter's late nights at the office; the password on his phone that he seemed to change every few weeks; his acceptance of their almost nonexistent sex life. As the months passed, she stewed. The family had moved to the Bay Area for Peter's career, after he'd lost a promotion at his investment bank in London and went on the job market. In moving, Maud had upended her own career, given up Monk's House, and given up England. Now she was back in the USA, where she didn't want to be, and back living close to her parents, which she didn't want either. She was completely dependent on Peter financially. And he was still fooling around.

One night as he slept, she groped through the drawers in his unlit study until she found the notebook where he jotted down passwords. She plugged the latest one into his computer, then skimmed his emails until she came upon messages to a woman who worked in the London office and who had recently been in San Francisco. The content was banal: *Want to meet for a drink? What time will you finish?* She correlated the email timestamp with Peter's credit card bill and found a charge for a hotel bar in the city. He must have met this woman for an afternoon of sex before coming home to Marin. The next evening, she asked her sister, Annette, to take the girls out to pizza and waited alone for Peter to return from the office. Without a word, she handed him the printed-out email and credit card bill. He blustered, denied, then confessed. Yes, just that one time. Twice. Two afternoons. Never before and never again. The affair hadn't started until after he left London—Maud didn't believe this, but she didn't press.

"My ego was still crushed from losing that promotion when we moved here," Peter said. "And you've been so distant. We barely have sex anymore."

"So it's my fault that you slept with someone else?"

"That's not what I'm saying." Suddenly Peter looked panicked. Usually, in their arguments, the two of them circled until Maud became dizzy and confused by his logic. But he knew not to get on that merry-go-round now.

"I'm sorry," he said. "I am. What can I do?"

Maud already knew what she wanted. She'd known when she went to his study the previous night. She said that she wanted to separate for the summer, to be away from him and out of their marriage. "We'll parent the girls together, but that's it. If you want to sleep around, feel free."

"I'm not going to do that."

"Well, I'm not going to stop you. No obligations. That's what being separated means."

A month later, when she saw the listing for a position at Montgomery Place, she applied.

———

Having run string around the circumference of the circular beds, she and Chris carved them out of the lawn that week, cracking their shovels through the net of roots and ripping out the plugs of grass. Maud had grown to like the calm of working with him. When she made a joke about the ground being stubborn, he looked at her blankly. He spoke in short, concrete sentences, and his gaze still landed below her eyes. But this was no longer unnerving, because she knew what to expect. On previous projects, she'd had to prove herself to the men on her team, show them that she could do the physical work as well as they could, that she could both flip the pages of a book and grind a tree stump. Chris didn't seem to care that she was a woman or that she was an uncommon hybrid of gardener and academic. He did care, though, about doing everything right.

"It's not straight enough," he said, when Maud laid down the hoe.

"We're not done with it yet," Maud replied. "We'll line the beds with the edging tiles."

Earlier, they had visited the dusty crypt of the coach house and found the terra-cotta tiles, which were shaped like scrolls and remained in surprisingly good shape.

"Grass climbs over everything," Chris said.

Maud showed him her garden design and explained that once they'd made the beds, they'd mark off the paths and all the lawn would be gone.

As they finished a bed, Ella's math teacher called. Ella had failed her final exam. She'd left for the bathroom in the middle of the test and was gone a long time. The teacher said that he was going to let Ella retake the test since she'd been sick but wanted her parents to know. Maud had no idea about any of this, and she assumed Peter didn't either. On the phone after school, having treated Maud to a dose of speaker silence, Ella erupted.

"Why did my stupid teacher call you? I already talked to him about the test. He's letting me take it again. Why do you have to get in the middle of everything?"

"He said you went to the bathroom and missed most of the class."

"I was freaking out. I got confused on one of the questions and thought I was going to bomb the whole thing. My stomach was upset."

"Is that why you told him you were sick? Did you throw up?"

"I had to take a shit, okay, Mom? I don't want to talk about this. Do you have to tell Dad?"

"He'll be fine about it."

"No, he won't. He's being a jerk."

"Ella, don't say that."

"He is. He got pissed at Louise this morning because she forgot her lunch in the house."

"He's a little stressed about work right now."

Maud knew Peter had an important presentation to give at the end of the week. He kept saying on the phone that everything was going well at home, but last night he'd texted that if Louise brought up getting a puppy one more time, he was giving her away to an animal shelter.

"He's always stressed about work," Ella said. "Work's all he cares about."

"That's not true. You and Louise are the number-one priority for both of us."

"Then why is Dad staying here this summer?"

Maud's throat closed. "Because his work is there. He'll visit us."

"For one weekend in August," Ella said.

Peter had said he'd miss the girls too much to be away from them so long and had insisted on coming to Montgomery Place at least once.

"A long weekend," Maud told Ella. She'd walked away from Chris and was standing under a black locust tree, bees storming the creamy flowers. The sweetness turned her stomach. She was being deceptive and manipulative. She knew where this summer was headed, and when she and Peter eventually told the girls, Ella would know too. She would remember her mother's reassurances and know that they'd been lies.

"What if you tell your dad about the test yourself tonight?" she said, to change the subject. "Would that be better?"

"I guess so. But not if he's being a jerk."

Maud's discomfort lasted all morning. Even if she and Peter thought they hid their problems, even if the girls were used to their parents being apart, this summer was the start of an end. As she returned the tools to the coach house, Peter's arguments drummed in her head. Divorce screwed up children. "Look at me," he'd said. "It's a miracle I got married after what I lived through." Maud would be miserable not having the girls all the time. Money would be impossibly tight. And what about health insurance? Where would Peter live if he moved out of their rental in Marin— the Bay Area housing market was a nightmare. "Take the summer," he had said. "I made a dreadful mistake, and I'm sorry. When you come back, things will be better."

But they wouldn't be, Maud thought, as she hung a shovel on its hook and walked through the warren of rooms, past the decorations from the formal garden: cast-iron urns, a prostrate Diana still powdered with lichen. She didn't love Peter and hadn't loved him for years. More important, she couldn't pretend anymore. She couldn't be that woman with her eyes closed and her mouth shut, playing the contented wife. Nor could she be that woman in her husband's study, looking for evidence of infidelity to justify her escape.

Gabriel had asked her if she wanted to visit his site, so after lunch she walked through the woods toward the river. In the canopy above her head, invisible birds competed for the loudest song. On the forest floor, golden mushrooms popped from a musty clutter of leaves, needles, and twigs.

"You came," Gabriel called. He got up from the test pit where he'd been kneeling. He's so glad to see me, Maud thought. That full smile held nothing back. When had Peter last looked at her that way? Had he ever?

The site had spread since she'd last been here, with test pits flagged and tarped and buckets filled with the dirt that Gabriel screened for artifacts. She walked with him around the chessboard of shallow squares as he pointed out where he'd found the charred acorns and fragments of lustrous green flint that he'd brought to the table the previous night. After, they went down the path to the Hudson.

"I want to take the girls canoeing," Maud said, as she gazed out at the water. She knew that she'd be a better mother here, out of Peter's shadow. She'd focus on Ella and Louise, serve them pancakes in bed, take them on excursions, fill the farmhouse with laughter.

"I bet they'll love that," Gabriel said.

The Hudson flowed by, sullen and murky and throttled with algae, poisoned by PCBs and heavy metals, abused, dammed, disdained. But Maud could see the other river that had once cut through mountains to find the ocean, tiled by oyster beds, running with sturgeon, herons plucking along its shores. And as she stood next to Gabriel, she felt less lonely to know that he could see that other river too.

3

The evening before the girls arrived, Frazer invited Gabriel and Maud to a barbecue at his farm across the road. The property was a mess of corroded equipment and overgrown fields with a house that looked as if it had been kicked in the stomach, the roof sagging and porch buckling. In a wire enclosure, chickens stalked grubs in the grass, and a comatose pig nursed ravenous piglets. A lone cow, haloed by flies, stared at them over a crooked fence. Maud wished she and Gabriel hadn't accepted the invitation. The farm's decline made her sad, and these were her last hours alone with Gabriel. As much as she couldn't wait to pick up the girls tomorrow, she'd miss their nightly dinners.

"Let's slip out early," he said, as if reading her thoughts.

"Deal. What's our signal?"

"Spill your drink."

She laughed, stepping over a clump of manure. "I usually end up doing that anyway."

"I know. That's why I'm making it the signal. We'll be gone in twenty minutes."

"I'll make sure we're out by dessert," Maud said.

Frazer's wife, Lydia, a thin woman in a denim muumuu with accordion wrinkles on her forehead, came out of the house and threw her arms around Maud.

"Finally," she said. "I've heard so much about you." She kissed Gabriel on the cheek and pointed at the backyard. "You go say hi to Harriet. She's been waiting for you."

The inside of the house was as chaotic as the outside. Columns of newspapers and magazines teetered in corners. A bicycle, turned upside down in the living room, waited for its flat tire to be fixed. One of the kitchen walls was covered in crusty ribbons, freckled by grease. *Best Sheep, 1975*, one of them read. *First Premium Holstein, 1950*, read another.

"My parents bought this place after the war," Lydia said when she saw Maud looking at the wall. She took the casserole that Maud had made, her mother's recipe of canned mushroom soup, green beans, and egg noodles, and set it on the counter. "We milked cows, then Frazer and I raised them for meat, and now our doctors only want us eating plants. My kidneys, his heart." She turned on the oven. "He isn't doing too much over there, is he? Chris keeps an eye on him, but I worry."

"I don't think he exerts himself too much," Maud said. In fact, she rarely saw Frazer out of the cart in which he prowled the property, unless he was clipping the boxwood hedge, seemingly one leaf at a time. She took the glass of wine Lydia offered.

"He had a coronary a year ago," Lydia said. "Gone four full minutes. I wanted him to retire, but he couldn't, you know? Chris was between jobs again, and it turns out he's good with plants. So Harriet made it happen."

The two women, Maud learned, had been friends since high school. Out the window, Harriet was in culottes and a tank top, smoking a cigarette as she chatted with Gabriel. Maud hadn't recognized her at first, her ballerina spine curved into a lawn chair with one flip-flop dangling from her toes.

"I couldn't do this project without Chris," she said.

"It means a lot." Lydia put the casserole in the oven. "My boy having something he's responsible for, having people depend on him. That doesn't happen much." She shut the oven with her hip. "People don't understand the way he is and most of them don't bother to try. He lost oxygen when he was born. So did Frazer with the heart attack, but a baby's brain can't come back from it the same way." She glanced out the window, where Chris was wiping down a picnic table. "I haven't seen him this good in years. He wants to start a flowerbed behind the house. He talks about it at dinner."

"He's a huge help, and the garden will be all his when I go," Maud said.

Lydia hugged her again. "I mean it," she said. "Thank you."

Outside, by an empty firepit, Frazer and Lydia's daughter sat in a folding chair with a toddler, who was naked save a diaper, as her husband wrangled a pacifier out of a baby's grip and into his screaming mouth. Two other grandchildren, dressed in bathing suits and pirate hats, ran in circles through a sprinkler. Seemingly oblivious to the noise, Chris was now meticulously smoothing a checkered cloth over the table. The food that Maud helped Lydia bring outside—Swedish meatballs in a Crock-Pot, a spiral ham—

was familiar from her childhood, and her mother's casserole fit right in.

After they ate, Frazer and Lydia played folk music from the sixties on guitar and banjo, as Harriet sang the lyrics in a wavering, mellifluous voice. During the chorus, the older children joined in, screechzing out the refrains, jumping up and down to "Puff the Magic Dragon" and "Mr. Tambourine Man." On the porch, where he'd gone to sit on a rocker bench, Chris closed his eyes and nodded to the beat.

"Let's take ten," Harriet announced. She lit what seemed to be her hundredth cigarette. Lydia suggested starting a fire to ward off mosquitoes, and Gabriel said he'd grab some logs from the stack by the porch. Maud had hardly spoken to him; he'd been sitting between Harriet and Lydia, the women talking to him and past him.

"Want to help?" he asked Maud.

"He knows my destructive tendencies," Maud said as she got up.

The baby wailed, and his mother gave him her breast.

"You two are the cutest couple," she said to Maud.

"Oh, we aren't a couple," Maud blurted. Then she went on too long, explaining that she had two daughters and a husband back in the Bay Area. "The girls get here tomorrow," she said.

"And Gabriel here is a lone wolf," Harriet added. She tilted back her head and let out a howl that sent Lydia into hysterics.

Eight-thirty arrived with no sign of dessert. The fire danced drunkenly in the pit. Maud kept catching Gabriel's eye through the flames. Who knew how things would go when he met Louise and Ella? Who knew if they'd like him?

Or if he'd like them—and if he didn't, she wouldn't like him anymore. He was only a few yards away, but he already seemed long gone. He was mouthing something at her. She tried to read his lips. Spill the drink.

"I should probably get back," she said. "Need to get ready for the girls."

"Looking like rain anyway," Lydia said.

"When did rain ever stop you from sitting outside?" Harriet said.

"You think?" Gabriel said. The cloudless sky looked stoic.

"We're old," Lydia said. "We feel it in our bones."

"And we read the weather forecast," Harriet added.

Sure enough, as Maud and Gabriel walked away from the house with the umbrellas Lydia had insisted they borrow, Maud felt a drop on her forehead.

"They're sweet," she said, as they waited to cross the road, the raindrops turning to glitter in the headlights of a passing car.

"A little too sweet, maybe."

"Too much love?" Another car swished by, windshield wipers squeaking.

"Too much everything. Did you see that kid pull off his diaper and pee against a tree? And everybody talking at the same time. I don't think I had one actual conversation."

"If you figure out how to have enough love without too much love, let me know," Maud said.

They crossed to the other side. Maud hadn't meant to say something so serious. The chaos at the farm reminded her of family gatherings in Burlingame, with her elderly aunts clucking over the latest Hollywood scandal, her father and uncles roaring with laughter as a football game blared on the TV, nieces and nephews racing each other between the rooms, tripping on the carpet, skinning their knees, and crying, her mother barking orders at Maud and her sister from the kitchen. An only child, Gabriel had no idea. Peter, when he first met Maud's family, had been shell-shocked, though in time, somehow, he'd adjusted. Even when they were divorced, Maud thought, as she and Gabriel passed through the gates, Peter would be in her life. She belonged to an equation in which Gabriel had no part. And how could he ever? They'd been playing house these weeks, and that was coming to an end.

"I didn't really want to go over there tonight," Gabriel said. "I wanted us to have a last dinner together in our usual spot."

Maud swallowed her fear. "I'll miss spending time with you," she said.

"Your husband will probably prefer it, though," Gabriel said. "It doesn't bug him that we're always together? He knows, right?"

They were passing the orchard, its cherry leaves buffed by the rain. Neither of them had opened the umbrellas, and Gabriel's face glistened. Maud knew what he was really asking.

"Peter and I are separated," she said.

"Separated like you were in England?"

"No. Really separated. He thinks it's temporary. I know it isn't."

Gabriel stopped. "So, what does that mean?" He was an arm's length away and he was looking at her softly, and it was up to her to decide what would happen next. For a moment, Maud thought she could do it. She'd take his hand and go with him to the farmhouse. She'd pull up that T-shirt, unbuckle that belt, open her mouth to his mouth, be with him as she hadn't been with anyone for ages. But the most this could be was a fling, and if it went poorly, she'd still be here all summer living close to him, working on the same grounds. And right now her children were boarding a plane and heading her way.

"It means my life is about to become very messy," she said.

"But isn't yet," Gabriel said.

"It is in here." Maud tapped her head. "And everything changes tomorrow."

She saw him readjust, take a step back. "We can meet up late," he said. "Right? To talk. Your girls sleep, don't they?"

"They sleep," she said. "Sort of. But you might not like me as a mother."

"How are you as a mother?"

"Boring. Distracted. Often worried. Sometimes grouchy."

"That sounds exactly like you."

"Does it?" She smiled, glad to have the tension relieved. "Good, then. You won't be surprised."

She was going to ask him inside for a drink, then he said, "Do you want to go for a swim?"

She looked at him blankly. "In the Hudson?"

"In the swimming lake. I've wanted to ask, and this might be my last chance." He shrugged. "Plus, you know, we're already wet."

Maud laughed, feeling giddy. "Why not?" she said.

Gabriel headed toward the cottage. "See you in five minutes, boring, grouchy, distracted mother."

"See you in five minutes, lone wolf."

———

They met in bathing suits, towels around their waists, and walked through the woods, flashlights swishing. The rain pattered on the oak leaves, then dwindled. Side by side, they moved deeper into a cool, shadowy world that croaked with frogs and chirped with crickets. The lake, pictured in an archival sketch with a gazebo and two bonneted women rowing a boat, was now hemmed in by weeds, but the surface was silky and inviting. Maud slipped off her towel, adjusted her suit, and lowered herself into the water. Wincing at the cold, she wondered if Gabriel noticed her body the way she'd noticed his. His chest, as she'd imagined, was muscled and sculpted, but his body wasn't perfect. She liked that he had a slight belly.

"Race you to the other side," he said once he was in the water.

"I thought this was supposed to be a relaxing dip."

"It'll be a relaxing race. And this water is freezing. I need to move." He dove and started to butterfly toward the opposite shore.

"You're cheating," Maud yelled at him, laughing. "I refuse to participate."

"Fine," he called back. "I'll race myself."

She twisted onto her back and floated. Eventually Gabriel returned and floated too. Together, they looked up at the moon, blooming in its bed of sky. Everything would change tomorrow, Maud thought, but maybe not too much.

On the drive from the airport the next morning, she stopped with the girls in Tarrytown for lunch at a tavern with time-clouded windows and a boot scraper by the door. A woman in colonial petticoats and Birkenstocks led them to a table.

"Go see if you can find the mermaid," Maud told Ella and Louise, pointing to a hearth covered in cornflower-blue-and-white Delft tile. She'd read about the building the night before to collect details that might intrigue them. In the car, she'd spilled out a history lesson about the people who first had lived by the river, the arrival of the Dutch, the Hudson River School of painting, realizing too late that Ella was wearing earbuds and hadn't heard a thing.

"What do I win?" Ella said. She'd spotted the mermaid languishing on a bed of kelp and tulips.

"Lunch?" Maud said.

She was so happy to be with them. She'd almost started crying when she saw them walk off the plane. Louise wore her fluorescent-orange backpack on her chest, a stuffed turtle peering its head out of the front pocket. Ella was chewing gum for her stopped-up ears, but her jaw stilled and she smiled when Maud ran up to them.

"Let's play the anachronism game," Louise said now.

"Too tired." Ella perused the menu. The girls had slept through the flight but were still on California time.

"You go first," Maud told Louise.

Looking around the room, Louise began: ice in the water, granulated sugar on the tables, the server's braces.

"The air-conditioning," Maud added.

Ella laid down the menu. "I think I'll just get a piece of cornbread."

"At least try the cider," Maud said.

"Does it have alcohol?"

"If it did, they wouldn't serve it to you."

"I was just asking." Ella rolled her eyes. She could slip so easily from the childish pleasure over finding the mermaid—"Look! Right there in the corner," she'd said to Louise—to adolescent scorn. In a couple of years, with that same group of girls from her school, would she be drinking and partying as Maud's sister, Annette, had done? Maud doubted Ella would follow her mother's example and hide out in the library.

After lunch, she drove the girls to Montgomery Place. "All that fruit's for us," she announced when she parked by the orchard. "I already bought the jamming jars." At Monk's House, the three of them used to spend summer afternoons picking peaches, gooseberries, and plums, and canning, pickling, and preserving cucumbers and beans. "And that's our creek." By the cottage, Gabriel's truck was gone. He was out for the day, on a dig with an archaeologist from a nearby college. *Hope they love it!* he'd texted Maud that morning.

"It does look like Monk's!" Ella said as she walked into the farmhouse.

"Told you," Maud said. "Only missing the hedgehog in the walls. Surprises on your pillows when you find your room."

She'd spent the previous few afternoons getting the house ready. She refreshed the wildflowers in a mason jar on the coffee table, the columbines like red umbrellas in a storm of periwinkle forget-me-nots. She'd washed the girls' sheets, cleared the dead stink bugs off the windowsills, strung daisy garlands over their beds. At an overpriced shop in town, she'd bought them earrings: small brass hoops for Ella and brass hearts for Louise wrapped in tissue-paper cocoons. They put them on now, and Ella took a selfie with her phone—the ultimate compliment.

"We'll unpack later," Maud said. "I want to show you the grounds first."

Louise jumped off her bed. "Straight to the pond with the frogs, please."

"What's the Wi-Fi password?" Ella's thumbs were busy on her phone.

"Later," Maud said.

"I want to post this picture."

"Come on. Posting can wait. Frog time!"

They stopped at the office to meet Harriet, who gave the girls pencils with the Montgomery Place logo and chalky-looking caramels from a tin in her purse.

"I'm glad you two are here now to keep an eye on your mother," she said.

Maud wondered if she and Gabriel had left a wake of gossip last night when they went home.

"She's nice," Louise said as they cut through the orchard toward the mansion.

"She only likes you because you're the cute one," Ella said.

"You're cute too," Maud said and gave her a hug.

As she followed the girls through the trees, time folded, and they were back at Monk's House. Weekdays, Maud would disappear into Virginia Woolf's letters and journals and Leonard's careful lists and gardening books. She wrote papers and articles and led tours. She was always inside and outside, planting or trimming or reading or writing. Her gardening boots stood ready by the kitchen door, which opened onto a brick path that flashed with zinnias and jolted with lavender. She and the girls established their own routine when Peter wasn't home: tea parties by the pond, wet slickers dropped in a heap in the hallway after puddle-jumping in the orchard, sleepovers in Maud and Peter's bed. If only they'd never left, she thought, as the trees retreated and the mansion appeared against a watery sky.

They couldn't go inside because the building was sealed off for an asbestos abatement on the second floor. All of the rooms, save the archives, were now stripped bare. But Maud showed the girls the dining room and library through the windows, Louise climbing on Ella's back to see. The two of them weren't as wowed as Maud would have liked by the size of the formal garden, but what did she expect, with no flowers yet? The conservatory, however, they found cool, "like a spaceship," Louise said. She galloped from one end to the other, yells echoing off the glass walls as Ella walked around with her hands over her ears. Down by the pond, the frogs stayed hidden despite Louise's attempts to find them by flipping over the lily pads with a stick.

Ella wanted to go online the minute they got back to the farmhouse, so Maud showed her where to find the Wi-Fi password, then helped Louise unpack her suitcase.

"It doesn't work," Ella said from the doorway.

"Hmm?" Maud dropped shirts into a dresser drawer.

Ella held her phone in front of Maud's face. A message— *FaceTime Failed*—showed on the screen.

"Let me put these away, then I'll take a look."

"I knew something like this would happen," Ella said. "You guys just wanted me off my phone and away from my friends."

"Are you sure you got the password right?" Louise said. She was arranging her socks on the bed in a rainbow, her version of unpacking.

"I know how to type a password, Louise!"

"Don't yell at your sister," Maud said. "This isn't an

emergency. Why don't you unpack and then we'll look at it together?"

"There's nothing to look at. Because the connection sucks!"

Steadily, Maud put away another shirt as Ella ranted: she only had two real friends anyway, and now she would lose them because they wouldn't be able to FaceTime. Texting wasn't enough. You had to see people's faces. She'd go back to school with no friends at all. Plus, she didn't want to live in the middle of nowhere. "I'm going to die of boredom."

Maud shut a drawer. "You're not going to be bored. You'll have camp."

"I'm too old for camp. I told you guys that."

Ella's jaw jutted and her cheeks flared. She was having an updated version of the tantrums she used to have as a toddler, when she'd lie prostrate on the kitchen floor, pounding her fists and feet and wailing because she didn't want a nap. And Maud felt that old irritation, that internal battle to stay patient.

"Give me the phone," she said.

"What are you going to do with it?"

Throw it in the Hudson, Maud thought. "See if I can figure it out. You unpack."

She had no idea what the problem could be with Ella's phone. Hers worked fine in the farmhouse, although she never used FaceTime—few people her age did, and she'd never been good at technology. As for using the internet, Harriet had advised her to plug her computer into the modem with an ethernet cord. She called Peter to see if he had any ideas.

"FaceTime uses more bandwidth," he said. "But if the router's dodgy, she should be able to use cellular."

He told her to check the indicator, which showed only one square at the farmhouse, so she headed down the hill toward the offices, watching the phone like a divining rod. Past the table, two bars showed. By a dogwood tree, four.

"Bingo," she said.

"I'll FaceTime her phone to try," Peter said.

Behind his stippled face, San Francisco skyscrapers loomed through the window. His office was on the top floor of a building that resembled a needle jammed into the streets near Chinatown.

"Too bad," he said. "You'll never get her off that thing now."

"I'm so happy to have them here," Maud said. "And I'm already tired."

She was also disappointed in herself for losing her cool with Ella so quickly.

"I miss them already," Peter said. "Even the pouty one."

"We'll try you again tonight when Ella has calmed down," Maud said.

She said goodbye and hung up, feeling guilty. Peter missed his daughters. Of course he did. There were these windows of connection with him when she forgot herself, forgot their history, when the problems of parenting distracted from the problem of themselves. But if she didn't stick to her intentions and leave him this summer, she feared she never would.

Not wanting to reward a fit, she waited until she and the girls had finished eating dinner to tell Ella about the hot spot. They were sitting outside at the table—with Harriet's approval, she'd dragged a barbecue from behind the farmhouse to grill burgers.

"You can go to that tree if you want to call," she said.

"It's not called calling," Ella said, as she got up from the table with her phone. "But thanks."

By seven, Maud was starting to wonder why Gabriel hadn't texted. His truck had been parked at the cottage for two hours. As she drew the girls' bedroom curtains shut, Ella said, "What's that noise?"

"Crickets."

"If there are deer, are there mountain lions?" Louise said from her bed.

"No. Once upon a time, there were wolves. But they're long gone." Maud kissed her on the forehead, then kissed the back of Ella's head. "Don't worry. It'll feel more like home in a couple days."

She closed their door most of the way and turned on the hall light, glancing again through the window. Maybe Gabriel had decided to stay away now that Ella and Louise were here. Maybe the feelings were all on her side and she'd imagined what they'd really been saying last night.

"Stop it, you idiot," she whispered out loud. She put her phone in the kitchen, opened her laptop, and worked on copy for the explanatory placards about Alexander Gilson, trying not to phrase certainties where there was doubt.

An hour later, when she checked her phone, there was a message from Gabriel. *How is it going?*

Warmth rushed through her body. *Good. Minor internet catastrophe but all fixed now.*

Drink?

They're still wide awake. Jet lag.

She'd been down the hall twice, once to bring Louise a glass of water and again to open the window, because Ella was hot.

I'll wait up.

At ten, when the girls were finally asleep, she went outside to meet Gabriel, trying to tame her smile. He placed a squat candle on the table. "Figured we could use this now that we're meeting in deep night." He struck a match. "Do they like the place?"

"I think so. The Wi-Fi is too weak for Ella."

"You could borrow my router."

"It's better if she can't get online easily." Maud handed him a beer. "She might actually stay off her phone for five minutes."

"I can't wait to meet them. I researched children while eating dinner. Took copious notes."

"Lower your expectations," she said. "You'll be lucky if Ella says two words to you."

"I plan to try for three."

Even in the dark, she could see the lines by his eyes that creased when he smiled.

"Do you want to have dinner with us tomorrow night?" she asked quickly, before she'd regret it.

"I'd love that," he said.

"Don't expect caviar and coq au vin. I'm grilling hot dogs."

"And here I thought you didn't cook."

The chair was a comfort under her legs. The candle flickered with the stars. In such little time, they'd created this neutral territory together: not his and not hers, free of boundaries save the obvious one. As they drank their beers, she wondered if it was possible that the girls would slip easily into those two other chairs tomorrow night. Maybe it wouldn't be as hard as she'd thought to keep spending time with Gabriel.

4

The next morning, having dropped the girls at their camp down the road, she and Chris started to plant the beds in a colorful symphony of bearded irises, snapdragons, and asters. As if an announcement had been broadcast through the grounds, butterflies coasted to the site to flirt among the petals and a cardinal couple perched in a black locust tree, waiting for seeds.

"I like these best," Chris said. He teased the roots of a sweet pea into the soil. "Maybe because they're the smallest."

"And the prettiest, I think," Maud said.

"I like the geraniums too."

He was learning the names of all the flowers. He tamped the soil in a careful circle. It had been an unexpected miracle of this summer, Maud thought as she knelt next to him, to get to know Chris. She wanted the girls to meet him and make that same discovery. It seemed an important lesson, especially for Ella.

In the parking lot after camp, they filled her in on their day.

"It's super-fun," Louise said. She'd done a ropes course, gone swimming in the lake, and made a suncatcher—a popsicle stick frame around multicolored tissue paper—that she hooked on the rearview mirror.

"Pretty lame" was Ella's verdict. Fishing was the most boring thing she'd ever done, and also totally pointless when you just threw the fish back. The ropes course was stupid too.

"What did you do when everyone went swimming?" Maud asked. Ella had forgotten to bring her bathing suit from Marin.

"Sat under a tree and got eaten by mosquitoes."

"We'll buy a suit tonight."

"I'm having my period." Ella clicked on her seat belt. "Can't swim until it's over."

"I can teach you to use a tampon."

"I don't want to use a tampon and I definitely don't want you to teach me."

With further questioning, she revealed that her group had also taken a hike in the woods. "That was okay." But, she continued on the drive home, the other kids in her group were a-holes.

"Why do you say that?"

"I can tell by their clothes. Who wears a polo shirt to camp?"

"Not all people in polos are a-holes," Maud said, slowing the car as they approached Montgomery Place. "Look at your uncle Kevin."

"If he weren't your brother, you'd think he was a total a-hole," Ella said.

This was true, Maud thought, as she parked by the farmhouse. Sometimes Ella nailed things perfectly.

Dinner that evening with Gabriel went much better than

Maud had expected, mostly because Louise talked non-stop, a counterweight to Ella's silence and Maud's nervousness. After returning Gabriel's hello, Ella studiously painted ketchup on her hot dog. Maud was glad that she'd prepared Gabriel for Ella's aloofness. He listened to Louise's torrent of anecdotes about camp, asking her questions, seeming somewhat dazed. Done with eating, Ella asked Maud if she could FaceTime at the tree.

"Go ahead," Maud said. "Have fun."

"Nice meeting you," Gabriel said.

"Yeah, sure, you too," Ella said without turning around.

"That was four words," Gabriel told Maud.

As the girls got ready for bed in the farmhouse bathroom, Maud asked them what they'd thought of Gabriel.

"Nice-o," Louise said. She scooped her head into a nightgown.

"We just met," Ella said. "I don't know. Seems okay." Already in her pajamas, she had her face close to the mirror and was squeezing a pimple on her chin.

"So, you don't mind if he eats dinner with us sometimes? We won't talk about work too much so we don't bore you."

"Sure," Louise said.

"I guess," Ella said. Mournfully, she opened a tube of acne cream. "If this zit is still around in the morning, I'm going to camp with a bag on my head."

Once Ella and Louise were settled in their room, Maud texted Gabriel. *I hope that wasn't too much for you.*

Too much? Are you kidding? It was fun. They're great. Louise is adorable and Ella has your smile.

She smiled at you?

No, not yet.

I guess that's tomorrow night's goal!

You'll make it out again tonight, won't you?

See you there.

She packed the next day's lunches for the girls: two swipes of peanut butter on Louise's sandwich to three swipes on Ella's, strawberry jelly for one and grape jam for the other, crusts cut off but included to eat on the side for Louise, her carrots sliced into rounds and Ella's into sticks. When Louise called for water, she brought her a glass. She rinsed Louise's bathing suit in the sink and hung it up to dry. It had been nice to take a break from these duties, but it was also nice to do them again.

"You're good with them," she told Gabriel when she sat down at the table.

"You sound surprised." He lit the candle.

She laughed. "I am."

"Maybe because they're yours." He'd texted earlier that he'd gotten sunburned that morning, and she could see the dark blotch on his forehead. She almost reached over to touch that tender place. "I was a little worried they'd hate me and I'd never see you again," he said.

"I was a little worried when you didn't text yesterday," Maud admitted. "I thought you'd run away before even meeting them."

"I wanted to text," he said. "I was trying to leave you alone. Let you have some time with your girls."

The candlelight brought out the angles of his face. His eyes looked sad. Maud gripped the seat of her chair for courage.

"You don't have to leave me alone," she said. "I'd rather you didn't."

"But you don't take me seriously." Gabriel shook his head. "You think I'm a player."

"It's not that," Maud said. "I mean, it's not only that."

He laughed wistfully. "I love your honesty."

She wanted to walk around the table and put her arms around his waist, tuck her head into that space between his neck and shoulder.

"I'm not honest," she said. "I've been pretending in my marriage for years."

"But now you're getting out."

"I'm trying," she said. "It isn't only about me, though. I can't mess this up."

Gabriel leaned across the table, the candlelight on his throat. "I'm not asking you to mess anything up. I'm not asking you for anything. Just time with you. However that's possible. I like how I am with you."

"How's that?" Maud said, and she heard the hope in her voice.

He thought for a minute. "Honest."

"I feel that way too," Maud said. "Even if I can't do anything about it."

"Well, that's something, I guess," Gabriel said.

"Yes," she said. "That's something."

Lying in bed later, eyes closed but fully awake, she left for another life in Turkey. She saw the minareted mosque that Gabriel had described, the bats swarming out of the hilltop caves, the ruins of the ancient city soon to be drowned by the Tigris. She imagined a garden atop one of those hills, filled with pistachio and Judas trees and beds of native tulips. She'd work all day under that new sun while Gabriel was at his dig. Nights, she'd put her feet into the hot springs next to his. She'd sit at a fire with him and his colleagues, eating roast lamb. And when the moon came out, the two of them would say good night, then walk to their tent, take off their clothes, and zip out the world.

With Gabriel's help a few days later, she and Chris moved the garden's original statues from the coach house to the conservatory. They placed the urns in the center of the beds and filled them with chartreuse sweet potato vines and scarlet begonias.

"We're getting as close as we can," Maud told Chris as they drove in his truck to the hardware store one morning. She had snaked an irrigation system through her garden design and they were getting supplies. "But you can't haul water to those beds twice a day."

"I could do it," he said.

"Plus, we'd have to redig the well."

"We're good at digging."

She thought he might be making a joke, so she laughed and was happy to see him almost grin. They returned from town with a truckful of pipes, sprinkler heads, and tubing, and spent the afternoon installing a buried drip system.

Gabriel came to dinner that night with a boxed kit to make gigantic bubbles. "Thought you guys might like this," he told the girls. He'd texted Maud earlier that he'd googled "best presents for kids," then gone to a toy store in Rhinebeck. *Nice!* Maud had texted back. She didn't reveal that she was unsure how this present would go over with Ella. She had taken the girls out to eat the night before, and when the server offered Ella a children's menu, she had been insulted, a stern grimace on her face for the rest of the meal.

After they ate, Ella went to the tree, but eventually she joined Maud, Gabriel, and Louise by the orchard as they competed to make the biggest bubbles, applauding and cheering when the bubbles escaped the branches and headed toward the moon like gigantic, quivering jellyfish. Gabriel joked that Ella's bubbles were smaller than his and pretended he was trying to burst them when they drifted by. Although Ella played along, Maud saw her face harden.

"Bubbles?" she said, when they were back inside with the dishes. "Does he think I'm five?"

"I'm not five, and I like them," Louise said. She set her plate on the kitchen counter.

"You don't have to do it if you don't like it," Maud told Ella.

"Then you'd say I was being rude."

She went to the bathroom, banging the door shut. Maud scraped the plates into the trash. Montgomery Place couldn't be like Monk's House, she thought, for many reasons, including the fact that Ella was no longer a little girl who liked to make mud pies and dance on the kitchen table.

Sunday was the Day of Our Lord for Maud's parents, and the day of Maud's parents for Maud. When she'd lived in England, she phoned them after they got home from Mass. Living in Marin, she and the girls visited them in Burlingame on Sunday afternoons. So, on Sunday, as the girls slept in, she steeled herself and dialed their number. Her mother picked up the call in the defunct commercial garage near the house. She was sorting food for the parish pantry, cans clunking in the background. "Your dad's doing doughnuts with the Shriners, so you're stuck with me," she said.

"How are you, Ma?"

Another can clunked down. Maud could see her mother in the pungent garage, wearing the same slacks she'd been sporting since the 1980s, white hair cut into a mushroom cap. The phone on the wall, still gummy with oil, stretched to the space where Maud's father and brother had once repaired cars, and which now hosted shelves of mixed vegetables, soup, chili, and infant formula.

"I left dinner on your front deck for your husband last night," her mother said, ignoring Maud's question. "Relieve some of the burden."

"He told me," Maud said. "Thanks."

Peter, she knew, had called her mother to say thank you and then dumped the casserole in the trash and ordered takeout.

"All alone in that house," her mother said. "He must be miserable." She sniffed. "The ladies were asking about you at Mass this morning." The ladies, like Maud's mother, were in their seventies. Maud had grown up in their mildewy, wood-paneled club rooms at gatherings for wakes and First Communions. Their part of Burlingame used to be called Little Ireland. "No one understands," her mother continued. "New York State? What's she doing there? I didn't try to explain."

Maud let out her held breath quietly so it wouldn't sound like the sigh that it was. "They didn't have careers, Ma. Not that there's anything wrong with that."

She heard the squeak of the shopping cart used to transport the food down the street to the parish. "Mallory Brown's daughter left her husband, and now she's on food stamps."

"I haven't left Peter."

"Did I say that you had? I'm sharing news about people you know. Or used to. Have you talked to your sister lately?"

"We text every day."

"She's been standing on her head. It'll give her a stroke."

"I should let you get that food to the parish," Maud said. "Tell Dad I said hi. Talk next Sunday. Love you."

Immediately she called Annette, who always knew how to release the frustration of these conversations with their mother.

"Mom says don't stand on your head," she said.

Annette laughed huskily. "I should have never told her I nailed my headstand. She's also worried I'm going to become a Buddhist. They all go to hell or get stuck in limbo, apparently. I told her since I'm already confirmed, I'd probably squeak through."

"Better a Buddhist than a daughter who abandoned her husband," Maud said. "She seems to like Peter so much better now that she thinks I've left him."

"Thinks you left him? She knows you have."

"She'll still feign chest pain when I announce it in the fall."

"Every family has a leaver," Annette said, echoing their mother's proclamation when Maud had gotten a scholarship to Amherst twenty years before. "How's Ella doing?"

"The same. She's so thirteen."

"I promise I didn't give her any tips while you were away."

At thirteen Annette used to climb out their bedroom window to meet her boyfriend, Dale, for make-out sessions in the Burlingame cemetery. They eloped their senior year of high school and went to community college together. Now Dale was dead, and Annette was an administrative assistant at a law firm in San Francisco, her hair dyed its original red to cover the gray it had turned in her twenties, bitten-down nails hidden under gel tips, always on a diet, always dating another questionable man. As she described her dinner date the night before with a neurologist who had demonstrated lobotomization on a bread roll, there was a knock on the door. "Hang on a second," Maud said.

Gabriel was heading out for the day and wanted to know what he could pick up for dinner. "Do the kids like pizza?"

"They love pizza. Pepperoni for them, something else for us?"

"Done," he said.

"Sorry about that," she told Annette, watching Gabriel walk away into the morning light.

"Was that your boyfriend?"

"Ha, ha." Maud shut the door. "He's trying with the girls but Ella's unenthusiastic."

"You should have fucked him when you could."

"It's not about sex, Annette. I actually like him. It's possible to be friends with a man without sleeping with him."

"You aren't getting feelings, are you? I know men like that."

"Yes, yes. You know how all the men are."

"I'm serious. Forty-six, never in a real relationship? Forget it."

"I don't want to be in a relationship," Maud said. "I'm trying to get out of one." She could hear the girls stirring in bed and lowered her voice.

"Just don't let on to Peter. He'll be a total shit about it. Right now you hold all the cards."

"You should have gone to law school, you know," Maud said.

"Yes, well, I learn tricks at work. And I've been waiting for you to leave this marriage for a decade."

That night, Gabriel watched Louise studiously peel all the pepperonis from her pizza slice and stack them on Maud's plate.

"I thought your mom said you like pepperoni," he said.

"I just like the flavor on the cheese," Louise replied.

"We have a system," Maud said, and added the pepperoni to her own slice. She glanced at the tree to check on Ella, happy to see her laughing with a friend as she ate—she'd been in tears several times today over a new crop of pimples. Earlier, on their way home from wandering the galleries of Dia Beacon, Maud had stopped at the old-fashioned pharmacy in town. She and Ella read the descriptions on acne products while, at the candy counter, Louise dropped fireballs and gummy worms into a bag that now sat on the table. Since Maud had allowed Ella to eat at the tree, Louise had been allowed to have dessert with dinner.

As Maud sat on the living room couch that night, reading a book on Victorian statuary and waiting for the girls to sleep, Ella came down the hallway.

"Louise is snoring," she said.

"Really? She must have a stuffy nose."

"She sounds like a warthog." Ella's chin was covered in pimple patches. She seemed to have used the entire box.

"Want to sleep with me tonight?" Maud asked. She put down her book.

"Sure," Ella said.

Maud couldn't remember the last time Ella had climbed into her bed. She was grateful to Louise for snoring, a sound audible from the hallway as she and Ella passed the door. In her bedroom, she pulled back the comforter. "Scratch your back?" she asked.

"Okay," Ella said, letting Maud tuck her in. When she was little, Maud would tell stories on her back with her fingers, tracing the outlines of the pond in "The Frog King," thumping her hand down her spine as she whispered,

Fee-fi-fo-fum. But this, she thought, as Ella pulled up the back of her T-shirt, was close enough.

"Why does Gabriel want to have dinner with us every night?" Ella said after a while.

"He likes us," Maud said carefully. "But he doesn't have to. We'll eat alone tomorrow night."

"Are you and Dad fighting?"

"No." Maud paused in her scratching. "Why?"

"You guys never talk on the phone."

What now? Maud thought. How not to lie? How not to alarm her?

"We've never been phone people," she said.

"And he keeps asking me about you," Ella said. "Like how does Mom seem? What's Mom up to?"

"He likes it better when we live together," Maud said. "But it's hard because our work is so different."

Maud saw Ella's shoulders relax; the answer had appeased her. Her back was still a child's back, with the same brown mole that had appeared one summer, the faint birthmark shaped like a sailboat. Maud snuggled closer.

"I'm so glad you two are here," she said. "I missed you. I love you so much."

Ella gave in to the hug. "You'd love me even if I was an axe murderer. You said that once."

"It's true," Maud said into the fruity thicket of her hair. "I wouldn't approve of the murders, but I'd love you the same."

"I don't know why." Ella's voice wavered. "I'm not that good at school. I'm not that good at friends. I'm not that good at anything. Don't say it isn't true. It's how I feel."

"Friendships will get easier as you find the things you love to do. You'll meet other people that love them too."

"When?"

"It takes time. You will. I promise. Want more scratching, or ready to sleep?"

"Sleep," Ella said, and she burrowed deeper into the covers.

Maud left her hand on Ella's back as her breaths lengthened. Being good but not good enough. She understood so well. Her entire childhood, she'd thought of herself that way. Attending Amherst on a scholarship hadn't helped. She'd realized her first year that her love of history was a love of stories and atmosphere. Theory left her cold. She didn't want to make and support arguments. She felt like an imposter. Then, the spring of her junior year, she'd interned at a historical estate near campus, working with a professor of archaeology on a garden restoration. In a letter written in 1890, she found a reference to a peony plant on an acre of the grounds now covered by pines. On her own, she'd discovered the peony under a honeysuckle blanket, still alive, more than a hundred years later. This, she knew that day, was what she wanted to do, whatever this was. Landscape history, her professor told her. There are graduate programs in the U.K. Not so much in the U.S. That conversation had changed the course of her life, sent her over an ocean and in Peter's direction.

Once Ella was asleep, she texted Gabriel that she couldn't meet tonight. *Sleepover with the girl.*

Which one?

The one who eats the pepperoni.

Let me take you to lunch tomorrow, he replied and sent a link to a restaurant in town.

———

At noon the next day, Maud drove to the restaurant, a French bistro called Catherine with photographs of Catherine Deneuve on the walls, all of them predating 1960 when Deneuve was young and in black-and-white, as if she'd died at thirty. Maud felt self-conscious in the airy room, with its zinc bar and burgundy satin banquettes, its chalk menu and cheese trolley. Walking to the table where Gabriel waited, she wondered if she'd tracked in dirt.

"I hope you like champagne," Gabriel said when she sat down.

"I do," Maud said. "But I'll have the arsenic, instead, please." She spread a starched napkin over her lap. "Sorry. I'm not very fun right now."

That morning, fertilizing the beds with Chris, she had worried about Ella. What was she picking up on about Gabriel? Why was Peter asking questions? She'd almost canceled coming to this lunch. And now she wished Gabriel had chosen to meet at the taco place a few doors down.

"You're fun even when you aren't fun," Gabriel said, as the waiter filled their glasses and nestled the bottle into a silver ice receptacle. "What's going on?"

"Ella's so down. And I don't know if I'm helping, if I'm saying the right things. It used to be so easy with her." Maud took a sip of champagne, barely registering the taste. "She was talking about her dad last night," she said. "I don't know how she's going to take it when we tell her we're splitting up. Or when I say we're splitting up. I don't even know how he'll react either. He's in denial."

"You think he'll fight it?"

"I worry he'll wear me down. When we discussed divorce before, he was totally opposed. And he's very persuasive."

"He doesn't want to lose you," Gabriel said quietly. "I'd fight it too."

Maud's breath stopped in her throat. "It isn't that," she said. "He doesn't really want me. He had an affair. He's probably had a lot of them. I only know about the one."

"And you can't forgive him?" Gabriel said. He was buttering his bread, not looking up at her. He feels vulnerable with me too, Maud thought.

"Worse than that," she said. "I don't care. It's as if when I had Ella, I grew a new heart, which got bigger with Louise. But the heart that loved Peter shrank to a pit."

"I thought mine was a pit too," Gabriel said. His eyes lifted from the bread plate and met hers squarely. "I think about you a lot," he said.

"I think about you too," Maud said.

The waiter set down their entrées, a welcome distraction from the heat consuming her face. Gabriel's mountain of french fries rose above a massive island of steak, and she regretted her Niçoise salad. Her appetite had returned. Gabriel always made her feel better. Simply being with him made her feel better.

He cut off a piece of steak and chewed it reflectively. "Ella doesn't like me, does she? I can tell."

"I wouldn't say that," Maud said. "She's not in a receptive phase." She hesitated. "But maybe no more presents."

"She's not into bubbles."

"It was such a nice thing to do," she said. "But she needs space from everyone right now. Especially me. Try to relax. Let her come to you. Be yourself but keep your distance."

"Be myself? A single man who has no idea how to talk to children?"

"You were a teenager once."

"I was cutting school and smoking weed at her age."

"Okay, don't remember that." She laughed. "I need to chill out too. Let's do dinner together every few nights. Let things evolve naturally."

"Like they have with us," Gabriel said.

"Sort of. Yes."

"But you and I don't play games," he said, pointing his knife at her. "And here you're telling me to play hard to get."

Maud stole a french fry from his plate. "As Ella is quick to point out," she said, "parents are major hypocrites."

5

With the laying of this last path, the garden was done. Maud dropped her shovel and walked backward to see. Since planting the final bed of lupine and roses, she and Chris had been emptying wheelbarrow after wheelbarrow of gravel and raking it into a smooth, glistering maze that slipped past one bed to another: irises to coneflowers, primroses to violets. Sweet potato vines spilled from the cast-iron urns under a conflagration of begonias. With its swirls and splashes of color, the garden was more like a brilliant, bold archipelago than the carpet Downing had described.

"What do you think?" she asked Chris. Side by side, they'd backtracked halfway to the mansion.

"It's the prettiest thing I ever seen."

He'd taken off his baseball cap, and his forehead sparkled with sweat. Both of them were drenched, the backs of their T-shirts sticking in the high heat. Bare-handed, not stopping for water, they'd shoveled gravel and raked without pause for the past three hours.

"We did it," Maud said. "Now we get to watch it grow."

"And water it and weed it."

"Yes, that too."

Gabriel came up from his dig to see, and that afternoon Maud brought the girls. Chris was still working in the beds, digging in the compost that Frazer had brought over in his cart.

"Don't eat those," Chris told Louise. She had picked a foxglove for a bouquet she was making for the dinner table.

"I wasn't going to," she said. "I don't eat flowers."

"Those ones can kill you." He went back to composting.

Maud saw Ella withdraw and cross her arms over her chest.

"That guy is so weird," she said when, out of earshot, they were walking along the drive.

"Don't say that, Ella," Maud said.

"You can't judge a book by its cover," Louise singsonged and waved her bouquet.

"I know that," Ella said. "It's just—he kind of freaks me out. The way he looks without looking."

"I see what you mean," Maud said. "But he's nice. I promise. He's just different."

Chris had looked at Ella the same way he looked at Louise, which was the same way that he sometimes looked at Maud or Gabriel or his father. There was nothing sexual to the gaze. But maybe it was enough to be stared at by a man for Ella to feel uncomfortable. As they took the shortcut through the orchard, Maud remembered visiting a public pool with her friend when she was eleven. There was one man on a plastic lounger who, every time they passed, would inspect them from head to toe with a half-smile on his face. She'd felt exposed, embarrassed, felt something was wrong, although she wasn't sure what. Thirty years later, she could still see it clearly: the Coke balanced on the man's hirsute belly, his thick purple lips and hungry eyes.

At five o'clock, as she skewered chicken and peppers on kebab sticks in the kitchen, she listened tensely while Louise told Peter about how Gabriel had helped her and Ella catch a frog in the pond the previous night.

"We let him go," she said. "Because, you know, freedom and liberty."

Things with Gabriel and Ella had improved since Maud's conversation with him at lunch. He'd eaten dinner with them several more times over the past week and had taken Maud's advice, bringing no gifts and no longer trying to joke with Ella. Last night, when Louise asked Gabriel to help them catch the frog, Ella jumped up and said she'd get a jar from the house, and the four of them went to the pond until dark.

"Sounds like your charming neighbor has become a regular," Peter said when Maud took the phone back from Louise. "I hope you're collecting rent."

She went out to the porch, shutting the door behind her. "He likes the girls," she said, "and the girls like him."

"Clearly, you like him too."

"We're friends," she said. She noticed a wasp nest tucked under an eave, like a gray papier-mâché outcrop of coral. "Anyway, Peter. We're separated."

"It's a trial separation."

"It's a separation." The phone weighed down her hand. "And my feelings haven't changed."

"Have you figured out how I'm going to support two households on my salary in the Bay Area?" Peter asked.

"I'll get a full-time job."

"That's been going well."

It was the first time he'd struck out at her in months, and she almost enjoyed the blow, because it was real.

"I'll stop looking for historical work. I'll be more open. I'll do landscaping."

"You'd hate that."

"Then I'll hate it."

"Is something going on with that guy?"

"No."

"Okay. I trust you. And you can trust me."

"Why? What's changed?"

"I don't want to lose you, Maud."

But I'm already gone, she thought. I left long ago and I never came back. And I never will. "We'll talk about it when I'm home at the end of August, like we said."

"Why can't we talk about it when I visit?"

"Because that's not what we agreed to. We can't have the conversation with the girls around."

"Don't ruin our life over one mistake."

"I thought you slept with her twice," Maud said, unable to stop herself.

"You know what I mean."

After she hung up, she walked across the porch to look more closely at the nest. She recognized the hexagons made by paper wasps—they wouldn't sting the girls, so she decided to let them be.

That weekend, she took Ella and Louise to the city. On the boat to Ellis Island, she thought about Gabriel. In the kaleidoscope of the gem room at the Museum of Natural History, moving up and down on a carousel horse in Central

Park, and walking along the High Line, she thought about Gabriel. *This place is a desert without you,* he texted.

"Bathing suit time," she told Ella on Sunday morning, as people bearing shopping bags rushed by them on the sidewalk. "Your period must be over by now. You can't keep sitting around doing nothing at camp when everyone's swimming."

"Fine," Ella muttered.

They were standing on Fifth Avenue in front of the flagship store of a clothing chain that Ella liked and Maud didn't, a source of previous shopping conflicts.

"I'd think you'd be happy I brought you here," Maud said, opening the door.

"I don't feel like getting a bathing suit."

"You can buy a few other things too."

Maud's impression of the clothing chain as overpriced, cult-like, and ridiculous (it had an urban cowboy theme) was not lessened by the sight of two shirtless white boys in ten-gallon hats who greeted them as they walked inside.

"Yuck," Louise whispered.

"Agreed," Maud whispered back, although there was no need to lower her voice given the cowpunk music blaring through the store. Ella gave the boys a nervous wave, then beelined for a wall of T-shirts. Maud stifled her opinions about the clothes that Ella heaped into her arms: a bandanna repurposed as a tank top, jeans that seemed to have passed several times through a shredder. Later, though, in the dressing room, when Ella parted the curtain to show them her first selection, Maud almost gasped as Louise applauded. In a spaghetti-strap sundress, her thick hair flooding her bare shoulders, her body all soft, delicate lines, Ella was stunningly beautiful.

"You look amazing," Maud said. "Do you feel good in it? That's the important thing."

"Pretty good," Ella said.

Instead of a bathing suit, she'd chosen a bikini top and board shorts from the boys' section.

"Why didn't you want a suit?" Maud asked as they walked back to their hotel, the sidewalk now empty.

"Board shorts are cool."

"Are you feeling self-conscious about your body, honey?"

When Ella didn't answer, Maud improvised a speech about loving yourself as you are and about Ella's body being healthy and strong.

"Strong means fat," Ella said.

"No, it doesn't." Maud remembered the math teacher's phone call about Ella staying in the bathroom during her test. Could she be making herself throw up? "Are you trying to lose weight?"

Ella rolled her eyes. "God. No. I'm not anorexic or something. I just like board shorts."

As they caught up with Louise, who was gawking at a Tiffany's window, Maud scanned Ella's body, looking for any change and seeing none. And Ella's appetite seemed fine as they ate dinner in the Theater District before a show.

"She does spend a lot of time in the bathroom," Peter said when Maud asked him if he'd noticed anything odd with Ella's eating.

"Check under the toilet lid for vomit splash," Annette advised. "That's how I knew with my housemate."

Back at Montgomery Place the following day, Maud looked under the toilet lid and saw nothing. A battalion of toner, moisturizer, concealer, and body spray lined the counter. Makeup tubes and boxes cluttered the drawers.

The bathtub caddy held three kinds of shampoo and conditioner. Ella's razor lay on the lip of the tub. Maud remembered being thirteen herself, and how terrified she'd been by the wiry hairs that poked out of her pubis, the fur that grew on her legs, the scarlet mountain ranges that broke the surface of her forehead, the crusty blood on her underwear. Everything erupting and oozing and out of control—the body becoming something that wasn't even yours.

They met Gabriel for dinner in the formal garden with the picnic Maud and the girls had picked up on the way home from the city. She kept an eye on Ella, but she polished off her pasta salad and caprese sandwich.

"Look," Louise said. "The mansion's on fire."

The sun had coated the roof in a golden haze. In the garden, a broken-winged Cupid pranced in a bed of white roses, arrow ready to strike, as a terra-cotta Psyche sank into a sea of bluebells. Come September, Montgomery Place would open again. Visitors would walk these paths, and their faces would brighten. Beauty, Maud thought, as the sunlight turned to embers. She was selfish and wrong about so much, but she helped to make beauty. She would never let that go again.

Although Maud had hoped that Ella would have adjusted to camp by now, several weeks into her stay she continued to complain, whereas Louise burst into the parking lot with delighted reports of the day's activities.

"Everyone else is twelve," Ella said. She slumped in the backseat as Maud pulled onto the road one afternoon.

"I thought it was their polo shirts," Maud teased.

"It's all of it."

Chronologically, Ella wasn't much older than the other

girls, but she'd passed a threshold they hadn't met. Their chests were still flat, their knees still knobby, and their hips narrow. One girl arrived each morning with a teddy bear.

"Let's talk about it tonight," Maud said. "It's our field trip afternoon."

She herself was determined to stop thinking so much about Gabriel. He kept invading her mind, distracting her from what she was doing. That morning, she'd dumped a bag of compost on the wrong bed. She'd cut new blooms off a yarrow. Every night, she looked too forward to ten o'clock, when they could be alone together.

Ella brooded on the drive to Washington Irving's house in Sleepy Hollow. She brooded on the tour. She brooded during dinner, furiously twirling spaghetti around the tines of her fork. Maud tried to stay out of her angry energy field and focus on Louise. But by the time they drove home, her patience had eroded.

"What is wrong?" she snapped at Ella, who was scowling in the passenger seat.

"Nothing. I'm just not jumping around like you guys."

"We weren't jumping," Louise said from the backseat. "We were skipping."

"You don't have to ruin the day for everyone," Maud said.

Ella's face collapsed. "I'm sorry."

One hand on the wheel, Maud reached out to hug her, but Ella slipped closer to the door.

"How can I help you feel better?" she said. And be less of a drag, she thought.

"I don't want to go to that camp anymore."

"It's the best camp around."

"Five stars on campers.com," Louise said.

"Whatever," Ella said.

Instead of calling Peter, Maud talked the problem through with Gabriel that night.

"I should have known better." She sighed. "When we got there the first day and the counselors were singing a good-morning song, Ella looked like she might kill someone. I wanted them to love it here so much."

"Can she skip it?"

"And stay around here all day? No way. She needs structure. She'd just be on her phone."

The camp that Louise and Ella attended did offer a half-day horseback riding program for teens. But, Maud explained to Gabriel, in that case she'd have to pick up Ella at noon and then return again three hours later for Louise. Her workday would be chopped in two.

"It sounds like the pain of having her unhappy in camp might be worse than the pain of picking her up early," Gabriel said.

"You might be right."

When, the next morning, she proposed the plan to Peter, he grunted. "Is it safe for her to be alone at Montgomery Place in the afternoons?"

"I'm so close by. The director is in and out of her office. Construction's done in the mansion, so no one else is around these days."

"What about that guy?"

"What guy?" Did he mean Gabriel? Peter hadn't mentioned him since that phone call on the porch.

"The one that helps you. She told me he freaks her out."

"Chris? She's misinterpreting signals. I hope you reinforced that with her."

"I've never met the man," Peter said icily. "I'm simply reporting what our daughter said."

"Anyway, I was going to tell Ella to stay inside when she's alone. That'll be one of the rules."

If Ella were a boy, Maud thought after hanging up, would they have had that conversation? During her childhood, she used to ride her bike, helmetless, all over Burlingame. The risks existed—that man at the swimming pool—but her parents didn't seem to register them. After school, they had no idea where she was, and as long as she showed up for dinner, no one worried. Even if she was late, no one worried; instead, they yelled at her for not checking her watch. Maybe her parents' generation had been naive about the dangers, but parenting now seemed to demand an unhealthy level of paranoia.

That afternoon, she offered Ella a deal. She could switch to the camp's half-day horseback riding program. "But your dad and I don't want you on your phone or watching TV all afternoon, so you're going to have to figure out a project."

Ella leaped up from the couch and hugged her. "I'll read half a book a week."

"A book a week."

"Thanks, Mom," Ella said, hugging Maud again. "Thank you, thank you, thank you."

By the following Tuesday, everything had been arranged, and Maud picked up Ella from the camp at noon. "It's still kind of lame," she said, "but way, way less lame."

Back at the farmhouse, Maud pulled peanut butter and jelly out of the cupboards as Ella unpacked her backpack.

"I'll make you a sandwich," she said.

"I can do it, Mom. I'll be fine. I'll eat something and then read."

"No going to the tree to FaceTime your friends, okay? Stay inside. It's only three hours."

"I guess I can make it," Ella said, feigning despair.

"You can always text or call me. Harriet's usually down in her office. And Gabriel gets back here around one to work in his cottage. So, if there's an emergency, you can find one of them. But call me right away first."

"Yup," Ella said, waving her off. "'Bye. Go to work. I'll see you guys at three-fifteen. I'll have read fifty pages."

On her way back to the site, Maud texted Gabriel:

Oh my God. She seems so happy. Horse camp saves the day!

On the Fourth of July, Maud organized a canoe trip with the girls, borrowing canoes from Frazer and Lydia. She wanted to find the remnants of a folly—a false ruin popular during the Gilded Age—on the island across from Montgomery Place. Guests at the estate used to take evening rowboat excursions to see the stone structure, which was lit by torches and contained plundered Mayan statues. When she announced the plan to the girls on Friday night, Louise jumped up and down.

"Gabriel was hoping to come," Maud said, "but it's up to you guys."

"Sure," Ella said. "Maybe he can rescue us if we drown."

"We're not going to drown. What do you think, Louise?"

"Yes! But I want to row."

The next morning, the four of them walked the canoes across the road from Frazer and Lydia's farm, wearing moldy teal life vests, flip-flops slapping on the asphalt.

"I don't get why you want to see a folly," Ella said as they navigated through the gates. "It's fake history in history. Just like Disneyland but back then."

"My parents boycott Disneyland," Louise explained to Gabriel. She was walking in the shade of the canoe that he was carrying over his head.

"There are more interesting places to go," Maud told Louise, then said to Ella, "Maybe you won't like the folly, but you'll like canoeing."

"I hate canoeing," Ella said.

"You've never been canoeing."

"I've been rowboating. Same thing."

"I thought you loved going to Stowe Lake."

When they'd lived in England and visited her parents, she used to take the girls to Golden Gate Park, as she'd once done with her favorite grandmother. They tossed pink popcorn to passing ducks on Stowe Lake, held their breath under the bridge with the troll living under it, and then strolled from the lake to the Japanese Tea Garden for sesame cookies and sencha served in thimble-like cups.

But Ella wasn't buying nostalgia. "Follies are fake history in history," she said. "That's all I'm saying."

"My parents wouldn't even let us get the Disney Princesses," Louise told Gabriel as she carefully matched his pace to stay out of the sun. "Everyone had them but us."

"Help," Maud said to Gabriel. "Mutiny."

"Drop the canoe and run," Gabriel said.

"Yeah, do that," Ella said. "Then we won't have to get in it." But her grumpiness this morning was almost playful.

The woods moved over them and, with them, mosquitoes.

"Shithead," Ella said. She stopped to stomp a mosquito off her leg, and Maud almost dropped her half of the canoe.

"Ella," she said.

"Well, they are. And I can't use my hands because I'm carrying this stupid canoe."

"Yes, yes, we know the canoe is stupid."

"They bite me too," Gabriel said. "We let off a lot of carbon dioxide, you and me. Let's move faster, maybe that'll help." He started to run, and Ella ran with him, pulling Maud down the hill.

At the river, Louise stood on the shore and surveyed the water skeptically before stepping into the canoe. "This river is pretty," she said, "but it kinda smells like poop."

"It'll smell better when we get out of the algae," Maud said, handing her an oar. They rowed through the chartreuse blanket. Ella and Gabriel were in the canoe ahead, Ella paddling hard, jerking her oar through the water.

"Who are you trying to impress?" Maud called.

"I want to get it over with," Ella said.

"You're making me look bad," Gabriel said.

Maud had a vague idea of where to find the ruins of the folly. She and Gabriel had figured it out two nights before, during one of those conversations where they got lost in their back-and-forth about her knowledge of Romanticism and the obsession with ruins and jungles and his knowledge of those jungles themselves and the real ruins being replicated. But a problem emerged as they approached the island. The shore was a marsh. When Gabriel got out of the canoe, his feet disappeared to the ankles in muck.

"Is this quicksand?" Louise peered over the edge of the canoe. They tried paddling farther down the shore but were met by impenetrable creepers.

"I think this expedition is doomed," Gabriel said.

"Explorers often meet with disappointment," Maud said.

"Then maybe they should stay home," Ella said.

"Let's go there instead." Gabriel pointed to the opposite shore, where a rope swing dangled from a tree.

"It's probably private property," Louise said.

"The swing is over the river. The Hudson's not private property."

Five minutes later, as they made their way through the water, Louise's paddling had been reduced to the occasional halfhearted swipe. Maud hauled them along, listening to the conversation that had started in the canoe ahead.

"I hate my school," Ella told Gabriel.

"I feel you. Middle school is the worst. But in another year, you'll be in high school and have lots of freedom."

He gave Ella an abbreviated, sanitized version of his teenage years, without the drugs and early sex.

"That's crazy," Ella said after he described his father, who had once tied him to a chair and shaved his head because he wouldn't get a haircut.

"Adults can be crazy."

"You're an adult."

"But I'm not a parent, so I'm a little better. No?"

"If you say so." Ella smacked her arm.

"Was that another shithead?"

"Yeah. They follow me everywhere."

"Then stop giving them directions."

"Ha, ha."

The rope swing dangled from an oak tree that jutted off the shore. After docking the canoe, Gabriel grabbed the end of the rope and swung himself out, landing with a splash in the river.

"Try it," he called, as he treaded water.

"No way," Ella said.

"It's fine if you don't open your mouth."

Maud did wonder about bacterial poisoning, but she grabbed the rope and swung out too.

"Mom," Louise shrieked delightedly, "you're swimming in poop."

"We are not getting in your shitty river," Ella said, laughing at the two of them as they strode out of the river, streaked with algae. "And I'm not going back in your canoe," she told Gabriel.

"Looks like we're stuck together," he said to Maud.

As they paddled back to Montgomery Place, Maud saw it clearly, like the final draft of a garden design. She and Peter would get divorced. She'd take on landscaping projects around the Bay Area, even if they didn't appeal to her and involved no history. She'd rent an apartment in Sausalito near the girls' school. She and Gabriel would email and text and talk on the phone when he was on his dig in Turkey. They'd become even closer. By the time he entered her life with the girls, Ella and Louise would have adjusted to the divorce, and Peter would have moved on to his own new life as well. Ahead on the river, Louise was paddling vigorously in her desire to compete with Ella, and the girls' canoe had almost reached shore. Maybe, Maud thought, one day the four of them would go canoeing at Yosemite. Or rafting down the Grand Canyon. They'd become one of those outdoorsy families with tents and dirt bikes in the garage. She moved her paddle in sync with Gabriel's and gave in to the fantasy.

6

Peter called one morning as Maud sat at the desk in the archives, scribbling notes. Two more weeks had gone by and the garden was filling in, leaves unfurling, petals multiplying, so she'd turned her attention to the conservatory.

"How's Ella?" Peter said.

"Good. Why?"

"You worried me when you said there might be something happening with her eating. I started to fret about it last night. She barely tells me anything when I call."

"You know how she is about telling us things." Maud closed a folder. "Her eating seems fine, and it doesn't look like she's lost weight. I'm sure she's not making herself throw up"—she'd checked under the toilet lid again several times—"and her mood is much better."

She had started to wonder, in fact, whether Ella was better because her parents weren't together. She now chatted with Maud on the way back from horse camp. Evenings, at the table with Gabriel, she told stories and made jokes. She still got crabby, and Maud caught her glowering at times, but overall there had been a real improvement.

"I don't like living apart from them," Peter said.

"You'll see them in less than three weeks."

He was coming for his visit, and she dreaded his arrival: his eyes on her garden, her conservatory, her farmhouse. She cringed at the thought of sleeping with him in that bed where she slept so well alone, where she lay in the stillness of night thinking about Gabriel.

"You aren't hearing me," Peter said. "I don't want to live apart from my children."

"It won't be like this. We'll work out a schedule."

"I'll want more time with them than you think. I'm not doing every other weekend."

Through the window, a moving van had pulled up to the mansion—rumbling, kicking up gravel on the drive—and was now backing up to the steps, where Harriet waited. Maybe being alone with the girls for those weeks in Marin had given Peter new confidence in his parenting. What if he asked for joint custody? Maud had never considered that possibility. She couldn't conceive of living without the girls half the time.

"We'll figure it out," she said, failing to keep her voice in line.

"I'll go to counseling like you wanted."

"I wanted that years ago, Peter. It's too late."

"You're being a child," Peter said, and like a blade cutting through her fear, Maud's resolve returned. Peter was the child, taking what he wanted, doing as he pleased behind her back with who knew how many women. She understood the urge to stop thinking and to let your body take what it wanted. She felt that way often with Gabriel. But it was always her job to be the responsible one, the patient one, the blind one in the marriage.

"I'm forty years old, Peter," she said, and hung up on him.

Dragon tree, date palm—she wrote down the names of the plants from Downing's letters. A grapery had once climbed up a glass wall, and the grapes, she decided, had probably been Concord. With each plant name, her body relaxed, but she still felt unsettled. Her work was also an escape, wasn't it? She was always running away. She was a leaver, as her mother said. She had run away to England. She'd run away to Monk's House. She'd run away here. She was still afraid of Peter, of his logic and coolheaded power, afraid of what he might do when he knew all hope was lost and they sat on opposing sides of a negotiation table. That young woman who thought herself so bold to go abroad at twenty-two had headed straight into a traditional marriage with a traditional man. The facts of her life clashed with her self-perception, but then wasn't it true, she thought, that in a marriage you grew into the space left for you? How might she have evolved if she'd chosen a partner like Gabriel?

He brought a bottle of champagne to dinner that night. "Hate to drink it out of mugs, but we have to work with what we've got."

"The first champagne cup was molded from Marie Antoinette's boobies," Louise said, cackling.

"Louise!" Ella yelped.

"Sad to say, that's not true," Maud said.

"She did get her head chopped off, though." Ignoring her sister's mortified expression, Louise was plopping macaroni and cheese onto their plates. The girls had wanted to make dinner tonight, and the result was a gooey mess.

"Yes, she did," Maud said to Louise. "What are we celebrating?" she asked Gabriel.

"Whatever you want. You said you liked champagne when we went out to lunch."

"When did you go out to lunch?" Ella handed Maud her plate.

"Oh, ages ago. At the restaurant with the snails that you and Louise rejected."

"Everyone cover your eyes!" Gabriel aimed the bottle at the orchard and popped the cork.

"Can they have a little?" he asked Maud.

"Sure," she said. He poured a finger of the champagne into a mug for Louise and another for Ella.

"Shouldn't I get more than her?" Ella said.

"In that case, I should get more than your mother."

"That's fine, as long as I get more than Louise," Ella said.

She sipped the champagne, holding the mug with her pinkie finger in the air. Maud had started to think that she might have developed a crush on Gabriel. She changed outfits before dinner into her favorite T-shirt and a fresh pair of shorts. Earlier, she'd repainted her toenails before they went outside. Maud once had a similar crush on the owner of the Burlingame movie theater where she'd worked as a teenager. She used to scoop the popcorn with extra flair whenever he walked by.

Gabriel had retrieved the cork from the grass and was holding it to his eye, making the girls chortle. Ella's laughter rose to a trill. Teenage girls could be such coquettes without even realizing it, Maud thought, as Ella swung her bare leg back and forth, talking about the champagne bubbles going up her nose. It was normal and harmless and also somewhat annoying.

For the next two days, rain pummeled the valley, foaming the Hudson and casting moody clouds over the Catskills. The girls' camp closed due to flooding. After breakfast, raincoats over their pajamas, umbrellas up, they went on a puddle walk and then stayed in the farmhouse, drinking malted milk, doing puzzles, and playing board games.

Having given up working at the muddy dig, Gabriel came by and joined them for Monopoly.

"You be the top hat because you're a boy," Louise said.

"That's sexist," Ella said.

"So should I be the thimble?" Maud said to Louise.

"I think you should be the ship," Ella told Gabriel.

"Nice. Why the ship?" Gabriel said. He was cross-legged on the floor, knees bent awkwardly.

"Because you travel all over the place," Ella said. "And there isn't a plane."

"That's fine," Louise said. "It's a battleship. And I'm a pacifist."

"A sexist pacifist," Ella said. She lined up her stacks of money.

Louise stuck out her tongue and lowered her face as if she might cry.

Gabriel looked from one of them to the other. "I'll be the dog, how about that?"

"I don't feel like playing anymore." Ella pushed herself off the floor and left for the bedroom. Music started to play on her phone, the volume turned to maximum. The words "fucking," "pussy," "ho," blasted down the hall.

"She listens to a lot of inappropriate songs," Louise told Gabriel, as she sorted her Monopoly cash.

Maud called to Ella to shut her door, which slammed in reply. A half-hour later, she stormed down the hall, studiously not looking into the living room. The refrigerator door banged, a glass clunked down, the faucet ran, the bedroom door slammed again.

"I might sleep in your bed tonight," Louise told Maud.

"I guess I should go talk to her," Maud said.

"I'll head out," Gabriel said. "Louise is gonna win anyway."

Maud walked him to the porch. The rain had washed the blue from the sky and was cascading off the roof.

"Sorry," she said.

"I should have stuck with the battleship."

"Ella's so hot and cold these days. She gives me whiplash."

"She has a lot going on," Gabriel said. He put his hand on her arm. "We have a lot going on too." His finger touched the crook of her elbow, a shock to her skin.

"I know," she said.

Gabriel appeared to have more to tell her, but he simply said, "See you later." He walked into the rain, head down to keep it off his face. Maud watched until he reached the cottage, wishing she could follow, then she went inside to talk to Ella.

Midafternoon, she took the girls to the conservatory to see the passionflower vine, which had opened the previous day on its iron trellis. Lemon and orange and palm trees stood by the door, ready to be potted. The air had turned fruity and steamy. Water pattered on the glass ceiling, slipping from drop to smear. The passionflowers spun their violet-and-white petals, decked with green stamens like spider legs.

"This is officially my favorite flower," Louise said.

"Cool," Ella said. Earlier, when Maud had knocked on her door and asked if she wanted to talk, Ella said no. Still thrown by that moment on the porch with Gabriel, Maud took the pass. Ella seemed fine now. Sometimes, Maud thought, it was better to not talk things out.

In the formal garden, the flowerbeds gulped the rain, rivulets boating pieces of gravel along the path. As they walked to the pond, they came upon Chris and Frazer, who were pulling leaves out of a drainage pipe. Once again, Ella shied away from Chris.

"We're going to find a turtle in the pond," Louise said. "Gabriel thinks he saw one last time we were there."

"Bring a boat," Frazer said. The pond had overflowed, taking down the pussy willows.

"It might all get washed away," Chris said, and Maud didn't know if he meant the pond, the mansion, the grounds of the estate, or the world.

"It has to stop eventually," she said.

As she walked behind the girls, she could feel that place on her arm that Gabriel had touched like a newly discovered valley of her body.

When she picked Ella up at noon the next Monday, the counselor told her that she was learning to trot her horse. "She got over the fear," the woman said brightly.

"I didn't know you were afraid," Maud told Ella in the car as they drove to Montgomery Place. It hurt her feelings that Ella had told this stranger instead of her.

"Not super-scared, but yeah, at first. Horses are huge."

"How did you get over it?"

"Concentrated on getting my foot in the stirrup and holding on to the horn and then getting the reins right. I didn't look at the horse."

Their phones dinged simultaneously. "Hey!" Ella said, looking at hers. "Dad says he's coming to visit a week early."

Maud clenched the steering wheel. "What a wonderful surprise."

She texted Peter the minute she returned to the farmhouse. *What's this about?*

I told you I miss the girls. Are you saying I shouldn't?

Of course not. You're their father.

Good, because I've already changed my ticket. And by the way, I'm also your husband.

At dinner, Ella told Gabriel the news about Peter right away. "That soon?" He took a long sip of beer. "Nice."

"He can rub your shoulders again, Mom," Ella said. She twisted a strand of her hair into a coil. "Did she tell you she has a bad shoulder?" she asked Gabriel.

"Not too bad," Maud said. "An injury from a bike accident decades ago."

She'd told him that story so long ago, back when they could be alone for hours. She missed having an expanse of time with him. And Peter never rubbed her shoulders. What was Ella talking about? Maud felt snared between their two faces: Ella's hostile, Gabriel's uneasy.

"What's with your husband's change of plans?" Gabriel asked her that night as they sat outside.

Maud looked out at the dark mess of orchard. "I think he can tell I'm serious now."

"Are you?" Gabriel said, something that sounded like pleading in his voice.

"Yes," she said. And for the first time she knew for certain that she meant it.

Arms hanging with baskets, Lydia came over one afternoon to help pick the cherries that had ripened in the orchard, leaving Frazer and Chris behind. Ella and Louise climbed into the trees without the ladder and spit the pits at each other through the tunnels of their tongues. They hung cherries over their ears to simulate earrings. Being in the orchard seemed to transport Ella back in time to the days when she led her little sister on outdoor adventures.

"Your daughters are sugar," Lydia said as they strolled under the trees behind Ella and Louise. She wore a wide straw hat with a bent brim and a pair of Frazer's boots. "Where's your charmer? I thought he'd come too."

"Gabriel? Working at his site. He lost so much time with the rain. Where's yours?"

Lydia laughed. "Frazer isn't a charmer. I love the man to death, but he was never handsome."

Maud reached for a handful of cherries. Again, she wondered if everyone at Montgomery Place thought that she and Gabriel were having an affair. It made her uncomfortable to imagine them discussing it, spinning a web of gossip around the two of them.

Back at the house, she and the girls set about making jam. They boiled six glass jars, washed the cherries, and added sugar and water. Standing on a chair, Louise stirred the pot. Once they'd poured the thickened liquid into the jars, they took photos and emailed them to Peter. By five o'clock, Louise was a juice-streaked mess and Ella was finishing the lattice top on the cherry pie she'd made.

At the sound of Gabriel's knock, Ella went to the door. "We've got a surprise for you," Maud heard her say.

"You made this whole thing?" Gabriel said of the pie. He'd come straight from his dig, his magnifying glass still slung around his neck on its leather cord.

"Yup."

"Incredible."

Ella beamed. Then Maud noticed Louise's frown. The jam, she mouthed at Gabriel.

"I hear there's jam," he said.

Louise gave him a spoon and pointed at the table.

"That," he said, after dipping into a jar, "is the best jam I've ever tasted."

"We made it all the time when we lived in England," Ella said. "From quince and plums. We had an orchard."

"Can you eat jam on pie?" Gabriel said.

"Why not?" Maud said. "There are no limits when it comes to sugar."

"You never say that at home," Ella said, and Maud felt her gaze scrape her skin.

"I get a lot of cavities," Louise explained. "The dentist thinks it's because they don't put fluoride in the water in England. Dad thinks he's loony for thinking that."

"Well, I'd like some of that pie with some of that jam for dessert tonight," Gabriel said. But Ella had soured the mood again.

As they ate outside, Maud and Gabriel kept snagging glances. Under the table, she could feel the warmth of his legs, his feet so close to her feet, the change of pressure on the chair when he sat back and laughed. With Peter's impending arrival, the atmosphere felt heightened.

Meanwhile, Ella smacked Gabriel on the shoulder, laughed shrilly, rolled her eyes, vied girlishly for his attention.

"You should come to camp tomorrow," Louise said when Gabriel got up to leave. "It's parents' and grandparents' day, but they said we could invite friends too."

"Yeah," Ella said. "You can see me trot."

"Fine by you?" Gabriel said to Maud.

"Great with me." She continued to stack the dishes.

"It's a date," he said.

"Since we don't have Dad yet," Ella said.

"That was nice of you," Maud told Louise when they'd returned to the farmhouse. "If I'd known you wanted Gabriel there, I would have asked."

"Ella told me to do it. She's giving me a dollar."

"I thought he'd like coming," Ella said, "but I didn't want him to feel like he had to."

"So you paid Louise to ask him?" Maud said.

They were all in the bathroom, Ella brushing her teeth, Louise stripping off her clothes to change into pajamas.

"It was between us," Ella said to Louise. "Don't be a bigmouth."

"Don't be a meanie," Louise said.

"It's nice he's coming," Maud said.

"Can you guys leave so I can change?" Ella said. She spat into the sink.

"Your sister needs to brush her teeth too," Maud said. "Why don't you go change in the bedroom if you want privacy?"

Go to bed, both of you, she thought. Go to bed and go to sleep so I can see him. After reading with Louise, she kissed the girls good night, then sat at the kitchen table waiting for them to collapse, which they finally did at eleven.

Outside, crickets were playing a high-pitched melody in the orchard. Gabriel sat in the dark without their usual candle. "I forgot our light source," he said. "Just wanted to get out here."

"I'll come to you." Maud picked up her chair and moved it closer, the metal table no longer between them, Gabriel inches away. She opened her hand and his fingers slid between hers like a puzzle locking into place.

7

Ella's toast was smoking in the toaster. Maud hadn't added enough coffee grounds to the pot, and her coffee tasted like water with a splash of cream.

"Earth to Mom!" Louise said, after asking again if she could put cookies in her lunch.

Maud couldn't look at Gabriel when he met them by the orchard for the drive to camp, her body so wrenched by yearning. She kept reliving the eternal stretch of time the night before when they'd held hands. Wordlessly, they'd sat next to each other, fingers joined, until Maud said she should go in. Even now, she could feel the callus on his right thumb, his rough palms, the friction of his skin.

At the camp, the girls joined their groups as Maud and Gabriel registered at a picnic table. When he leaned over to sign his name, she wanted to grab his shoulders and pull him in.

"You ready for this?" she said as they headed toward the ropes course, where Louise and her group waited in helmets and harnesses.

"I'm ready for anything," he said.

Louise stuck by Maud as they climbed the ladders, and then they were balancing on a wire twenty feet over the ground. Ahead, hair tufting out from under his helmet, Gabriel exaggerated his wobbliness, tightrope-walking clownishly to make Louise laugh. Following him, lining up one foot in front of another, Maud remembered reading the letters between Virginia Woolf and her lover Vita Sackville-West, and feeling a sad alienation because she herself had never felt that way. *I am reduced to a thing that wants.* She now knew exactly what that meant.

The horse show began down by the swimming hole. Ella and the other girls rode out of the stables, weaving their horses down a line of steel drums. Hands slack on the reins, they followed more than led—clearly, the horses knew what to do on their own. High on the saddle, talking to the horse, Ella looked proud.

"You'd never know how afraid she was," Maud told Gabriel.

She felt his hand on her elbow. His fingers ran down her arm, to her wrist, over her palm. Her breath staggered. His hand moved away. She returned his gaze. When she looked back at the ring, she saw that Ella was watching them, eyes small and mouth set.

That night, as Maud waited to meet Gabriel outside, Ella came down the hall. "Can't sleep. I'm gonna be up all night."

"You will," Maud said. "Just close your eyes."

"I had them closed. It doesn't work."

A half-hour later, Ella was still awake. At eleven, her eyes fluttered when Maud came into the room. Maud went to check at midnight again—Ella sat up and stared back at her before flopping onto her side. Finally, Maud texted Gabriel that she didn't think she'd make it outside.

The same thing happened the next two nights. Ella flipped and scrunched up in her bed and turned to look at Maud when she stood at the door.

It seemed clear that she was trying to keep Maud in the farmhouse. At dinner with Gabriel the following evening, Ella sat next to him, talked to him, and interrupted whenever he said anything to Maud. Again, that night, she wouldn't fall asleep.

I miss you, Gabriel texted.

Maud phoned him from the porch. "Ella's acting strange. But I don't think she could have seen us out there the other night."

She was sure that Ella had been asleep when they held hands, plus you couldn't see the table from the girls' bedroom window, especially without the candle on the table.

"I'll stay up as late as you need," he said. But at one o'clock, Maud finally fell asleep in Ella's bed after scratching her back.

When Louise tried to play with Ella's hair the next morning, Ella ducked her head away. "You'll mess it up."

"I was giving you braids."

"You do them crooked."

Louise's lower lip puckered.

"She's having the teens," Maud said.

"Don't patronize me," Ella said.

"We need to get you more sleep," Maud said.

"That's patronizing."

Ella was relaxed at dinner, but once Gabriel left, she became taciturn again. Later, looking into the bedroom, Maud saw that she was crying. When she touched her shoulder, Ella cringed. The sight of her contorted face filled

Maud with remorse. She sat on the bed until Ella finally fell asleep, as she used to do when she and Peter were training her to sleep alone in their London flat. Across the room, Louise was flung out on the bed, arms and legs akimbo. Maud opened her phone and texted Gabriel, *I'll come by your site tomorrow.*

She'd see him at his workplace in the light of day, not at their table in the dark. She'd tell him that they should no longer be alone with each other, because not touching him during those times felt impossible. She was a middle-aged mother of two children trying to extricate herself from her marriage. He was a lone wolf who rolled around the world, slept in tents, and had never lived with anyone. Annette had been right. There was no hope for anything but a mindless fling.

The next morning, she went to Gabriel's dig after dropping the girls at camp. He met her on the path, tense and bleary-eyed, as if he too hadn't slept well.

"We have to knock this off," she said. "My husband will be here in a few days. I'm not cheating on him, but I feel like I'm cheating on my children." Her voice was reassuringly straight and clear, but her body wasn't listening to her words. "Summer will end. You'll be in Turkey. I'll be in California trying to find a job and figuring things out with Peter."

"What do you mean by figuring out?" Gabriel said, and Maud realized he still worried that she'd stay married.

"Figuring out how to end it without making the girls suffer," she said. A woodpecker was hammering on a maple tree, its head a carmine flicker. "I can't feel this way about you right now."

"I can't feel this way about you either," he said.

He put his hands around her waist, and she hooked her hands around his neck. As they kissed, his lips, his tongue, his entire mouth felt familiar. She pulled up his shirt to feel the skin of his back and the trail of his spine, the furrows made by his ribs.

Hands linked, they walked to the river, the woods alive around them. Maud felt breathless and stunned. But as the water flowed by, reality set in.

"I really think Ella knows," she said. "I think she's trying to keep us away from each other."

"How could she know?"

"Kids sense things. I think she's waiting for me to go to sleep. I'm waiting on her, and she's waiting on me."

"Can't you stay up later?"

"We'd be up all night."

"Then we'll be up all night," Gabriel said, and they kissed again.

At dinner, Ella sipped her Shirley Temple and glared. "My new counselor is so fat, she can barely get on her horse."

"Ella, that's not nice," Maud said.

"You say that, but I saw you looking at her thighs when you dropped me off."

"I wasn't looking at her thighs."

"You think the same things I think. You just don't say them. Like you say smoking is bad and then you and Annette go to the garage and do it whenever we're at Grandma and Grandpa's house."

"You know about that?"

"Everybody knows about that," Louise said. She was fishing a cherry from her drink with a spoon.

"At least your mom isn't too uptight," Gabriel said. "I've told you what my dad was like."

"Why are you taking her side?" Ella said. She got up with her phone and headed to the tree.

Gabriel raised his hands in the air. "I'm on nobody's side," he called after her. "I'm Switzerland."

Ella had been reading Jane Austen's *Emma* that week. But Maud had started to wonder if she had actually been reading any of the books that she said she was reading during the day, or if she was simply looking up summaries. She never had anything specific to say about the plots or characters. The question returned later as they finished eating and Ella described the story to Gabriel. "She's this girl who thinks she knows everything, but she's actually an ingénue," she said, mispronouncing the word.

"It's ahn-génue, honey," Maud told Ella. "Like *on* the table."

She knew well because she had mispronounced the same word in a discussion her freshman year at Amherst and had been mortified when a fellow classmate corrected her publicly. After that, she never used a complicated word in class again.

"That's not how it's spelled," Ella said.

Where? Maud thought. On Wikipedia, where you read about the book? "But that's how it's pronounced," she said.

"No, it isn't."

"Could I borrow the book when you're done?" Gabriel asked Ella, clearly trying to defuse the tension. "I've only seen the movie."

Maud took out her phone. "Let's look it up," she said to Ella.

"The signal's too weak out here. You'll have to go to the tree." Ella's smile was a challenge.

"We'll go inside," Maud said stiffly. "Come on."

They walked to the farmhouse, where Louise was fetching ice-cream bars. Ella dragged after Maud, kicking at the porch steps. Inside, Maud typed the word on her laptop and played the pronunciation.

"So what?" Ella said.

"Why are you acting like this?" Maud said.

"You're showing off," Ella said. "You always show off in front of Gabriel."

Look who's talking, Maud thought.

In the girls' bedroom later, when Ella said she couldn't sleep, Maud told her that she'd scratch her back if she wanted.

"I'm too old for that."

"Do you want to talk about anything?" Maud said. "Is something wrong?"

"I'm trying to sleep," Ella said to the wall.

With her free hand, Maud took her phone from her pocket and awkwardly texted Gabriel. *Think won't make it.*

Try? He texted back.

"Who are you texting?" Ella asked.

"Your dad."

She sat on the bed for another twenty minutes, waiting for Ella's breaths to lengthen.

"I think I'll go to bed, sweetheart," she said finally. "Is that all right?"

"What do I care?" Ella said.

Twenty minutes later, Maud heard Ella walk down the hall and stand at the door. Twenty minutes after that, when she tiptoed to the girls' room, Ella was asleep.

By the orchard, Gabriel sat in the dark. Even if the girls

were to look through the windows of the farmhouse, Maud thought, as she made her way over the grass, they'd see only nebulous shapes. She sat in the chair next to Gabriel and took the hand that waited for hers on the armrest. All thoughts of the tension with Ella disappeared.

"Can we just go over there?" Gabriel said, nodding at the orchard.

"You know how we'd end up," she said. "Rolling around on rotten cherries."

His middle finger traced a circle in her palm. "Always the grown-up."

"Someone has to be," she said softly.

Gabriel squeezed her fingers. "Maud, I've never felt this way."

"I haven't either," she said. "But where can it go?"

"I'll do anything to make it work. I'll drop out of the dig in Turkey. I'll find something in California."

"You can't do that. That dig is too important to you." Her heart flipped; his saying he'd do so meant everything. "When I go back, I'm facing at least a year of hell," she said.

"Then I'll wait a year," he said. "I'll wait as long as it takes."

"This is crazy, you realize." She squeezed his hand back.

"No, it's not. We're good together. You know that."

Inside, after checking on the sleeping girls, Maud collected herself and called Peter.

"Ella's having such a rough time," she told him. "She still doesn't like camp. She misses her friends. Maybe she and Louise should fly back home with you when you come this weekend."

She'd had the idea between the table and the front door.

"It's only a three-week difference if they come back with you as planned," Peter said.

"It's not just that she's unhappy here. Managing her is starting to interfere with my work. I can't focus. I want to finish up well. Can you handle it? I'll fly back a week early, so I'll only be apart from them for two weeks."

The wait for his reply felt interminable.

"Of course I can handle it," Peter said. "They're my children."

She told him she'd make calls to find a camp in Marin that would take Louise during the day and see if there was a spot in the camp Ella had attended last summer.

"I thought she hated camp," Peter said.

"She liked that one. Or I'll find something else."

She said she'd call the airline to change the girls' tickets to match his flight home. She suggested that they tell the girls together when he arrived. Peter agreed. Hanging up, she couldn't believe how smoothly that had gone. She'd have two weeks alone with Gabriel. Two weeks to see if this impossible feeling was real.

Her mother called the next afternoon after Maud had dropped Ella back at the house and was spraying a rosebush for aphids.

"I hear you're returning your children," her mother said.

"My children are going home with their father. And then I'll be back."

"I thought you were done with your restoration."

"I'm still working in the garden."

"Hasn't that place been getting by without you for two hundred years?"

Then Annette called as Maud was putting away tools in the carriage house.

"Mom says you're sending the girls back with Peter," she said.

"How did she know about it in the first place?"

"Peter called her to ask if he could drop them off there on Saturday, because he's got some work thing. But she has a parish fundraiser, so she asked me to do it. Why didn't you tell me first?"

"It's been a little nuts this past week. Ella's being awful."

"You should come back with them. Forget about that guy."

"It's not about him."

"I don't believe you. You're being cagey."

"I'm not. I have to go. I'll call you tonight."

She hung the shears on the wall next to the shovel, along the tidy line of tools arranged by Chris. She only had to make it to the moment when the girls and Peter got on that plane, and then she could think clearly again.

She texted Gabriel. *Could we meet on the grounds tomorrow? She'll be up again tonight.*

Yes, where?

At the hedge? 2? After I drop her home from camp?

The reply came in a half-hour later.

Perfect.

The next day, she went into the farmhouse with Ella after picking her up from camp and made them both sandwiches. She brought hers to the living room couch instead of eating it on the walk back to the site, as she usually did.

"Don't you have to go?" Ella said.

"I wanted to spend some time with you. What are you reading today?"

"*O Pioneers!*"

"Do you like it?"

"No."

"We could go to the bookstore in town later."

"If you want."

"Or with your dad when he gets here tomorrow."

Ella didn't reply. The forced cheer was exhausting, and Maud was glad to finally walk outside and head toward the mansion. Chris and Frazer had been helping her in the conservatory, and they were still there. Frazer held a ladder as Chris attached the grapevines to their trellis. Maud wound a snail flower up a post. She thinned the ferns. Trapped in the glass, warmed by the sun, the spreading leaves and coiling vines sweated, dampening the air.

At two o'clock, she told Chris and Frazer that she'd be back soon. She hurried past the mansion and to the hedge, where Gabriel waited.

"I'm sending the girls home with Peter," she told him.

He looked surprised. "Will they want that?"

"I don't think they'll care much. Ella misses her friends. And I really think she knows something is happening with us. I need to get myself together. I can't think straight anymore."

"I can't think either," he said. "I'm going to head out for the next couple of days until he's gone. To my place in Ithaca."

"He doesn't matter," Maud said.

They stood there staring at each other, not knowing what to do or say. Gabriel spoke first. "I love you," he said.

"I love you too." The words came out as if they'd always been there, waiting to surprise her.

And then they were walking away from the hedge, through the trees, deeper and deeper into the forest. She pulled her shirt over her head and unclasped her bra. She didn't know who this woman was that leaned back against a trunk to tug this man closer, digging her fingers into his skin, but she let herself go and surrendered.

8

Gabriel slipped away from Maud's body, and she returned to the world. Her lower back burned from pushing against bark. Her ankles were caught in the grip of her pants. She pulled up the waistband and tucked in her shirt, but she was still floundering, unable to breathe. Gabriel kissed her neck below her ear. They said it again. "I love you."

As they walked out of the forest together, Maud felt both elated and overwhelmed. No one saw, she thought. It was all right. They were in love. And somehow they'd figure out how to end up together.

"I'll text you," Gabriel said before they parted at the hedge. The quick brush of his fingers on her waist steadied her again.

In the conservatory, Frazer and Chris were sweeping soil from the floor. As Maud tried to focus on clipping faded leaves from a fig tree, her phone buzzed.

You're sure you're OK? In the truck now, about to go. But if it's better that I stay, I'll stay. You tell me what to do. A bubble appeared and disappeared, appeared again.

She wanted to drop her gloves and run down the drive to the parking lot where he sat in his truck.

Yes, she texted. *Better than OK. I'll be waiting for you when you're back.*

I meant it.

I meant it too.

That evening, as she and the girls stood in the arrivals area at JFK, Maud anticipated remorse or pain at the sight of Peter's face, but she only felt numb when he walked off the plane. He was wearing a casual suit, as if he'd come straight from a meeting, with his reading glasses hooked on his shirt collar. His gray eyes mellowed when he saw the girls, and he set down his suitcase and computer bag to gather them into a hug. He pecked Maud on the mouth and they walked through the parking lot toward the car as Ella bolted ahead.

"I don't think she slept at all last night," Maud told Peter. "I heard her going to the bathroom twice."

"Looks like fresh air and sunshine weren't all she needed after all," he said.

She could make out the vein in his temple that swelled when he was upset. Maybe he didn't know that she'd been naked in the woods with another man hours ago, but he did know she was serious about a divorce.

On the drive, excited to have her father there or maybe nervous about the tension in the car, Louise pointed out the Hudson, the Catskills, the pharmacy in Red Hook with its old-fashioned candy counter.

"I can't wait for you to drop me at camp on Monday," she told Peter.

Maud glanced at Louise in the rearview mirror. She hadn't thought over this part of things carefully enough. She was sure that Ella wouldn't mind going home early, but that might not be the case for Louise.

As they pulled up to the farmhouse, Peter said, "I need to have a chat with your mum. You two head in."

"Why?" Ella said.

"We have something to discuss between adults."

Maud assumed that he wanted them to figure out how they were going to announce the early return to Marin. "Do you want to sit down?" she said.

Peter stayed by the car, looking at the cottage, where the windows were dark and the porch light off.

"Is that where he lives?" he said.

Maud almost said, "Who?" but didn't. "Yes."

"I can't wait to meet him."

"He's not here."

"Was he afraid I'd pack a sword?"

"I told you," Maud said. "We're friends."

"I gave you what you wanted," Peter said. The vein in his temple throbbed. "All the bloody space in the world. Let you take off with my children for the summer. And right away you start fucking some archaeologist."

"I'm not fucking him." Maud kept her face still and unreactive, feeling herself start to panic about the lie.

Peter blew out a stream of air. "I told myself, Okay, she needs to get back at me. Fair enough. But you're going too far now, sending the girls home so you can have a two-week shag fest."

"I'm not shagging him, and our problems aren't about him." Maud took a breath and said what she'd rehearsed on her walk home from the site that afternoon. "I don't love you, Peter. I haven't for years." She saw him wince. She didn't realize that she could still cause him pain.

"You want a fairy tale," he said. "You always have. We made a promise to each other."

"We were too young to make that promise," she said. "Neither of us is happy. I know you aren't either. I know you cheated on me in England. I don't care. And I don't care that you did it again in Marin."

"If you don't care, what are you doing here?"

"I'm here because I need my work," she said. "And because I want out of this marriage. The girls aren't little anymore. They pick up on things. I'm sure we've been part of Ella's problems. She knows more than we think."

"So suddenly this is about Ella."

"That's not fair."

Peter's eyes assessed her, measured her, as if she were a column on a spreadsheet. "Fine," he said. "Take your two weeks. Do what you have to do here. Whatever that is." He started toward the house. "We should go tell them they're coming with me. Louise keeps looking out the window."

Following him, Maud felt smaller and weaker with each step. Maybe she'd gone too far, telling him she didn't love him. That had been cruel. And he was right that she hadn't been thinking about Ella and Louise when she asked him to take them back home. She'd been thinking about Gabriel.

Inside, Peter took the lead. He told the girls that he'd missed them. "Your mum and I think it would be better for you to go back to Marin with me."

"I'll cut my time short and come home in two weeks," Maud said.

"No way," Ella said. She'd been on the couch, under a blanket, and now she stood up, flinging the blanket to the floor. "I'm not going."

"But you've missed your friends," Maud said. She was surprised by the intensity of Ella's reaction.

"What do you know? You don't know anything about me. I can't believe you're doing this."

"We both think this is best," Peter said.

"But what about the camp-out?" Louise said. "We have the camp-out next week, Mum."

Maud had forgotten about the "night under the stars" hosted by the camp. As Louise's mouth trembled, she scrambled for a solution, not finding one. "I didn't know you cared so much about it, sweetheart," she said. "I'll make it up to you."

"You can't do this," Ella yelled.

"We already got the plane tickets."

"Unget them."

"We're supposed to make s'mores and sleep in tents," Louise wailed.

"It's just a little change in the plan," Maud said.

"No, it isn't." Louise laid her face on her knees.

Maud stroked her hair. This is what it will be like when you tell them that you're divorcing, she thought. Only even more brutal.

"I'll take you camping back home," she said. "We'll go to the Headlands."

"We don't have a tent."

"We'll borrow one from Uncle Kevin."

"You don't know how to put it up."

"I'll learn."

As Louise cried, Ella stood by, fierce and silent. Peter looked at Maud as if asking her what to do. "I'm sorry you're both upset," he said, then moved into repair mode, telling the girls that he would do half-days at the office for the next two weeks for fun activities like the Exploratorium and Ghirardelli Square. "Pick something, Ella," he said.

"No."

"And when I get back, I'll take you guys to Big Sur," Maud said. "What do you think? We can stop to see the elephant seals on the way."

Louise's face was still on her knees, but her shoulders had stopped shaking. "Can we go to the Santa Cruz Boardwalk too?" she said in a small voice.

"Sure." Maud gathered Louise in a hug, feeling slightly better. She and Peter seemed to be working as a team. Maybe it would be all right. He'd calm down and see her perspective, see that he'd be happier without her too.

"I'm going to bed," Ella said.

When Maud started to follow her, Peter shook his head, so she let Ella go.

They sat with Louise at the kitchen table, playing Old Maid. Together, they tucked her into bed. Ella was asleep, and they kissed her forehead, one after the other. Then they were alone in the living room.

"I think that went okay," Maud said.

Peter's face cracked into a bitter smile. "It was brilliant. Just brilliant."

"It doesn't have to be awful."

"I already know what it's like."

"We aren't your parents." She touched his hand, and he yanked his arm away.

"Do not try to manage me." He spat out the words.

"Do you want help making up the couch?" she said. When he didn't answer, she told him there were sheets in the closet and left for her room.

Lying in bed, she felt emptied and eerily calm. She wanted Gabriel to hold her, but he was away in Ithaca. She held a pillow to her chest and fell asleep.

Someone was tapping on her shoulder. Moonlight pooled through the window. Louise stood by the bed in her pajamas. "Ella's gone," she said.

"What do you mean, gone?" Maud said.

"Not in her bed."

Blinking herself awake, Maud followed Louise down the hall. The alarm clock in the girls' room read 3:16. Ella's bed was empty, as was the bathroom. Then Maud noticed that her backpack no longer hung on a hook by the front door and her phone was gone from the charger in the kitchen. She woke up Peter.

"Ella went somewhere."

"Where?"

"I don't know. She's not here. She took her backpack and her phone."

Peter dialed Ella's number, but the call went straight to voicemail. "She must have turned it off," he said. "I should have downloaded that tracking app, goddammit."

Maud grabbed flashlights from the kitchen drawer, and they hurried outside, Louise trailing behind. The lights shone on the claw of a tree, the stump of a garbage can.

"What if someone took her?" she whispered to Peter. The quiet tempo of worry was becoming the fast beat of panic.

"I'll check the road," he said.

"I'll check the grounds."

Louise had walked to the edge of the orchard and was shouting out Ella's name.

"Don't worry," Maud called. "We'll find her. She was mad. She probably went somewhere to calm down."

But where would she go in this darkness? Peter was getting into the car and told Louise to come with him. "Your sister might have taken a walk," he said, as if that made any sense.

Maud ran down the drive toward the mansion, through the sticky, damp night, past clumps of trees, the empty lawn, the flash of eyes from a phantom deer. The conservatory glowed in the moonlight. No Ella. The mansion was locked, so she couldn't be inside. The pond? She looked down the slope, calculating shapes.

"Where are you?" she said.

She headed to the coach house, hurrying through its crepuscular rooms filled with two centuries of ice cutters and carriages. Nothing. No one. The gravel on the drive crunched like bones breaking. She stopped by the trail to the woods and phoned Peter. "Anything?"

"No. We're back. I'm ringing the police."

Down the trail into the trees she ran, stumbling over a root. "Please, God," she said. The blood whooshed through her head. An owl screeched. Would Ella come here? Why would she be in any of these places? But where else to look? If only she were around that bend, standing on the shore, looking at the Hudson. But the shore was empty. The oak leaves rattled in the breeze.

As she ran back up the trail, that terrifying thought rose again: a stranger, a kidnapping, Ella dragged from her bed.

She slowed down and texted Gabriel: *Ella's gone. Do you know where she could be?* She was crying by the time she reached the top of the trail. Please, God, she thought. Give her back. She would return home with Peter and the girls. She would stay in the marriage. She would never speak to Gabriel again. She would do anything.

Back in front of the farmhouse, Peter was talking to a police officer, a man with a goatee whose calm demeanor made Maud more frightened. He said they had sent out patrol cars to look for Ella.

"We almost always find these kids in the first hours," he said.

Maud heard only "almost."

"Has your daughter had problems lately?" the officer added.

"She's a teenager," Peter said. "But nothing out of the ordinary."

Maud had never seen him so afraid, his face so closed, his voice so wobbly. But this wasn't his fault. She was the one who had decided the girls should leave early. She had made Ella run away.

The officer asked her to list everywhere that she'd taken Ella, repeating the places into his walkie-talkie for the other officers who were searching. Sleepy Hollow. The Italian restaurant. "We also went to the city." Maud told him the name of the camp. "These places are all so far away."

"She might have hitched," the officer said. "Has she before?"

"No. No. She's never done anything like this."

Who was on the roads in the middle of the night? Men. Men who had drunk too much and wove their cars into the bike lanes. Men with guns in their glove compartments. Men with rope in their trunks.

"And no one around lately at this place?" the officer said. "Any strangers? Anything you've noticed?"

"What do you mean?" Peter said, and Maud saw Ella sobbing in blackness. Ella gagged, wrists bound. Ella calling out for her mother.

"There's just me and the archaeologist who lives down there," she said, her voice quavering. "He's away."

"Ma'am, I know it's hard," the officer said, "but I don't think she's been abducted. Your husband told me her backpack and phone are gone and that he locked the front door when he went to bed. I don't think you'd sleep through a forced entry."

"What about those people you know?" Peter said. "That guy you work with?"

"I'll go," Maud said, already turned to head down the drive, through the gates, across the road. She pounded on Lydia and Frazer's front door. Lydia answered in her robe, her silver hair flowing over her shoulders.

"We can't find Ella," Maud said.

Lydia called to Frazer, and the three of them searched the yard and in the barn. Saying he'd check the road, Frazer drove off in his truck.

"She's going to be okay," Lydia said. She hugged Maud, smelling like mothballs and rosewater. And now Maud had to ask the question that had sent her over the road to the farm. The fear that had intensified as she looked around the property with Frazer and Lydia roiled her body. What if she had been wrong about Chris? Maybe in shirking from him, Ella had recognized something she hadn't.

"Is Chris here?" she said.

Lydia looked confused. "Chris? He's at his sister's in Hudson for the night."

"Are you sure?"

"He left after dinner."

"Could you call?" Maud said.

Lydia's expression hitched. She understood what Maud was asking.

"Could you make sure he's there?" Maud added.

"He texted me when he arrived. He is." Lydia came down hard on the last word. She pulled her robe tighter. She had a long crease down her cheek left by a pillow.

"I need you to call your daughter and make sure he's there," Maud said. "Now, please."

She couldn't worry about what she was doing. All that mattered was finding Ella.

Lydia's lips folded. "I'll get my phone," she said and went inside. From the porch, Maud listened to her apologize to her daughter for waking her up and ask her to check on Chris. "The people across the way can't find their daughter," she said. "Okay. Thanks, babes. Yes, everything's all right."

She came back to the door. "Asleep in bed," she said. "Alone."

"Thank you." Maud backed off the porch.

"Good luck finding her," Lydia said, as she shut the door.

At the farmhouse, the officer had no reports of Ella. She wasn't on the streets of Red Hook or Tivoli. "And the emergency rooms are clear. That's good."

Maud hadn't thought of emergency rooms. She gulped down a breath.

"They're going to check her camp," the officer said.

"It's been four hours. Or more."

A man in a truck. A door opening for Ella. Rope and a blindfold.

Peter put his arm around her shoulders. "They'll find her," he said.

She clung to his arm. "Can you calm Louise down?" she said. "I can't."

He went to Louise, who was circling a tree, sniffling and talking to herself. The officer stepped away and murmured into his walkie-talkie. Above the orchard, the first layer of night had peeled off the sky. An engine slowed on the road, and Maud saw Gabriel's truck pull through the gates.

"I ate dinner and turned around," he said when Maud ran over. "I felt like I was abandoning you." He glanced at Peter and the police officer. "What's going on?"

Maud swallowed a sob. "You didn't see my text?"

"I've been driving."

"Ella's missing. We've looked everywhere."

"Did you check the grounds?"

"Everywhere."

"Have you looked at my place?"

"She can't get in."

"She knows where to find the key."

Without measuring his words, she took off toward the cottage. The door was unlocked. The table was cluttered with crystals and flint. A low hum of a refrigerator came from the kitchen. And there, on a sagging couch in the living room, Ella slept with her backpack under her head. Maud knelt on the floor and grabbed her into a hug. "Wake up, honey." The lights went on, then Peter was beside her with Louise.

Ella's eyes opened. "What's happening?" she said fuzzily.

"You were asleep. What are you doing here?" Maud said.

Ella's brow crumpled. "I started to walk down the road, but it was so dark"—her voice quaked—"I got scared. I was gonna wait here until morning since he was gone." She looked over Maud's shoulder. "Why are you back?" she screamed. "Go away!"

Gabriel stood in the doorway behind the officer, who had come into the room. "Ella," he said. He looked jarred, as if she'd punched him with her voice.

Peter scooped Ella up off the couch. "How did she get in here?" he said to Gabriel. "You don't lock your door?"

"The key's in the pot outside," Gabriel said. "She knows where to find it."

"What are you talking about?" Maud said.

"She came over here a few times to use the Wi-Fi."

"What? When?"

"Move," Peter said to Gabriel. Ella in his arms, he headed through the open door. "Take Louise," he told Maud over his shoulder.

She grabbed Louise's hand and followed him outside, blindly moving past Gabriel.

"Did something happen?" Peter said to Ella, who was crying now. "Did he do something to you, love?"

"Talk," Maud said. "Please."

Ella shook her head and sobbed. Ragged and short, her breathing sounded muffled.

"She's hyperventilating," the officer said. "Could you set her down for a minute, sir?"

Peter settled Ella on the grass, and, adjusting his duty belt, the officer knelt down. He talked to Ella gently. He told her not to panic and to breathe from her belly. She didn't have enough oxygen in her head, he explained, that's why everything was topsy-turvy.

"I'll count to five, and you breathe," he said.

"She just used the Wi-Fi." Gabriel's voice came from somewhere distant, although he was only a few feet away.

Peter swung around. "By herself? Or with you?"

"Make him go away!" Ella yelled. She reached around the officer and grabbed Peter's pant leg.

"When?" Maud said to Gabriel. His face was alien and terrifying. He's afraid, she thought. Why is he afraid?

"Folks," the officer said. "Let's all calm down." He gestured at Gabriel. "You go wait at that table, sir." He helped Ella stand up. "We're going to take you to the hospital to get you checked out."

"I don't want to."

"We need to be sure you're okay. Your mom and dad and sister will go with you."

Maud didn't even know where Louise had gone, then saw her, hovering next to Peter.

The officer headed toward his squad car. "You folks take Ella on to the ER in Rhinebeck. I'll radio ahead. My colleague will meet you."

"I don't want to," Ella said again from the grass. Gently, Peter picked her up, as if she were a baby.

"How many times did you go over there?" Maud asked Ella as Peter settled her in the car.

"Shut up," Ella told her.

Maud drove, since she knew the route, Louise's suncatcher swinging on the rearview mirror. Peter sat in the backseat with Ella. Louise was up front, her hands on the dash as if preparing for an accident. Panic kept seizing Maud, like the aftershocks of the earthquakes she'd experienced as a girl, when she'd crouch under her school desk until the shaking stopped. Why had Ella screamed at Gabriel like that? Why had she been going to his cottage? Why hadn't he said anything about it?

"Did something happen with Gabriel?" she asked Ella again, craning her neck to look into the backseat, where Ella was sheltered under Peter's arm.

"No," Ella choked through her sobs. "Stop asking."

"Watch the road," Peter said as the car lurched close to the shoulder. Next to her, Louise gasped.

"Sweetheart, did he ever touch you?" Maud asked again.

"Leave me the fuck alone," Ella said.

9

At the hospital in Rhinebeck, three women clipped through the swinging doors—a nurse, a police officer, and another woman in clogs and jeans with reading glasses on her head, who introduced herself as a social worker. Peter had coaxed Ella out of the backseat, and now she hung on his arm. She'd been whimpering since they'd left the parking lot. Sprawled in a waiting-room chair, a man held a bloody dish towel to his head. A coughing toddler bucked in a stroller, pushing away his mother as she tried to soothe him.

"You must be Mom," the social worker said to Maud. She squatted next to Louise. "And you must be Louise. Your sister had a rough night. The doctor's going to check her all out. Do you like cartoons? Do you want to watch some with me?"

"I want to stay with my mom," Louise said.

Maud put her hand on her head, then took it away so Louise wouldn't feel the shaking. "It's all right, honey. I'll come check on you soon."

"Why is Ella making that noise?"

"She's just upset. Go on." Maud gave her a quick, hopefully reassuring hug. "I'll find you."

"We'll be right down there at the nurses' station," the social worker said.

The police officer had hung back by the doors. The nurse asked Ella if she felt she could walk to the examining room. "I can get you a wheelchair if your legs feel wobbly."

"I don't want a wheelchair," Ella said. "I want to leave."

"They'll take care of you," Peter said. "You can trust them."

With glazed eyes, Maud filled out paperwork, box to box, line to line—date, patient name, insurance ID number. She sorted through her credit cards to find the insurance card in her wallet. She reminded herself to keep breathing.

The social worker returned. She murmured to Ella that it was all right. They'd take her to a private room. She and the nurse looped their arms under her elbows.

"I'll come get your mom and dad once you're settled," she said.

"Can't we go with her now?" Maud said.

"Let us settle her in. I'll be back soon."

Then Ella was gone through the swinging doors, followed by the police officer.

Peter grabbed Maud's arm, his fingertips boring into her bicep.

"Did you ever leave Louise alone with him? Even once?"

"No." She'd already done an inventory of all their times together. "Peter, he wouldn't do anything. I don't know why he didn't tell me Ella went over there. I don't understand."

"You don't understand," Peter hissed and dropped her arm.

Maud's stomach heaved. Two hours. There'd been at least two hours between the time that Gabriel got back to the cottage every day and the time that she herself arrived at the farmhouse with Louise. How long had Ella been going over there? How often? She had always been back on the couch, shoes off, when Maud returned, as if she'd been in the farmhouse the whole time. And Gabriel had never said a single word.

"Why is there a social worker?" she asked Peter.

"It's your bloody country. You tell me."

The social worker came back into the waiting room and took them through the doors and down a hall, where a doctor stood at the nurses' station, his bald head reflecting the lights.

"We'd like to give your daughter a sedative," he said without moving his gaze from his clipboard. Maud wondered why he wouldn't meet their eyes—did he suspect something terrible?

"Why? Can we see her?" she asked.

"Let's get her calmer first," the doctor said, finally looking up. "She's been hyperventilating. She doesn't want to be examined."

"Has she been abused?" Peter's voice quaked. "Did you hear where we found her?"

"One step at a time," the doctor said. "We've taken her vitals, but we're stopping there for now until she's calmer. Someone from psychiatry is on the way down."

He left them, and they sat down in two chairs lined up against the wall. Somewhere at the end of the hallway an alarm sounded, and two nurses hurried toward it. The PA system paged a doctor. A woman—the psychiatrist?—stern-faced and straight-backed as one of the nuns at Maud's elementary school, walked out of the stairway and entered Ella's room.

"The sedative should kick in soon," she told them when she came back out, joined by the doctor. "Ella was having a panic attack. I'll be back to check on her again. I agree about the genital exam."

"What genital exam?" Maud said. Her knees filled with air.

"It seems prudent," the doctor said. "Given the concerns that have been raised. If there was any abuse, we need to check for it now." He flipped a paper on his clipboard. "Do you know if your daughter is sexually active?"

"She isn't," Maud said.

An orderly wheeled a meal cart by, letting off the smells of stringy meat and plastic wrap. The hallway had become a funnel. The doctor's head gleamed.

Peter grimaced. "Are you sure this is necessary?"

"It's protocol."

"Isn't there a woman doctor?" Maud said.

"I'll have a female nurse with me," the doctor said.

"Will you have to use a speculum?"

Ella had never been examined before, never had her legs parted into stirrups, the piercing bluntness of the speculum, that invasion, handing over your body to someone who could see places of yourself that you would never see.

"Not unless I find signs," the doctor said.

"What signs?"

"Swelling, lacerations, petechiae."

"What's that?"

"Broken blood vessels."

"I want to be there," Maud said.

In the small room, Ella's shoulders were lifted, hands

knotted in her armpits, eyes bleary and unfocused. A nurse spoke soothingly as she checked the IV. "You're dehydrated," she told Ella, "so we're giving you fluids." Maud sat in a chair next to the bed. She took Ella's hand. The doctor told Ella that he was going to take a quick look at her privates. He sat on a rolling stool and put on a pair of gloves. Maud hated his calm, measured face, the way he sniffed as he turned on the examination lamp. He looked at the nurse, who, in a caramel voice, asked Ella to fold her knees, then open them.

"No," Ella said.

When the nurse touched her thigh, Ella let out a low, guttural howl. Maud started at the noise, then squeezed Ella's hand as bile climbed into her throat.

"Let's give this a little more time," the doctor said. He turned off the light and took off his gloves. He told the nurse to increase the dosage of sedative.

"What was that noise?" Peter said in the hallway.

"She didn't want to be examined," Maud stuttered. Her mouth and throat were ice-dry, her tongue stuck to her teeth. That noise had been wretched. What was Ella hiding? What would they see when they looked between her legs? What had Gabriel done to her?

"We should check on Louise," Peter said.

Maud swallowed hard. "Can you?"

She waited for him to go before hurrying down the hall to a restroom. She locked the door and with a trembling finger dialed Gabriel's phone number.

"What did you do to her?" she said when he picked up.

"Jesus," Gabriel said. "Maud. Nothing. She came over to my place to use the Wi-Fi. I worked in the other room."

"How many times?"

"Just a few afternoons. I was going to tell you."

The white tiles of the bathroom flashed like strobe lights. Maud heard again that howl that had come from her daughter's mouth like an animal caught in a trap.

"You're lying," she said. "You're a liar. Why wouldn't you have told me?"

"She didn't want me to tell you. Listen"—his voice rose— "I'm at the police station right now. What is Ella saying? You need to get her to tell the truth. Nothing happened. I never touched her."

"I'll kill you if you did," Maud said.

"Make her tell the truth."

"I'll kill you, Gabriel."

She spat in the sink and splashed water on her face. Back in the hallway, she sat in one of the chairs near the nurses' station, sandwiching her hands under her legs.

"I called him," she said when Peter returned. "I don't think he did anything."

"Don't talk," Peter said.

The nurse beckoned Maud into Ella's room when the doctor once again arrived. Ella's eyes were now half closed. Again Maud took her limp hand. With a soft snap, the doctor's gloves went on. The nurse said she was going to open Ella's thighs. When Ella didn't respond, she put her hands on Ella's knees. Maud stared at the metal tubing that encased the bed. She heard the squeak of wheels as the doctor's stool moved closer, the creak of the light as he shone it between Ella's legs.

"All done," he said. "You did really well, Ella. I'm going to go talk to your mom and dad for a minute now."

Ella had closed her eyes, and the lashes glistened with

tears. Maud kissed her forehead. "I love you, baby," she whispered.

Peter jolted up from the chair when Maud and the doctor came into the hall.

"I don't see any signs of abuse," the doctor said.

The hatred Maud had felt toward him washed away in a tide of relief.

"What does that mean?" Peter asked.

"No bruising. No swelling. No abrasions. So we'll hold off on an internal exam for now." He paused. "There's something else, though. Are you aware that Ella has been self-harming?"

"What's that?" Peter said.

"Cutting her skin. She has a fresh wound on her inner thigh and scars that suggest this has been going on for a while."

"Cutting her skin with what?" Peter said.

"Sometimes it's a razor," the doctor said. "Or scissors."

"They're probably scratches," Maud said. "She's been riding horses at camp. Couldn't a saddle do that?"

"They aren't abrasions, I'm afraid. They're cuts."

"I don't understand," Peter said.

"Let's have my colleague talk to you," the doctor said. "She'll be right down."

Silently, Maud and Peter sat in the chairs. This, Maud thought, was why Ella hadn't wanted to wear a bathing suit and insisted on board shorts. She was keeping her thighs covered. This was why she spent so much time in the bathroom. Head whirling, Maud reviewed what she knew about self-harm and self-mutilation, which wasn't much: Saint Mary Magdalene de' Pazzi burning herself with hot wax, the needle girls of nineteenth-century England who stabbed their arms as they embroidered. Then she had an awful thought. What if Ella had hurt herself because she'd been molested by Gabriel? Maybe he'd managed to leave no trace, using the meticulous precision of an archaeologist. Her teeth chattered. What had she done to her daughter?

"We should get Louise out of here," Peter said. "I'll take her to breakfast."

"Will you?" Maud said. "Please. Can I stay?"

"Call me the minute they tell you anything."

"I will. I promise."

Why, she thought when he left, if nothing had happened, had Ella screamed at Gabriel to go away? What had gone on in that cottage? Why hadn't he told her?

The psychiatrist sat down next to Maud. She said that Ella had denied the self-harm at first, then admitted she'd been doing it for a few months.

So before she'd come to Montgomery Place. "Did she say why?" Maud asked.

"That'll take some time to understand," the psychiatrist said.

"Did she say anything about him?"

"She told me she's been going to his place in the afternoons for the past few weeks."

Maud broke into a cold sweat. "Every day?"

"Yes," the psychiatrist said with a concerned nod. "She says she went back there tonight because she didn't know where else to go. She was trying to run away. I think only to scare you. She was upset her father was taking her home. She told me again that Mr. Crews didn't touch her. But the police will want to talk to her before she's discharged. We need to be thorough. It's odd that he hid it from you."

Maud's eyes filled. "I had no idea. And I didn't know she'd been hurting herself."

"Now you do," the psychiatrist said gently. "And you can get her help."

Maud called Peter to tell him what the psychiatrist had said. "Is Louise okay?" she asked.

"She fell asleep. I'm driving around the block in circles."

Voices equally robotic, they'd moved into emergency mode.

In Ella's room, the nurse had folded the gown around Ella's waist and was swabbing her leg.

"Don't want you here," Ella said to Maud, drowsily and icily.

"Ella's agreed to let me disinfect her cut," the nurse said. "Why don't you wait outside? I'll get you when I'm done."

Peter texted that Louise had woken up and that he was getting her breakfast. Eventually the nurse told Maud that Ella was asleep if she wanted to go into the room.

Eyelids swollen, mouth ajar, Ella's pale face blended into the pillow. Maud stood at the foot of the bed. After folding back the sheet and blanket, she lifted Ella's gown and carefully peeled back the large gauze bandage on her left leg. Row upon row of ridges ran down Ella's thigh, some glossy and pink, some weathered to scars, others still crusty, each one straight and spaced precisely. She stared at the devastation, memorizing each line before replacing the bandage, lowering the gown, and pulling the sheet back up.

While Ella slept, she changed the three plane tickets home for a flight that evening, adding a seat for herself. She called Annette and told her what had happened, omitting that she'd had sex with Gabriel. She called Lone Pines, the psychiatric hospital near her parents' house, and made an appointment for an assessment. She called Ella's pediatrician and left a message. She called the insurance company. Her finger dialed numbers. Her voice said words. Her mind swirled.

The police officer who had met them when they arrived at the hospital came back midmorning, after Peter and Louise had visited. Ella had gathered herself to give Louise a hug.

"Let's switch," Peter said to Maud.

"Please let me stay with her," Maud said. "Please."

"Fine," he said.

She needed to hear everything. She needed every piece of information Ella gave. She was still anticipating another blow, some horrible truth about Gabriel. Again, she sat next to the bed in the room. The police officer pulled up a chair. The psychiatrist stood by the window with a clipboard. The social worker sat with her hands folded over her crossed knees.

"We'd like to understand why you left in the middle of the night," the officer said.

"I was mad." Ella gazed out the window at the hospital incinerator. "My parents said my dad was taking us home. I thought if I ran away, they wouldn't do it."

"But you went to Mr. Crews's place instead."

"I got freaked out. It was so dark. He was supposed to be gone."

"And you said you'd been there before?"

"I already told the doctor and the other doctor," Ella said. "I went there after camp when my mom was working. I used the internet. When he got back, he got me a Coke and, like, chips or something and we talked about stuff before he worked in his room."

"How many times did you go there?"

Ella adjusted the pillow under her head. "Every day."

Maud's chest contracted.

"How long did you stay?"

"I had to be back at three."

Because she knew I'd be home soon, Maud thought. Both of them knew I'd be home with Louise.

"And what did you do, exactly, during that time?" the social worker asked.

"I told you. We talked. Then I FaceTimed my friends."

"Where did you talk?"

"On the couch."

The officer took notes. "Always on the couch? Did you ever go into any of the other rooms? How about to the bedroom?"

"No. On the couch. I was on my phone while he took a shower and changed." At the word "shower," Maud flinched.

"Where did he change?" the officer said.

"In the bedroom."

"Did he shut the door?"

"Yes."

"You never saw him without his clothes on?"

"No." Ella sat up. "Why are you asking me these questions?" She looked at Maud. "Did you tell them we did something?"

"Ella," Maud said, "I can't tell them anything because I don't know any of this. Please say what happened."

"I am," Ella said.

"Whose idea was it for you to go to Mr. Crews's place when your mom was away?" the social worker said.

"His. He said the connection from his router was better."

"And you never told your mother. Did he tell you not to tell her?"

Ella tucked the blanket tighter around her waist. "He didn't think I should. He knew she wanted me to be reading instead. He didn't want me to get in trouble."

"When did this start?" Maud asked Ella.

"I don't know. Like, after we all went canoeing."

Three weeks. Fifteen weekdays. Fifteen times, and not one word from Gabriel.

"Why didn't you tell me?" She tried to keep the agitation out of her voice, but it pushed through and Ella raised a stubborn chin.

"You wanted me to read. You'd get mad."

"Did you tell Mr. Crews about the self-harm?" the psychiatrist said.

"No."

"What did you talk about?"

"I don't know. School. My friends. Sometimes my parents."

"Did you talk about boys?"

"A little. Not really."

"About private things?" the police officer said.

Ella's face buckled. "Why are you making it gross?"

That afternoon, she was discharged, and they drove to Montgomery Place. Ella had become upset again as they left the hospital, so the psychiatrist prescribed another sedative. In front of the cottage, Gabriel's truck was gone. The light that Peter had turned on when they'd found Ella shone through the window. Maud moved around the farmhouse, throwing out leftover food in the refrigerator, packing her suitcase, helping Louise find her sandals under the couch. As Peter put the suitcases in the car, she went to the office. Harriet, who must have seen her coming, opened the door.

"There's been an emergency with Ella," Maud said. "I'm going to have to leave early."

"I heard," Harriet said. "Lydia texted me during the night. And a policeman was here first thing this morning. I told him that I hadn't seen your daughter alone with Gabriel."

"It seems to have been a misunderstanding," Maud said. She gave Harriet the key to the farmhouse.

"Many misunderstandings." Harriet's eyes shone with anger. Lydia must have mentioned Maud's question about Chris last night. Harriet put the key in her pocket. "I'll send you an updated paycheck."

At JFK, Peter answered a call from the police officer who had first come to Montgomery Place. He told Peter that Gabriel had been questioned extensively, but between what he said and what Ella had said, they didn't suspect foul play.

"Thank God," Maud said. "Thank God nothing happened."

"One more week, and it bloody well might have," Peter said.

Still absorbing the words, Maud picked up her suitcase and followed her family onto the plane.

THE PRESIDIO

2014

10

Mist pearled the air of the shallow valley, shutting out the morning sun. The cold singed Maud's ears, which were newly exposed by the haircut she'd gotten a few weeks ago. She regretted the decision now ("Just get rid of it, please," she'd said to the stylist as soon as she faced the mirror), not only because the haircut made her eyes look waifish, but because hair, it turned out, was also a blanket. She coaxed yet another flag into the dirt. She was crouching in the adobe footprint of a walled garden that had once fed the Hispanic settlers of Tennessee Hollow. Halfway up the slope lay a second archaeological dig—the footprint of a house—surrounded by screens, buckets, and prostrate shovels. Below, past a veil of winter-crisp grasses, a stone trail marked the bed of El Polín, the stream that split the valley and had once watered this garden.

She dug up another clod of soil with the trowel and plopped it into a plastic bag, which she sealed and labeled. Ten samples this morning—she'd count that as good enough. Her chapped hands could barely move, even in a pair of gloves so torn up and caked by dirt they seemed themselves to be relics. As she walked the wooden pathway with the bucket of samples, a seagull wheeled and cackled overhead. Two joggers swerved around her on the path that led out of Tennessee Hollow and into a eucalyptus grove that flanked the Main Post, a grassy esplanade lined by brick buildings from the years when this national park was an American military base.

The archaeology center occupied a nineteenth-century stucco building on the short end of the green rectangle. Inside, the rooms smelled of clay from the artifacts spread out on tables waiting to be cleaned: coins from the Presidio's days of Spanish rule, tile shards from the Mexican years, chunks of adobe, a Coke bottle tossed into a landfill during the 1950s. After dropping off the bucket of samples to the archaeology office, Maud stopped at her mailbox and found a hoped-for envelope from the laboratory that analyzed her soil samples. Two weeks ago, she'd mailed off a shard of bark from a tree stump near the garden footprint. Now she ripped open the envelope. *Punica granatum.* Native to the Himalayas. Praised in the Babylonian Talmud. Grown in the gardens of Alcinous. Brought to California by the Spanish. If she planted a new tree soon, it would blossom this spring and lure hummingbirds and swallowtails from the meadows to its crimson flowers.

She knocked on the frame of the director's open door and held up the paper. "Maria," she said, "it was a pomegranate. Can I go ahead and plant it?"

"Maybe." Maria looked up from her laptop. "I've got news for you too. Could you shut the door?"

Under an asymmetrical bob, Maria's round face was punctuated by chunky black glasses. Her office—the epicenter of a proposed restoration at El Polín—abounded with maps and diagrams, sticky notes and charts. She moved a stack of files off a chair so Maud could sit down. "I think I've found us a donor," she said. "Have you heard of Alice Lincoln?"

"The artist? The one with the basket at the de Young?"

Woven from wrought iron, the basket towered on the lawn outside the museum café.

"Yup," Maria said, "that one. Turns out she's from old Boston money."

Alice Lincoln's father, she added, had died six months ago and left his daughter a fortune. "She's giving it all away as fast as she can to Bay Area nonprofits run by women. I managed to schedule a meeting with her. How quickly can you put together a garden design?"

"I can improvise something now," Maud said, "but it'll be sketchy. I'm still waiting on lab results."

"Sketchy's fine. I want to give her an idea of what it would look like. I'm asking for the entire budget, the house and garden restoration, the school programs, the garden maintenance, summer camps. Everything."

"From what I know of Alice Lincoln," Maud said, "you'd think she'd be interested."

The placard at the de Young described Alice Lincoln as a "feminist icon and lesbian pioneer" and the basket as a "monument to matriarchy." This would seem to make her the perfect donor for Tennessee Hollow, which had belonged to the family of Juana Briones, an entrepreneur and healer known as the "Mother of San Francisco."

"It's not so easy to predict with her," Maria said. "So far, she's a pain. Totally controlling and totally indifferent. She's some kind of Luddite hermit. She and I exchanged three letters to set a date for this meeting—and I mean letters on paper with stamps. Apparently she doesn't have a cell or even internet. She called me from a pay phone in town this morning. And she made it very, very clear that she wants to remain anonymous, so I'm only telling you and the archaeology team."

"Is there anyone else we can ask if she says no?"

"No one who could get us the money fast enough," Maria said. She frowned. "If we don't secure funding by next month, I'll have to close the digs."

Maud hadn't known that was a possibility. Maria was so savvy and forceful, she'd been sure she'd convince the Presidio Foundation to keep the project running until she found a donor.

"I'll start on a design tonight," she said.

Driving across the Golden Gate Bridge later, she mapped out the garden in her head. Thus far, she had found traces of tomatoes, pumpkins, blackberries, and yerba buena, a native mint Juana Briones used as a healer. And now she could add that pomegranate tree.

Four months ago, she'd driven in the opposite direction for her first day on the job, nervous that she'd never find the garden she was meant to restore. She had spent hours in the Presidio archives, then at the Stanford library, where she read about an 1850s painting of Tennessee Hollow that now hung in San Francisco's city hall. The faded canvas, which Maud found in a busy hallway above a drinking fountain, showed the flat, bare landscape of the Presidio before eucalyptus groves and lawns. She recognized the

Briones house—a chalky square of adobe, and the well near El Polín. And downstream, standing on her tiptoes, craning her neck, she made out two faint brushstrokes in that same adobe white. Maybe an animal pen. Maybe a walled garden.

For weeks, she paced the ground with the archaeology team, looking, measuring, digging test pits, hoping that they'd see the pale flash of adobe. And one afternoon, they did. But without funding, Maud thought, as she quit the freeway for Sausalito, the dream of the garden would go up in smoke. And I'll be here again, she thought, cresting the hill that led to her house, back and forth to the grocery store and the dry cleaner's, caught between the drumbeats of guilt and worry.

The house that she and Peter rented stood up a zigzag staircase. On the redwood deck, a container garden of ferns and succulents shimmered with constellations of dew. The garden had been Maud's great pleasure when they first moved to Marin, but it no longer needed her attention, save for the occasional clipping of a withered frond or a handful of fish compost to kick-start the nasturtium flowers that climbed a string ladder to the roof each spring.

Inside the house, the living room was all clean lines, with frost-colored paint and indifferent bamboo flooring. Their antique furniture from England hulked in every room—armoires cut into windows, bookshelves jutted from door-ways. At the kitchen table, Ella and Louise were clumped together, doing their homework

"Smoothie, anyone?" Maud said. She opened the freezer. "How was school?"

"I'm making a Sphinx out of sugar cubes for history," Louise said.

Maud dropped frozen strawberries into the blender. "Fun. Good thing it doesn't rain a lot in Egypt."

"I made a Big Ben out of sugar cubes before we left England," Ella told Louise. "Where did that go?"

"I think we gave it to your grandmother," Maud said.

"She probably threw it away," Ella said.

"Or used it in her tea," Louise said, making Ella laugh.

"How did the presentation on Gaza go?" Maud asked through the whir of the blender.

"Okay." Head balanced on her fist, Ella was plugging numbers into a calculator for her math assignment. She and Louise had been in the house for ten minutes before Maud arrived: a baby step toward independence planned with her therapist. Soon Ella would stay here on her own for several hours, and Maud didn't feel ready. Only recently had Ella been allowed to shut herself in the bathroom, after months of Maud sitting on the tub as Ella used the toilet or shaved her legs. As she watched her daughter take a sip of smoothie, Maud's stomach tensed. There had been so many relapses. When Ella had come home from Lone Pines Psychiatric Hospital, she had to be weaned from self-harming, putting ice cubes on her skin instead of a blade when she got the urge. She was out of intensive treatment now, but a mere six months ago she'd cut herself again. Maud only knew because she'd found traces of blood on the sheets.

Peter came home at five-thirty; he rarely stayed at the office now. "Good day?" he asked Maud.

"Yes, yours?"

"Good," he said.

Maud went back to beating eggs for an omelet. Peter had aged visibly in the past two years, time marked by the further retreat of his hair from his temples and the whittling of new lines on his forehead. He emptied a bag of spring mix into a salad bowl and poured on dressing. They organized their menus now, alternated who did the shopping week to week, moved around each other in the kitchen.

At dinner, Peter asked Ella how her presentation had gone.

"Brilliant!" she said. "I got the map to stick on the whiteboard, and I didn't mess up once, not even that part we practiced last night."

"Told you it would go well," Peter said.

"And I might go out for the spring tennis team," she added.

This was the first time Ella had mentioned an extracurricular activity, joining something, becoming part of the world of school again beyond classes. Maud and Peter exchanged an upbeat glance. But Maud felt stung. Ella had saved the information for her father. With Peter, her voice relaxed and her face opened. With Maud, she still seemed to be speaking from atop a glacial summit.

"We can bundle up and start practicing together at the Mill Valley courts if you like," Peter said.

"Are you good? I don't want to be crushed."

"He'll make mistakes on purpose," Louise said. "Like he does during Trivial Pursuit."

"I do not," Peter said.

"Yes, you do. I want to win for reals."

"Your dad was an excellent tennis player when I met him," Maud said.

"In your eyes, since you didn't really play." Peter laughed.

On a cracked tennis court behind his family's decaying manor, he had taught Maud to return his serves as his mother watched from the overgrown shade. This summer they were going back to England for the first time in three years. Peter would play on that court with Ella, hitting the ball back and forth with that ease between them, as Maud sat with Peter's mother, drinking Darjeeling, eating digestive biscuits off chipped china, and talking about novels. Once, Maud had pitied Peter's mother for the years she'd wasted with Peter's philandering father, but she didn't now. There were many ways to do this thing called marriage.

After clearing the table, Ella and Louise went to the living room to watch TV. Maud wiped down the table as Peter loaded the glasses in the dishwasher. Then she'd take over with the plates and bowls. The car needed servicing. The heating system hadn't been checked this winter. For some domestic activities, they had worked out compromises; others, they'd abandoned.

"I think I'll tuck in early," Peter said. "Can you do drop-off tomorrow morning?"

"Sure," she said. "I'll be up late. Need to hash out a design for a possible donor."

Peter left for his study. She'd join him in bed when he was already asleep, turned toward his own nightstand. They hadn't had sex in almost a year, after trying for a few months while they did marriage counseling at the start of Ella's treatment. There'd been no conversation, no analysis, no decision. They simply stopped.

She turned on the dishwasher, which she'd loaded as Peter liked—dirty sides facing the sprayers. It wasn't a hard thing to do, and she should have tried to do it long ago. Peter too made efforts. He had stopped his overreliance on the imperative, and when his jaw stiffened, he retracted, took a breath, and regained his self-composure. Ella had terrified them both into good behavior.

On her laptop, Maud opened the garden design software that she'd recently learned to use. She added the pomegranate tree, typing the scientific name. That tree was a fact. Those walls were a fact. She wouldn't think about the white pomegranate that grew in the hills of Turkey. She wouldn't think about the archaeological dig at Hasankeyf, with its mineral springs and caves. She focused on the glowing screen, which became a coffee-colored square of soil. She needed to help Maria convince Alice Lincoln to fund this project. She needed to restore this garden. She needed to crush the thoughts about Gabriel that were sprouting again in earth she'd thought scorched.

11

Over the first six months that had followed their return from the Hudson Valley, Ella gradually told Maud and Peter about her self-harm. She had first cut her thigh the winter before they went to Montgomery Place. She hadn't been happy at school since the start of seventh grade, and one afternoon, sitting on her bed, feeling rejected by her friends again, she clenched her leg with her fingers and dug nails into skin, leaving half-moons. Pressing harder, she dragged the moons into comets. Instantly the sick tension in her body released. Two days later, she did it again, this time in the school bathroom. By January, she'd moved from her nails to an X-Acto knife blade from the art room, wrapped in tissue paper in her pocket. Every day, during lunch, she'd wait in a stall for the bathroom to empty, then tug down her jeans.

At home, she sat at the dinner table, her only desire to lock herself in the bathroom with a fresh patch of skin. She didn't reflect on what she was doing. "I wasn't thinking about it," she said. "I just did it." If that bone-bruising dread came over her—in the lunch line at school, sitting on the couch watching television—if that voice said, *You're ugly, you're stupid, no one likes you,* she'd get up, relief descending before she'd even reached for the blade.

By spring, she became more daring, pushing deeper, harder, teasing out more blood. After stanching the cut with toilet paper, she'd tug up her pants, open the door, and go back to the classroom or the kitchen feeling better than she had when she'd left. There was excitement too. It felt good to get away with it. When she couldn't fall asleep, she ran her fingertips over the ridges, remembering where she'd been when she'd made this cut near her hip bone, that one by the peach-colored mole.

A few days before the flight to New York, her period came early, and she bled through her jeans at school. Mortified, she went to the nurse for a pad. In the bathroom, she took off one of her hoop earrings, dug it into her thigh, and yanked. The next morning, the cut was infected. "I was mad at myself for not doing it right," she said. She couldn't find antibiotic cream in the medicine cupboard so she used rubbing alcohol. The cut wept that night and the redness had spread by morning. On her way down the stairs to the car, she clenched the railing until she felt the bite of a splinter. Later, she showed her hand to Peter, who removed the splinter and got a tube of the antibiotic cream that Ella hadn't been able to find. That night, she used the cream on her thigh. While she and Louise flew to New York, the wound had only started to heal.

Ella's treatment began soon after their return to Marin, every pointed object in the house locked in a drawer in Peter's study. Ella barely left her bed. Since that first night off the plane, Maud couldn't sleep. She kept going over each interaction with Gabriel, each conversation, each look he'd given Ella. The questions pounded: What possible innocent reason could there have been for his behavior? Why had Ella screamed for him to go away when she saw him in the doorway that night? The morning of the intake at Lone Pines, she asked Ella again if more had happened, and Ella had lashed out, "Don't talk about him anymore."

"Stop bringing him up," Peter said. "You'll trigger her." Already they were becoming fluent in this new language.

"But why?" Maud said. "If nothing happened, why does it upset her so much?"

"Don't ask me, Maud," Peter said. "He was your 'friend.'"

At Lone Pines, having checked Ella in at the front desk, they sat in the waiting room until the psychiatrist called them to his office. On a wan couch, Ella picked at a thread on her sweater, as the doctor's tight mouth moved slowly and assuredly around the words Maud knew he'd said over and over to other families.

"I believe that we are dealing with several issues," he said. "Depression. Self-harm. Cognitive OCD, meaning that instead of washing her hands repeatedly, Ella clings to unsettling thoughts and can't let them go."

The entire time in the waiting room Maud had barely breathed, and now she blurted out the question.

"Did you talk about Gabriel Crews?"

"Ella told me about the secret meetings, yes," the psychiatrist said.

Ella's head shot up. "And he believes me that nothing happened."

"It isn't about believing you," Maud said.

But it was. Whenever her mind was still, the idea that Ella wasn't telling the whole truth resurfaced. She felt her daughter holding something back.

"Your mother's right," the psychiatrist said. "You wouldn't have done anything, Ella. Mr. Crews would have done something." He shifted his equanimous gaze to Maud and Peter. "I've talked to Ella about going inpatient, and she's agreed that it would be a good idea."

"You mean live here?" Maud said. "Sleep here?"

"For now. While we work on mood stabilization."

"Is that what you want, love?" Peter said to Ella.

"I guess," Ella said.

They drove to the house to pack a suitcase with the list the hospital provided. No shoes with laces. No hoodies with drawstrings. No cutting tools of any kind, including nail clippers. Give me back my child, Maud thought, as she folded Ella's shirts into a suitcase. She knew that Peter was feeling the same emotions down the hall in the bathroom, where he was filling a cosmetics bag with trial bottles of shampoo and toothpaste from their last trip to England.

Back at Lone Pines, they hugged Ella goodbye.

"I changed my mind," she said.

"You can do it," Peter said.

"You're so strong," Maud said, feeling sick.

She didn't want to let Ella go, but she didn't trust herself to take care of her. She had missed so many signs and misread many more. All those months when she thought Ella was being a snarly teenager, her daughter had been suffering. Her anger masked pain. And Maud had sensed that something was wrong—checking under the toilet seat, looking at Ella's arms to make sure they hadn't gotten skinny—and done nothing about it. She'd been blinded by her own desires, blinded by her feelings for Gabriel, and blinded by Gabriel himself. Gabriel, who had deceived her, lied to her, withheld and dissembled. And maybe worse— that fear kept returning, a furor that swept her up, kicking and struggling for breath.

A nurse arrived to tell them that the room was ready. As Ella disappeared through the steel door, Maud saw the metamorphosis that had taken place over the past year, how her hips had winged out, how her waist had narrowed. From the back, she could be mistaken for a grown woman. And that, Maud thought as the door closed, was what Gabriel would have seen when Ella walked away from the table.

Over the next week, she lay in bed while Peter slept and continued to think through what had happened with Gabriel, the actual and the imagined. She counted twenty-one weekdays at Montgomery Place between the canoe trip and Peter's arrival, so twenty-one times that Gabriel might have returned to the cottage and spent at least an hour with Ella. Twenty-one nights that he and Maud had sat together, talking, being intimate, with him saying nothing to her. And who knew what else he had lied about? Maybe he'd been manipulating her from the start. Maybe he'd played the same role of reformed lone wolf with all of those women he'd mentioned. Or maybe those women, too, had been fabricated, characters in a narrative meant to lure Maud in by making her feel special. She'd thought that they had been carried away when they walked into the forest from the hedge, but Gabriel might have planned the whole thing, knowing that she was close to cracking, just as she'd seen him slowly, gently crack Ella's resistance to him. And Maud had helped him, given him advice. She cringed when she thought of it. Maybe he'd had some sick fantasy about a threesome.

One night, she got up and paced the living room, as fog pressed on the windows. She couldn't stop her mind from churning. In the unlit kitchen, she did internet searches: Men/teenage girls. Pedophilia. Molestation. Everywhere, men were molesting children—girls and boys. But she'd known this already. In the very parish that she'd attended as a child, there'd been the "Father Chambers fiasco," as her parents called it. Four former altar boys revealed in their twenties the abuse they'd suffered in the sacristy. Maud had known that Ella was poised on that tricky edge between girlhood and womanhood. She'd even considered that Ella was flirting with Gabriel. And it had annoyed her. She remembered dragging Ella back to the cottage to look up that pronunciation, cutting her off when she became snippy at dinner. She'd been competing with Ella for Gabriel's attention, she realized now. And had he been flirting with both of them with his jokes and asides, his lazy-eyed grins?

Still, she hoped that she was getting it wrong. She hoped that there was another version of this story, one in which she was less culpable and Gabriel less questionable. As the weeks passed, though, the lack of word from him seemed to confirm his guilt. Why wouldn't he try to contact her to explain? In her more paranoid moments, she'd think that he and Ella were still communicating, that Gabriel knew Ella was at Lone Pines, that he was waiting—waiting for Ella—still in her life somehow: a clandestine email account, a burner phone hidden in Ella's suitcase.

Finally, one evening, she looked Gabriel up on the internet.

Nothing new appeared. He was still listed on the Ithaca College faculty page. By now he might be in Turkey, where he could molest other girls. But he hadn't molested Ella, she reminded herself. He'd only wanted to. Maybe.

She and Peter started family therapy with Ella. The first session was a misery of Ella in one corner and Peter and Maud in another as the therapist coaxed Ella to speak. Maud and Peter told her how much they loved her, how terrified they'd been that night she disappeared, how they thought she was smart and tough and could do anything. They spilled out words while Ella clenched her knees to her chest and stared at the floor.

"She won't talk to us," they told Ella's psychiatrist, who said that right now Ella was struggling with the desire to self-harm and the inability to do so. All of her energy went into that effort.

A few sessions later, when Ella did start to talk in family therapy, Maud missed her silence. Right away she brought up Gabriel.

"You're sick," she said to Maud, her eyes burning. "How could you think I would do something like that with him?"

"The doctors and police were concerned, Ella," Peter said, "not only your mother and me."

"I thought he was the only person in this world who understood me," Ella said. "But nobody does. You don't. You never have."

The family therapist, a ponderous man with gutted cheeks, tried to redirect.

"Ella," he said gently, "your depression and the self-harm started before you went to New York and met Mr. Crews."

Watching a storm cross Ella's face, Maud felt muddled

and panicked. There was no timeline, no logic, no perspective that organized this story into clarity.

"The higher antidepressant dose should kick in soon," Peter said on the drive home. He had been reading about the structure of the teenage brain, about norepinephrine and serotonin, and cognitive behavioral therapy. "We need to get into her head and try to understand why she would do this."

But Maud had understood viscerally in the hospital room when she saw the scars on Ella's thighs: The dangerous secret that makes you feel alive. The secret that gives you control.

Ella lived in the concrete block of the inpatient unit for seven weeks. Peter, Louise, and Maud had to be buzzed in and out of the steel door. Visiting hours ran from seven to eight p.m. Hair unwashed as if she'd neglected it in the shower, body listless, Ella sat in the lounge with other girls, scrunched up in a chair upholstered in plasticky fabric. Her nails were clipped short to keep her from scratching, but she managed to anyway, and bandages often encased her arm. They tried to play Scrabble; Ella watched and never touched her tiles.

"When will she be better?" Louise kept asking. She herself seemed smaller now, more hesitant in her speech, her steps whispering down the hall instead of clumping. Eventually Maud and Peter decided that Louise should visit only once a week and dropped her at Maud's parents' house before going to Lone Pines.

"You stopped her before she killed herself," Maud's mother said one day as Maud was leaving, patting her on the shoulder. "That's the important thing."

The difference between self-harm and suicide seemed

impossible to explain. Maud felt incapable of understanding or interpreting anything. Besides, her rigid, exhausting mother had been right. She should never have gone to Montgomery Place. She should have stayed home and paid better attention to her troubled daughter.

Gradually, over the next few months, Ella improved. She sat up straighter, no longer bent toward the floor, refusing eye contact. She told Louise she'd missed her, hugged her goodbye during visits, and made a couple of friends in the unit. She talked more calmly in family therapy, although mostly to Peter.

Maud and Peter started marriage counseling. Each week, for an hour, they sat next to each other in a room with a potted plastic ficus and reviewed the history that had led them to this point.

"Why are you here?" the counselor said the first day.

"We have to stay together," Maud said.

The counselor looked at Peter. "Is that your main goal too?"

"I want us to love each other again," he said, and Maud's stomach caved with guilt.

The counselor gave them exercises: cooking dinner together, telling each other one thing they'd done well at the end of the day. Dutifully, they did their homework. They were getting along better, but they were so miserable over Ella that it didn't seem to matter.

One night, Maud felt Peter's hand on her thigh in bed. She'd dreaded this moment. ("Just try touching each other again for now," the counselor said when they'd discussed their sex life.) Another fear had started to percolate—she was on the pill, so pregnancy had never been a concern, but what if Gabriel had given her an STD, and she, in turn, gave it to Peter? For all she knew, Gabriel never used protection and slept with women right and left. She should have a panel. As she turned in the bed, she was prepared to say: I'm not ready yet. But Peter spoke first. "This is the last time I'll ask. Nothing happened with him? Nothing at all?"

On the pillow, his face looked near pleading. "No," Maud said with all the force of conviction she had. "We were friends. Or I thought we were."

They kissed for the first time since she'd picked him up from JFK.

The next afternoon, at a Planned Parenthood clinic in the Embarcadero, she sat in a waiting room under a poster about HIV, then lay on a table in stirrups as a nurse practitioner swiped her cervix. She remembered that awful moment in the Rhinebeck hospital when the doctor had looked between Ella's legs. She felt woozy with relief over what hadn't happened, over what could have been, over the hell she'd escaped and would continue to escape by being careful and responsible and focused on her family. The night after she got the results, she undressed while Peter slept and caressed him until he grew hard and awoke. She parted her legs. They made love, slowly and timidly. As Peter moved inside her, Maud thought of erasure.

Winter went by, and her terror quieted to a dull background thud with the decrease in Ella's relapses. Maud drove her to Lone Pines in the morning for outpatient treatment, and then picked her up in the afternoon. She found a tutor so Ella wouldn't fall behind in school. At home, the scissors and razors stayed locked in their drawer. Only with Louise did Ella sometimes become lighthearted. The peal of her laughter one night from Louise's bedroom made Maud stop in the hall and put her hand to her mouth.

Then Ella had a bad day and self-harmed again with her nails.

"This happens," her psychiatrist said, but back home, Maud hid in her closet, a sweater clenched to her face to muffle her crying, while the girls did their homework in the kitchen.

When Maud and Peter returned Ella's phone, she didn't seem interested in contacting her friends. Running down the screen were almost a hundred texts that oozed over missing her, studded with the heart emoticons. *Love u!* the girls wrote. *You got this!* If any of the sentiment was sincere, Ella didn't believe it. "I'm done with them," she said. Peter thought they should monitor her emails, texts, and browser history to make sure that there were no bullying messages or worrisome searches. One or the other of them checked her phone every week. They agreed that they wouldn't mention anything to Ella unless they found something problematic. Ella mostly texted with one of her cousins and a couple of friends from treatment. She never seemed to email anyone. Her internet searches were all related to music or school.

Then one night Peter told Maud, "She looked up that tosser this afternoon." There he was, Peter said, in Ella's search history: Gabriel Crews, archaeologist.

The old vortex rose around Maud again, scenarios flying by: Ella thought she was in love with Gabriel. Gabriel was in love with Ella. They communicated via that secret email account. Gabriel was living in Mexico, waiting for the day when he could pick up Ella and drive her over the border.

Maud told Peter that she'd bring up the search with Ella's therapist, Rita, the next day at Lone Pines.

When she sat down in Rita's office at the end of the session, Ella was playing with a fidget, a stress-relieving toy shaped like a snake, the rainbowed segments clicking as she ran them through her fingers.

"Anything you'd like to discuss?" Rita said to Maud.

"Ella did an internet search yesterday," Maud said. She couldn't say his name.

"Yes." Rita folded her hands over her knees. "She told me." She turned to Ella. "Maybe your mother needs to hear what we discussed."

"I don't care what she needs to hear," Ella said, as the snake clicked. "I thought you said what we talked about stayed between us."

"It does, but if your mom doesn't hear, she can't understand. It's your choice, though."

This is when and where it happens, Maud thought, grinding her teeth. This is where I learn the truth.

Ella blinked at Rita, then glanced at Maud. "I wanted to see a picture of him. See what he looked like again."

"And can you tell your mom why?"

"Why should I have to?" Her hands moved faster, the clicking louder.

"You don't have to, but I think she'll worry if you don't." Rita tilted her head at Maud. "Is that right?"

"Yes," Maud said. She felt a gratitude for Rita that was close to adoration.

"Because I don't understand why I liked him so much," Ella said bluntly. "At Montgomery Place, he didn't seem so old. Or disgusting."

"Why disgusting?" Maud said.

Ella shrugged. "He just is."

"Could I have a quick word with your mom?" Rita asked.

After Ella had left for the waiting room, Maud said, "Disgusting sounds alarming."

"She knows she had a little crush on him," Rita said.

"She's said that to you?"

"Not in so many words. He listened to her when she was vulnerable. That gave him power. And she understands that his keeping their meetings a secret was inappropriate."

"I keep wondering if more happened with him," Maud said. "I feel she's not saying something. It's this worry that won't go away."

"Maud," Rita said, "if I had any suspicion that more had happened, I wouldn't only tell you and Peter, I'd tell the authorities. Ella is trying to let what happened last summer go. I'm not surprised that she looked him up."

"I can't let it go," Maud said.

She had pieces of evidence that no one else did. Gabriel had said that he loved her and slept with her, while meeting her daughter in secret over and over. But if she told Rita all this, she would eventually have to tell Peter. And he'd be enraged by her lies. Their marriage wouldn't survive the blow.

"It's going to be hard to trust Ella again." Rita leaned forward in her chair, her face both tough and sympathetic. "Self-harm does that. But you'll have to, eventually. For both your sakes."

Two months later, Maud sat with Peter in the waiting room at Lone Pines as he typed on the laptop balanced on his knees. It had been nine months since Ella was first admitted to the hospital, and they were at their monthly family session with Rita. Soon they would walk down the hall to Rita's office, where Ella would talk to Peter and barely say a word to Maud.

"I need to start working again," she said.

Peter glanced up from his laptop. "Are you looking?"

"No. But Ella hasn't relapsed in a long time. I'll do something part-time until she's out of treatment. I've been reading more about the landscape here. I think I'll be more marketable now."

"She may never be out of treatment." Peter went back to typing.

"So I shouldn't go back to work? Ever?"

"I didn't say that."

"You implied it."

"No," he said. "You inferred it." He sighed. "We said we wouldn't have those old fights."

"I know," Maud said. "We won't. But I'm finding a job."

Rita came to the door, and Maud got up from the chair. She followed Peter down the hall. The drama was over. The crisis had passed. Ella was getting better. Ella would be all right. Maud would go back to work doing something. Eventually she'd stop feeling guilty. Eventually the terror would subside. Eventually she'd be able to think of Gabriel without her body surging with confusion and rage. Eventually, she told herself as she walked into Rita's office, she'd look back on this time in her life and it would be so distant that she'd barely be able to see it.

12

The day of the meeting with Alice Lincoln, Maud put on a pantsuit that she'd ordered online. Her one suit from England no longer fit. She'd gained weight over the past year, thirteen pounds, according to the scale at the doctor's office, mostly in a band around her stomach. The contours of her body had melted; her rounded shoulders hid their muscles; her legs dropped straight from her hips to her ankles. In the bathroom, having mussed her short hair so it would look less like her mother's, she rubbed on a layer of the moisturizer that Annette had given her for Christmas, made from seaweed and apple stem cells.

"Fancy, Mom," Louise said when Maud came into the kitchen, where the girls were eating cereal.

"Nice," Ella said. "There's still a price tag on the sleeve."

Peter got up from reading the paper to fetch a pair of scissors recently reintroduced to a drawer. Maud raised her arm, and he snipped off the tag.

"You look splendid," he said. He kissed her cheek. "Break an arm."

"Dad, it's a leg!" Louise protested, mouth full of cereal.

"I know. I was joking."

My sweet family, Maud thought, as she drove away from the house. Peter truly had changed. He was a better father now and a better husband. And that was enough. It wasn't the worst thing in the world to live in one of those sexless Victorian marriages, a woman on one side of the house with her husband on the other, meeting in the middle for the children, kissing each other on the forehead at night before going to their separate rooms. Lust and passion had deserted her body. Her brain was back in charge. And soon she'd open her laptop and convince Alice Lincoln to fund the Briones house and garden.

Maria called as she drove over the bridge. "Change of plans. She doesn't want a presentation."

"I don't understand."

"When I called earlier to give her driving directions, I mentioned that you and I had prepared presentations. And she said she didn't want presentations. She just wants us to tell her, and I quote, 'what it is and how much.' Try not to think about the hours you spent on the PowerPoint slides."

"But I'm not good at winging things," Maud said.

She had indeed spent hours on the PowerPoint slides, plus hours learning how to use PowerPoint itself. On top of studying the landscape of California for the past year, she'd been trying to update her technical skills.

"You'll be fine," Maria said. "You know what you're talking about. Are you okay with dogs? She didn't need the driving directions because she and her dog are somehow coming here on a bus."

"I'm fine with dogs," Maud said despondently. But she was truly bad at winging things. From kindergarten through graduate school, whenever she was called on, a cork slid into her throat and words became goo in her mouth.

"I'm taking her over to the dig now," Maria said. "Meet us there if you can. Otherwise, I'll see you at ten for the meeting. We'll improvise something."

By the time Maud had reached the Presidio's gates, she was sweating so much from the stress that the fancy moisturizer had run into her eyes, and she had to blink compulsively to see the road. This stupid suit betrayed her desire for approval, and her ballet flats pinched. She stopped at Tennessee Hollow, but Maria and Alice had already left— not a good sign of Alice's interest. Careful not to muddy her suit, she took another round of soil samples.

"We'll keep it quick," Maria whispered as she walked Maud down a hall at the foundation's headquarters. "She's exhausting."

In a windowed conference room, Alice Lincoln sat a foot away from the table with a mountainous Dalmatian at her feet. The dog tilted its head at Maud, to assess her with skeptical blue eyes, before returning its head to its paws. Like the dog, Alice was large—big-boned, broad-shouldered, even taller than she looked in the photograph on her Wikipedia page, maybe because in the photograph she was standing in a vacuous warehouse that warped scale. Masses of black hair, marbled with gray, coiled over her shoulders. She was in her early fifties, and her face showed her years—grooves across her forehead, parentheses by her mouth—but her skin glowed as if backlit. In the Wikipedia photograph, that soft mouth arched belligerently and most of her face was shadowed by the welding mask pushed on top of her head.

Maud went around the table to shake hands with Alice after Maria introduced her, but Alice didn't move, so Maud simply said hello and sat down. Chris came to mind, although Alice's gaze was as blunt and direct as his had been detached.

"I didn't know garden historians were a thing," Alice said.

"It's more common in England," Maud said. "That's where I trained."

"Yeah, I was told."

Alice kicked off one of the sandals she was wearing with socks and tucked her foot into the space between the dog's body and paw, digging in her toes. Maud didn't understand her energy—was she being aggressive or indifferent or judgmental? Her expression was inscrutable; her mouth and cheeks and forehead barely moved when she spoke.

Maria began. She described how Juana Briones had spent her teenage years at Tennessee Hollow, where she lived in the adobe house and tended the garden with her sisters. In 1820, eighteen years old, she married a soldier from the nearby fort, and they bought a tract of land now buried by the manicured streets of Pacific Heights. They went on to have eleven children, eight of whom lived to adulthood. On top of farming and caring for her family, Juana Briones was a curandera, a healer; she calmed fevers, set broken bones, and cured illnesses with native plants like the yerba buena that she foraged in the hills around the Presidio.

In 1844, she made a formal request to the Catholic Church for a separation from her husband, who had become abusive. Receiving no response, she left with her children and constructed the first private house between the Presidio and Mission Dolores. There, she started her own successful farm in what became North Beach. She died in 1889 on her large cattle ranch in the hills near Stanford University a respected community leader.

"She was one of the first three settlers of San Francisco,"

Maria said, "a founder of the city, and all she gets is a plaque in Washington Square. I grew up in the Mission and I never heard a word about her in school."

Alice's face barely moved as Maria described the vision for Tennessee Hollow. The adobe house would contain exhibits about the lives of Juana Briones and her sisters. Educational programs would run year-round, with summer camps for disadvantaged children. The re-created garden ("Maud will tell you more about that") would be cultivated by students from a bilingual charter school and its produce sold at the Mission Dolores farmers market.

Listening to Maria steadied Maud's nerves until it was her turn to speak. But four sentences in, she was back in her plaid uniform in front of a classroom at Holy Conception, reciting a poem she couldn't remember, every missed word a five-point deduction. At first she sped too quickly through her description of how she'd located the garden, then she slowed down painfully on its design. "Once we've finished the soil testing, I'll know more and then I can decide what exactly to choose," she said, trailing off.

Alice's eyelids lowered, as if Maud had bored her to oblivion. At least with the PowerPoint there would have been pictures.

"Well," Maria said, ending the fiasco, "that wraps things up here. The folks from development will arrive soon."

"Great," Alice said dryly. The dog moved its head from its paws to her foot.

"It was nice meeting you," Maud said.

"You have dirt on your shoes," Alice said.

Maud looked down. Her flats were crusted with mud on the toes, a rippling line of brown like a trim on the black leather. "Gardeners often do," she said.

"Good for them," Alice said with an approving nod.

On the way back home, Maria called. "Nice job," she said. "I told you she's a piece of work."

"I blathered. Does she ever smile?"

"I don't think so. She's the spider. We're the flies. I hate this part of the job. And her insistence on anonymity is annoying. She doesn't seem to realize that people barely know who she is now. She was so hot in the nineties. I guess she thinks if word gets out that she's giving away all this money, journalists will swarm her compound."

"Do you think she'll fund it?"

"No clue. We have another meeting next week. But I'm moving that one to the archaeology center. I don't think the foundation office is helping our case. She ate the development people alive. Anyway, you're on salary until the end of the month."

No, Maud thought. It can't be over. "Can I go ahead with the pomegranate tree?" she asked. "The soil's warm enough for planting now."

"Sure." Maria sighed. "We can afford that, at least."

Ahead of the car, the Marin Headlands undulated at the foot of the bay, tawny and smooth as sleeping hounds. Maud had grown up less than an hour away, yet she had never walked those hills as a child, merely glimpsed them on excursions to the city. For months when Ella was in treatment, she had relearned this landscape and unlearned the history she'd been taught about it as a girl. She read everything she could find about the hundreds of communities, each with their own territory and language, that lived here before Juan Gaspar de Portolá and his expedition of two hundred men first saw the bay. Every commonly used nomenclative term—Ohlone, Indian—was wrong. The primary documentation—observations of Spanish explorers and missionaries—was warped by racism, and much of the secondary documentation contained elegiac, exoticized descriptions. Finally, in the spring, she gave up reading and hired a naturalist from a local tribe to teach her what he knew. Following him along a trail in the Headlands, she learned that bracken fern could be an umbrella, cattail made strong baskets, the smoke of California bay leaves staved off fleas. Plants as medicine. Plants as food. Plants as survival.

And Juana Briones, Maud thought, as the Headlands disappeared in the rearview mirror, found survival in those plants. She made a full, vigorous, loving life on this hard, unforgiving landscape. Beaten by her husband, dismissed not only as a woman but as a woman of color, she had shown a force of character that had thundered through Maud as she sat doing research in a cubicle at Stanford. The document had been transcribed and translated from Spanish, but it nonetheless rang with Juana Briones's voice: *I do not fear to shoulder the conjugal cross that the Lord my Father and my Mother the Holy Church have asked me to bear, being in a state that I have freely chosen. What I truly fear is the loss of my own soul forever, and what is more, I fear the destruction of my unfortunate family due to the scandal and bad example of a man who has forgotten God and his own soul. . . .*

Maud had applied to the project at Tennessee Hollow still lacking knowledge, still learning, aware that she was too white and too privileged for the position. But she came with a plan to find the garden, so Maria had taken a chance on her. And that garden mattered, she thought now. The history of the people who watered it and tended it mattered even if the only lines they'd left behind were adobe bricks in the ground. She would order that pomegranate tree tonight. And she'd trust that the rest would follow.

Sunday morning, she awoke feeling as if her head were stuffed with cotton. It was the day of the experiment that Ella's therapist, Rita, had suggested. Maud and Peter were going to take Louise to Stinson Beach for a party hosted by his firm and leave Ella alone in the house for the first time.

"Are we sure she's ready?" Maud asked Peter, who was shaving in the bathroom. "I could stay."

"We have to try it sometime." He tapped the razor against the sink. "And everyone else has their spouse at these things."

He said "spouse," but he meant wife. His firm was almost exclusively male, save the administrative assistants. Maud always dreaded these events, but today the dread weighed down her shoulders.

To wake Louise, she pulled back her curtains and let the light spill onto the bed. The suncatcher from the camp in the Hudson Valley dangled in the window. When Louise looked at it now, Maud wondered, did she remember days at camp, climbing the ropes course, swimming in the lake? Did she have good memories of that summer? All Maud could see was the suncatcher swinging on the rearview mirror as she drove to the emergency room.

In the car, Peter barked at Louise about buckling her seat belt. He was stressed too, Maud realized, and probably listing the same worries that were ticker-taping through her own head. Ella had never been deemed suicidal. Maud's mother had been wrong when she made that facile comparison. Then again, what was the difference between a shallow cut to the thigh and a deep cut to the wrist? A little harder, a miscalculation even, and a vein could open.

You OK? she texted Ella.

Yup.

Peter glanced over. "She'll be fine."

"I know. Don't miss the exit."

The Oyster Shack on Stinson Beach had once been an actual salt-cured shack where paper plates of oysters and shucking knives were handed out. Now it was à glitzy restaurant with valet parking, brushed aluminum tables, and good-looking young servers in canvas aprons who took orders on electronic tablets. The firm had rented out the entire space for their staff and select clients with portfolios over a million dollars.

Louise joined the other children in a back room to watch a clown attempt to balance a bowl of goldfish on his head. Peter put on his work face and got Maud a mimosa. The head of another division came over and slapped Peter on the back. Maud hauled up her mouth. She clinked glasses. Twenty minutes later, she set down the glass to text Ella again, *Still doing OK?*

Still wishing you wouldn't text every five minutes!

She swilled the mimosa. As happened at these events, the room divided into suits and dresses, and now she found herself standing with the wife of Peter's boss and another woman as they lamented their difficult house remodels. One of them hadn't had a working stove in weeks. Maud tried to look interested. Ella was home alone, and there were knives in the kitchen. She glanced at her phone as the women talked about paint swatches and shower fixtures. With the same honeyed highlights in their shoulder-length hair and the same pampered hands, they looked like twins. Maud felt that she had nothing in common with them, but of course she did—she simply didn't want to.

Honking a rubber horn, the clown was now leading the children out of the restaurant to the beach, a sack over his shoulder. "Kite time," he hollered as they passed the buffet table where their fathers were huddled. The mothers set down their drinks, put on their coats, and followed.

On the ocean, the dots of two surfers bobbed in the waves. The children ran after the stick-and-polyester falcons that soared over the sand, seeking prey in the wrong habitat. The wind whipped Maud's face. The woman next to her buttoned her designer coat and knotted a silk scarf around her neck. "Who the hell came up with this idea?" she said. "Did they really think we were going to stay inside drinking while some creepy clown takes our kids into the cold?"

"They wanted to get rid of the women and children," another woman said.

"They're probably smoking cigars in there."

Maud texted Ella again.

I'm fine MOM!

With a final blast of his horn, the clown waved goodbye, shift finished. Still holding her kite, Louise took over leading the group. The other children followed her down the beach, skirting the clutching fingers of tide toward a cluster of objects that, Maud saw as they all drew nearer, weren't rocks or washed-up redwood trunks as they had seemed. Three baby sea lions, ribs pushing though their mottled skin, eyes dull, lifted their heads, squirmed, dropped back down to the sand.

"They're starving," someone said. "Poor things."

In a chorus of alarmed exclamations, the children reeled in their kites. A woman called a ranger on her phone and alerted the fathers, several of whom now materialized on the beach.

"Climate change," a woman said. "They come in too far to find food."

"We need to go back to Ella," Maud told Louise.

"We can't leave them," Louise said. She had tears in her eyes. "Can't we do something? Like carry them back into the water?"

"Let's wait for the experts," Maud said. She texted Peter, who was still inside, and he replied that he'd take a cab home to Ella.

Finally, two rangers arrived. They loaded the sea lions onto stretchers, explaining that they'd release them back into the water when they were strong enough to swim again. As the truck drove away, the children cheered, save Louise, who stayed quiet on the walk to the car.

"What if they don't find their mothers?" she said.

"Their mothers will find them," Maud said, and Louise nodded resolutely, as if trying to convince herself that this was true.

Back home, she plopped down next to Ella on the couch to tell her what had happened, giving the story a happy end. But as Maud made dinner with Peter, she couldn't get the image of the sea lions out of her head. And when she kissed Louise good night, she knew her daughter was haunted by that image too. The way the pups had thrashed and churned in the sand. The way they looked up at the sky as if confused, as if they thought it should be water.

13

In the winter of 2007, Maud had attended a conference in Oxford and sat next to a woman who worked for the National Trust, which administered England's historic gardens.

"Would you ever consider moving?" the woman said.

"The odds are slim," Maud said, "but tell me about it?"

Monk's House, the home of Virginia and Leonard Woolf, had recently been vacated and a gardener was needed to live in the house to manage the grounds, conduct tours, and write about the Woolfs' passion for gardening.

Maud was flattered, but she explained that her husband would never be able to find work in Suffolk, and London was two hours away, an impossible commute. Plus, her career in London had been going well with a full slate of garden restoration projects—she'd recently finished rehabilitating a potting garden on a major estate. Still, over the next week the idea started to bubble, fed by the yeast of her imagination. In London, she constantly switched projects.

At Monk's House, she'd live in a garden year-round. She could invest in the beds from season to season, see the bulbs she planted in the fall break open in the spring. She'd live through the freezes of winter, the fruiting and blooming of summer, the rusting of fall. She'd be part of a landscape, part of its history. And she had always loved Virginia Woolf's writing.

When she mentioned the conversation to Peter, she expected him to confirm that it wouldn't work. He had a busy career as a manager in risk assessment at an international investment bank, not something you could do outside of London. He frequently had to travel abroad—half the time he seemed to be away, and the other half recovering from jet lag. Surprisingly, though, he wasn't opposed. After the four of them visited Monk's House that spring, Ella and Louise became excited about a potential move. They liked the village with its flint-and-thatch cottages, the lambs in the fields, the 99 Flakes from the ice-cream shop in the square. Peter said he could commute on the weekends from London to be with the family. He even seemed to think the change was a good idea. He worried about money, although they had plenty, and he liked the addition of a second stable salary. "And we're good being apart," they decided, having such different interests. Peter, for instance, hadn't read a novel since his university days and found Virginia Woolf's writing tedious.

The plan, when Maud announced it to her friends and family back home, seemed bold, innovative, and modern. The fact that her mother thought it strange ("What couple lives apart all week?") was a plus. What she hadn't realized was how much joy and peace she'd feel without Peter, without his flares of grumpiness, his work stress, his whiskers in the bathroom sink. Since Louise was born, she'd felt the gap between the two of them grow into a chasm, but she thought: This is marriage. Still, as the months went by and she fell more in love with her new life, she wondered if this was *her marriage*. When Peter came home to Monk's House, she stuck close to the girls. She pretended to be asleep when he reached for her at night. She no longer tried to ask chipper questions when he talked about work. She kept a mental log of his flaws. He walked straight down the path to the house without ever glancing at the flowers she'd planted. He called her friends the "gabbers," and had no close friends of his own. Despite his progressive social views, his reflexes were sexist. He always chose male doctors, hurried to open doors for women with a gallantry that suggested they couldn't push a handle, and constantly used the word "lovely" when describing his assistant. What had once seemed quaint and fixable now seemed oppressive.

Maud started to spend Friday nights out with her friends and away from him, joining a chorus that met over pints at the local pub to complain about men and marriage. No one was having good sex. Everyone was sick of putting down the toilet seat. But Maud's complaints ran deeper. She no longer wanted to be with Peter. And eventually he noticed. He stopped kissing her good night. He repeatedly asked her if she was listening to anything he said. They bickered over mundanities like who had left the cap off the saltcellar.

"Maybe we should go to counseling," Maud said half-heartedly after a failed attempt at sex, during which her vagina stayed dry and Peter lost his erection.

"What's the point of counseling if we no longer know how to talk?" Peter said.

"Isn't that the point of counseling?"

But she didn't insist. Together, they gave up. And, as she both knew and didn't know, Peter started cheating.

Then, in the spring of 2010, the head of his division retired, and Peter—the clear successor—was passed up by a junior colleague. He was devastated. "Kicked in the head," he said when he called Maud from London to tell her. He was his usual quiet on his weekends home, but crankier, even with Louise and Ella. He drank too much at night, which made him nicer but in a messy, slurring way that reminded Maud of her father. As the orchard blossomed and the tulips emerged, he turned his resentment on Maud. If he hadn't received the promotion, he said, it was the fault of the commute and the complications of a split existence. He said that Maud should never have taken the Monk's House job and put him in this position.

"You're rewriting history," she said. "You agreed to this."

"Stop talking about bloody history."

"Stop blaming me for your failure."

The two of them were in the potting shed, where they now went to fight to be out of earshot of the girls. Maud had thrown the word "failure" at Peter like a rock, and she saw the impact on his face. They didn't speak for the rest of the weekend.

The following Thursday evening, after she picked him up from the train station, he asked her to pull over. She'd never seen him cry, not even when his father died. It was disconcerting to watch his face crumble.

"I'm sorry I've been an ass," he said. "I feel lost. There's one thing I'm good at, and I don't even know if I am any-more." He couldn't take it, he said. He couldn't go back to that office. He was humiliated. He had to quit. "And I need you to believe in me."

"I do," Maud said, feeling ashamed. She had loved this man once. She had to figure out a way to love him again.

She expected Peter to find another job in London, but by the end of the summer he had an offer from an interna-tional bank that wanted him to head their risk management division in San Francisco. "It's perfect," he said. "We'll be near your family, and it's a million times better than what I had. Thank you for encouraging me." Maud was stunned. She didn't want to leave Monk's House or England. Peter reassured her that the move could be temporary. "Even a few years would reset my career," he said. He was so thrilled over the offer, and so relieved, that she felt there was no choice but to go.

Three months later, Maud was living in Marin as their furniture floated across the Atlantic. She started immedi-ately to look for work. The next spring, she was still looking. Eventually she found a short-term job at a winery in Napa Valley and drove there and back one day a week. She vol-unteered at the conservatory in Golden Gate Park. But she couldn't find a significant project. Most people in the U.S. didn't even know what "garden historian" meant. She kept having to explain and define herself until she stopped using the term and simply said "gardener."

One morning, she came home from the grocery store and stood in the kitchen, the bags cradled in her arms. This was her life, and she couldn't change it. She had no sav-ings in her name. Everything she owned she shared with her husband. She had no work and might not find any. This move hadn't been temporary, and she'd been stupid to think that it could be. She was now what she'd never imagined herself being: a stay-at-home mother, preoccupied with finding the right-size blinds for her oversized windows, checking the mileage on the cars to see when they needed service, doing laundry, mopping floors, cleaning baseboards that, it turned out, gathered alarming amounts of dust, although she'd never noticed such things at Monk's House. She would end up as a bitter version of Mrs. Dalloway and Mrs. Ramsay, without their interest or ability in the domestic arts. She had no room of her own, and even if she were to find one, she had nothing to do in it.

This was the recent history of Maud's marriage to Peter as the two of them unpacked it during their six months of marriage counseling in the early days of Ella's treatment.

"You're right that I drifted away a long time ago," Maud told him. "And I shouldn't have said that I didn't love you. Of course I do."

As my children's father, she thought.

"You're right that I didn't take your needs into account," Peter said.

During several tortuous sessions, they discussed Peter's cheating. He admitted to another affair and gave Maud the details when she asked: work colleague, hotel rooms. "I never brought her to the London flat," he said.

The tears in Maud's eyes were unexpected, tears of grief and humiliation.

"I thought I didn't care," she said.

"This is good," the counselor said. "This is real communication."

But even as Maud recognized her part in the marriage's disintegration, even as she forgave Peter for his infidelity, she willfully, intentionally, resolutely kept a secret. She never told Peter that she'd slept with Gabriel or about how she'd felt about him. Despite all her own questions about Gabriel, despite her belief that she'd been foolish and reckless at Montgomery Place, she still held the lie close, protecting its glow.

The gates of Lone Pines Psychiatric Hospital opened onto clipped grass islanded by stucco bungalows. The outpatient center, a modern, mirrored building, shone in a ring of palm trees. Several days had passed since the trip to Stinson Beach, and Maud and Ella were arriving for Ella's weekly therapy appointment with Rita.

"Everything okay?" Maud asked in the waiting room when she saw Ella roll her eyes at her phone. Since they'd sat down, she'd been scrolling through texts.

"It's this stupid guy in science. He keeps messaging me."

Maud already knew about the boy, because the night before, she'd read his long line of messages and Ella's monosyllabic replies.

What's up?

Not much.

Wanna hang out this weekend?

Can't.

Peter had stopped monitoring Ella's communications months ago, but for Maud, sneaking the phone from her daughter's nightstand felt as natural as checking her breathing when she slept as a baby. She didn't even know what she was looking for anymore.

"You should mention it to Rita if he's harassing you," she said.

"He isn't harassing me. He likes me. Whatever."

Ella unwrapped a stick of gum and folded it into her mouth. A hoodie bagged below her knees, zipped to the neck. Her style had changed since treatment, her clothes monochromatic and unrevealing. From what Maud could observe, she showed no interest in boys at all. Or in girls, for that matter. Was this normal? Could it be a sign of sexual abuse? Sitting in this room stirred up all the old, paranoid questions.

Once Rita called Ella's name, Maud went outside to escape the stale air of the building. An irritable sky threatened rain. Spreading for acres, Lone Pines had been built in the 1890s as an "asylum for the insane" that catered to the wealthy of California. Film stars, heiresses, and tycoons used to arrive by night in limousines for hydrotherapy and electroshock treatments. As a girl, Maud rode her bike down the busy street from her house and along the stone walls. She'd pull up to the gates to gaze at the original Gothic castle with its turrets and towers, the windows of the top floors barred, imagining women in nightgowns walking barefoot through cavernous rooms like Bertha in *Jane Eyre.*

Now, on the tennis courts, a group of teens from the eating disorders unit were tossing beanbags into a hoop, their eyes too big, their ears too prominent, their bodies dry as fossils. At least Ella didn't have that illness as well, Maud thought as raindrops flecked the sidewalk. She remembered checking under the toilet lid to see if Ella had been making herself throw up. What if she had taken her to a therapist then and found out about the self-harm? The secret meetings with Gabriel would never have happened. She kept walking until she had to return to Rita's office with damp socks and sodden pant cuffs.

"I want to congratulate you both on Ella staying by herself at the house," Rita said. "It's a big step for her to be completely alone with her thoughts and to not act on them. And for you and Peter to let her do that."

"It wasn't easy," Maud said. "I only texted five times."

"Six," Ella said.

"Is there anything you'd like to discuss?" Rita asked Maud.

Yes, Maud thought, Gabriel's name having followed her into the room. I want to hear everything Ella just told you. I want to look into her memory and find out exactly what happened with him. I want to see his face when they were in his cottage. I want to know what he said and what he was thinking. I want to know why I still think that Ella is lying.

"Not really."

Rita crossed her hands on her knees. "Ella has something she'd like to talk about."

Maud tensed. Sometimes these post-therapy debriefings felt like an ambush.

"Stop checking my phone," Ella said.

"How did you know?" Maud said.

"You left the browser open. You do that every time. Do you think I'm doing drugs or something?"

"No," Maud stuttered. "It's a habit from when you were sick and your dad and I wanted to make sure everything was okay."

"Well, he was better at it," Ella said with a withering glance.

Maud looked down and fiddled with a button on her sweater.

"Ella," Rita said, "would you mind giving your mom and me a minute?"

"Fine," Ella said and stalked out of the room.

"I'm sorry," Maud told Rita when the door closed. "I guess I shouldn't do that anymore? I don't know what I'm supposed to do."

Rita held out a tissue box. "She didn't mean for it to come out so harshly."

"I think she did," Maud said, taking a tissue. "She's different with me than with Peter. She's still so angry. It's like our relationship gets worse as she gets better."

"You're the mother. That makes it more complicated," Rita said. "I've mentioned this before. If you think that you could use extra support, I can give you names. You need to take care of your mental health too."

"Thank you." Maud wiped her eyes and picked up her purse. "I know. I'll consider it." But she didn't want to go to therapy. She didn't want to tell anyone about Gabriel.

She and Ella ran from the office through the rain. "I'll stop checking your phone," Maud told her when they were in the car. "I did it because I love you."

"Please love me without invading my privacy," Ella said.

"Please try to talk to me more."

"I talk to you, Mom." Ella pointed at her mouth. "See my lips moving?"

Maud headed out of the parking lot, but as they passed through the city, she exited the freeway and drove quickly up the steep streets.

"Where are we going?" Ella said.

"Annette's," Maud said. She needed a hug from her sister.

Annette's condo sat high on Twin Peaks in a lopsided building where she'd moved to after her husband, Dale, had died. Buddha statues, patchouli candles, and Tibetan prayer flags from Pier 1 Imports filled the sunny rooms. Crystals sparkled on the windowsills. In the first years of her grief, Annette had made a one-hundred-and-eighty-degree spiritual turn from Catholicism to a hodgepodge of watered-down Eastern religions. Yoga and this paraphernalia were all that remained.

"Surprise!" Maud called from the hall.

"Kitchen," a voice—not Annette's—called back. Their mother was at the table drinking instant coffee. Four opened packets of artificial sweeter lay on the saucer.

"Hi," Maud said. "Where's Annette?"

She usually got home by four, but maybe she'd stayed at the office late today and Maud would be stuck here alone with their mother.

"Basement. Doing laundry. Getting ready for one of her dates." Her mother turned to Ella, who was rummaging in a refrigerator stocked with diet sodas, protein shakes, and single containers of cottage cheese. "I finished sewing your sister's costume for the St. Patrick's Day parade. Are you sure you don't want one?"

"I don't dance anymore, Grams," Ella said. She popped open a can of Fresca.

"Maybe you should."

"It's kind of a little-kid thing."

"Your mom and aunt did it through high school."

"We didn't really have a choice." Maud took a Tab for herself. Annette's soda preferences were stuck in the 1970s.

Her mother frowned. "No one held a gun to your heads."

Ella gave Maud a look—solidarity? compassion?—and said she was going to chill out in the living room.

"How was it today, then?" Maud's mother asked when she'd left.

The closest she ever got to delving into Ella's illness was

this one question that she posed occasionally about Ella's therapy sessions. She barely said it like a question at all.

"Good," Maud said.

"I'm just glad she isn't living at that place anymore. Those girls were like zombies. No wonder they feel down, when all they do is sit around all day."

"They're sitting around because they're depressed, Mom. They aren't depressed because they're sitting around."

"Depressed." Her mother scoffed. "People didn't used to get depressed. Life's hard. You have bad days."

"People did get depressed," Maud said. "They just didn't get help."

Annette bustled into the kitchen with a laundry basket, wearing a bathrobe, her wet hair cocooned in a towel and gel patches under her eyes. Maud gave her the warm version of the hug she'd given her mother.

"I guess you two want to complain about me," their mother said, "so I'll go home and get your father's steak in the oven."

"We were taught to only say nice things about our parents." Annette set the laundry basket on the table.

"Sure." Her mother picked up her puce pleather purse, which resembled a bowling bag. "Be careful tonight."

"Ma," Annette said, "I promise you I don't date psychopaths."

"You know nothing about them."

They waited for their mother's steps to retreat into the living room and out the front door.

"Holy shit," Annette whispered. "She calls to say that she's stopping by for a chat, and I feel like I should be a good daughter and keep her company, even though I have a million things to do. Then she just sits there like she wants to go. Like *I* asked *her* to come over. I finally told her I needed to take a shower, and she said I was drying out my skin by washing it too much." She pointed at her face. "Does my skin seem dry to you? Because what she meant was, I'm looking worn out."

"You're radiant, as always," Maud said. "And don't ask me for advice about how to deal with Mom."

"'How was it today, then?'" Annette said, imitating their mother's high voice.

Maud laughed, shaking her head. "I don't know. I feel like shit. Ella caught me checking her email."

"Want to distract yourself by doing my makeup?"

"You know I'm no good at that."

"Yes, you are. Your lines are always straight."

Annette's bathroom was an arsenal of anti-aging devices meant to relax wrinkles, promote elasticity, and restore youthful glow. A plastic mask loomed next to the mirror like a prop from a horror movie. Plucking the patches from under her eyes, Annette sat on the toilet lid. The skin between her brows was now perfectly smooth from the injections she got every few months, her forehead and cheeks burnished by lasers. She'd erased the furrows of her grief, but they were still there, under the surface, carved into her cells. Maud drew liner on Annette's eyelids. Despite all the men she dated, her sister was still married. And to a ghost. Lanky and gap-toothed, Dale had been a delivery room nurse with a passion for baseball and guitar and, more than anything, Annette. When they were growing up, he had always been at their house in Burlingame, the brother Maud wished their real brother, Kevin, would have been: gentle and supportive and kind. His laughter was a train leaving the station, slow at first, then so loud and forceful that it picked you up and made you laugh too.

Ten years ago, when Dale and Annette had finally visited England, Maud stayed up late with them in the Monk's House orchard, talking and laughing, the girls curled up in sleeping bags on the grass. Annette casually mentioned on that trip that Dale had a weird-looking mole on his foot but that he wouldn't listen to her about going to the doctor. A year later, he was a skeleton draped in parchment skin. On their Christmas visit to California, Ella said, "Is Uncle Dale going to die?" when Maud tucked her into bed. In April, he did. Maud had grieved through her grandparents' deaths, but Dale's death was a horror. He'd been so young and alive. Even now she could see his jaundiced, hollowed-out face in that hospital bed, and the devastation in her sister's eyes.

"Look up," Maud said now, teasing a mascara wand along Annette's lashes as Ella came into the room.

"Perfect," Annette said once she'd examined the results in a hand mirror. She hopped off the toilet. "Help me decide what to wear tonight," she told Ella.

In the bedroom, three red dresses lay on the bed, necklaces lying on invisible necks, earrings lined up to invisible ears, matching shoes in invisible feet on the floor.

"The red one," Ella said.

Annette air-smacked her. "Very funny. Long, short, or fitted? Pumps, heels, silver, or gold?"

"Short, heels, gold," Ella said.

"You could have asked me," Maud told Annette.

"No offense, but look what you're wearing."

"It's Marin boho," Ella said.

"What's that?" Maud said. "Did you make that up?"

"It's what all the moms wear," Ella said. "You're the only one who actually does something besides Pilates in those clothes."

Maud was glad that Ella had become lighthearted enough to mock her. And maybe that had almost been a compliment?

After dinner in Peter's study, she debriefed him on the session with Rita. The air here smelled different from the rest of the house, more chemical, maybe from the guts of Peter's enormous computer, where numbers marched across two monitors. On the wall hung a drawing that Ella had done after they'd brought Louise home from the hospital. Peter was a tall stick figure next to the short stick figure of Maud, while Ella—the only one with hair—towered over both of them, Louise in her arms like a misshapen potato.

"You handle all this better than I do," Maud said. She was sitting in a chair made with two pieces of leather stretched on a steel frame.

"You handle it fine," Peter said. "It's hard."

She sighed. "Will she ever stop hating me?"

"She doesn't hate you." Peter swiveled in his chair and moved closer.

"She's so cold to me," Maud said. "You should have seen the way she looked at me today. I think some part of her will never forgive me for failing her."

"We both failed her," Peter said.

They'd discussed their guilt in marriage counseling, wondering if their problems had contributed to Ella's self-harm, although Ella never brought up their relationship.

"I failed her more," Maud said. "I was right there."

And I'm failing you now, she thought. I'm failing this marriage.

"It's not a competition," Peter said.

She imagined getting out of the chair and going to him, unbuttoning his shirt, unfastening his belt. When they were young, before the girls, they spent weekend afternoons on the couch. She read novels as he worked. An open window. Dimming London traffic. The roar from across the street when the pub door opened. Her head on a pillow on Peter's lap.

"I'll let you work," she said.

In the kitchen, she opened her laptop to her latest design of the garden at Tennessee Hollow. She added the bed of native herbs that she wanted to include, a triangle next to a square. Then her hand moved to the mouse and to the internet browser, and she typed the words "Gabriel Crews archaeologist." She clicked on a link that had appeared since she last looked a year before. He was now a lecturer at the University of Nevada. There was that same photo from his faculty page at Ithaca College. He taught two courses at the Las Vegas campus and directed a summer program in archaeology near Death Valley. Why was he there? He'd said he didn't like teaching. She made her hand drag the mouse, erase the history, and put the laptop to sleep.

14

The morning the pomegranate tree arrived at the archaeology center, Maud drove it straight to Tennessee Hollow. She'd left the stump of the original tree exposed, to be marked with a plaque. A few feet away, she dug a hole in the earth. What a labor it must have been, she thought, plunging the shovel into clay, to garden in such intolerant ground through summer fogs, erratic sun, salty ocean wind. Every plant that thrived and grew and fruited must have seemed like a miracle.

She dug as fast as she could, as if Maria might arrive at the site and tell her she had to stop because there was no more money. Despite another visit to the Presidio, Alice still hadn't committed to funding the project. She'd been back this morning to go over the budget, and Maria had texted Maud a string of exasperated emoticons and the message *Still didn't say!*

Torquing the handle, Maud strained and heaved. She flung off her jacket to move more freely, then stood on the metal lip again and ground the shovel down. Sweat stung her eyes. Her shoulder throbbed. She remembered working with Chris and the rhythm they'd found. Then she saw Lydia in her robe the night Ella disappeared, Harriet at her office door, hand open for the farmhouse key. Maud had written Lydia and Frazer an email a few weeks after leaving Montgomery Place: *I should never have asked about Chris. I'm so sorry.* Lydia replied a week later: *You were panicking about your daughter. And people have always thought the worst of Chris. We're used to it.*

The collateral damage of that heedless summer. Maud gritted her teeth and emptied the shovel, flinging the clay aside. How had she ever thought she could leave her marriage without wreaking devastation? How had she let herself go like that? Like a teenager, mooning over Gabriel. To say you loved someone after less than three months. That wasn't love; it was lust. And who had Gabriel actually been? When she'd looked at him across that table, had she been looking at him or looking at herself? The self she wanted to be: interesting and cultured, spontaneous and fun.

She dropped the shovel and glugged from her water bottle. Only then did she notice Alice Lincoln on the walkway, unleashed dog at her side. Maud called out a hello, and Alice waved vaguely. Maud wondered how long she had been standing there, watching. Alice patted the dog on the head. When it looked up, she pointed with two fingers. Its nose angled at her, head cocked to the side, then it started to walk with her toward Maud.

The dog was deaf, Maud realized. "I didn't know they could use sign language," she said. She wiped her forehead with the tail of her shirt.

"I wouldn't say 'use,' but they can understand it."

Alice wore the same outfit she'd had on that first day, a hybrid of jumpsuit and overalls made of canvas.

"Is he old?"

"Clark? Not too old. Blue eyes in a Dalmatian mean endless health problems. Usually they're murdered as puppies."

Maud picked up the shovel, shifting it between her palms. "I don't have a lot to show you here. Maria probably told you the rest of the soil tests came in. There were peppers in that bed over there." She wondered what Alice was doing at the site if she was so uncommitted to the project. "I'm planting the pomegranate tree."

"I can see that," Alice said. Her mouth flickered in what might be a smile.

"Do you want to see the final garden design?" Maud said. "I'm almost done. I can print it out and mail it to you."

"I wanted to ask you about a consulting job at my place," Alice said. "There's a plant in one of my fields that I can't get rid of. I'd pay you, to state the obvious. You can show me your design then if you want."

Maud wasn't sure how she was supposed to reply to this request. Would doing this consultation help Maria make their case? Saying no didn't seem like a good idea, so she said sure, she'd be happy to.

"Can you do Wednesday at ten?" Alice said without first asking about convenient days or times or windows. Maud thought about saying that day wouldn't work, just to prove a point, but clearly you didn't play games with Alice, or if you did, she set the rules. Maud found such breezy belligerence refreshing in a woman, but Maria was right that Alice was exhausting.

"Park on the shoulder, climb the gate, and come straight to the house," Alice said, having given Maud an address on Highway One. She patted Clark on the head. "See you then."

"Climb the gate?" Maud called.

"It's low," Alice said without turning around.

That Sunday morning, as Maud and Peter were reading the newspaper in the kitchen, Annette stopped by the house in a cocktail dress with a box of cinnamon buns from a bakery in Mill Valley. Louise, still in her pajamas, grabbed pastries for herself and Ella to eat in front of the TV.

"Why are you so dressed up?" she asked Annette as she headed back to the living room.

"Last night's date lives in Tiburon," Annette said. "The guest room had an amazing view of the water," she added, winking at Maud.

"I'll leave you two to gab," Peter said. He evacuated the kitchen with his coffee and the business section of the paper.

"Did I embarrass him?" Annette kicked off her shoes.

"He's probably jealous," Maud said. "It's been over a year for us." She gave Annette a mug of coffee.

"You do realize that's insane."

"Turns out giving up sex is like giving up sugar. After a while, you lose the taste."

"Are you sure he's not finding it somewhere else?"

"He wouldn't do that again. Anyway, not now."

At the table, Annette put her feet in Maud's lap, a ritual they'd started in their teenage years, imitating their elderly aunts. Maud cracked Annette's toes and massaged her heels. They went only that far, whereas their aunts shaved each other's calluses with a razor.

"So, what?" Annette said. She took another minuscule bite from the cinnamon roll, having scraped off the frosting. "You've taken a vow of chastity?"

"I'm not thinking about it."

"When women don't have orgasms, they keep all their negative energy in their cells. It can cause cancer."

"Jesus, Annette," Maud said, kneading her arches. "Where did you read that?"

"It's true! It's too much unreleased energy. Remember what almost happened in the Hudson Valley."

Maud dropped Annette's feet to the floor. "I can't forget what happened in the Hudson Valley."

"I don't mean Ella. I mean the archaeologist."

"I don't want to talk about that." Maud took her mug to the coffeepot and refilled it. She didn't want to talk about it, but she was remembering it: the musk of the woods, the feeling of Gabriel's hands on her skin, the taste of his mouth.

"I'm sorry," Annette said. She came up to the counter. "I just want you to be happy. It doesn't seem right for you to give up sex. Maybe you should try again with Peter."

"I don't want to try again with Peter," Maud said.

She was back to pretending, back to going through the motions, as she'd done for years. Only now she knew better the stakes of not pretending well.

"Forgive me," Annette said. She kissed Maud's cheek. "Subject closed forever."

"Yeah, right," Maud said with a weary laugh. "Subject closed until you can't contain yourself again."

Out the window, the planters on the deck teemed with ferns and grasses and soon the nasturtiums would start to climb their string ladder to the roof. She should have told

Annette about sleeping with Gabriel. She could still tell her now, but her lips wouldn't budge. Everyone was moving on from that summer at Montgomery Place, but she was still stuck there, and worse, she was starting to realize that she didn't want to leave.

The night before her meeting with Alice, she did some research. Alice had been raised in a wealthy Bostonian family, the daughter of a philanthropist and his socialite wife, who died of leukemia when Alice was two. She found a photograph in *The Boston Globe* of a pigtailed girl in a velvet dress on the steps of Symphony Hall next to her tuxedoed father. The next appearance was in 1988 in a *New York Times* article. "She was raised on the inside," the journalist wrote. "She chose to leave for the outside." The article described how Alice had moved from Boston to New York at sixteen after graduating early from high school. While working in one of the last sausage factories in the Meatpacking District, she took night classes at Brooklyn College and discovered sculpture with Louise Bourgeois.

Over the next five years, Alice made four sculptures in a series, one of which now stood in the Philadelphia Museum of Art, the second in Chicago, and the third at the de Young. The first basket was thirteen feet high and thirty-nine feet wide. Each ensuing basket was larger than the one before. To shape them, she hammered and welded strips of steel, crossing them in a technique that resembled weaving. She had no training in basketmaking and used no particular cultural model. In interviews, she said that she knew how to weave a basket instinctively because she'd been raised as a woman and had "many inherited skills that I don't care to have, like playing nice and caring about people's feelings and wiping the corners of my mouth with a napkin."

A 1989 feature in an arts journal discussed Alice's unique blend of conceptualism and crafting, her subtle critique of gender roles, her connection to and refutation of Louise Bourgeois's own sculptures. There were photographs of her at Studio 54 with Andy Warhol, arm draped around her shaggy-haired girlfriend. In interviews she called her father a Nazi and said that money had crucified the art world. She spoke freely of doing cocaine and heroin. She made broad metaphorical statements about her sculptures: *I'm interested in the way metal dissolves in fire, in the heaviness of steel submitting to the lightness of a flame.*

In 1992, when *Basket 3* was purchased by the de Young, an article in the *San Francisco Chronicle* described Alice on the stage in sunglasses, smoking a pipe. "The artist declined to answer any questions." Following that article, news about Alice stopped, as if she had vanished from the earth.

Now Maud drove along Highway One, the printed design for the garden in a cardboard tube on the passenger seat. Ahead, the road rolled hypnotically, teasing the ocean as if it would dive into its waters, before once again cleaving to the brindled hills. The Pacific disappeared from view behind a cloak of mountains. When the GPS announced that she'd arrived at her destination, Maud pulled the car onto the shoulder. A battered metal sign read "Esperanza," and another read "Keep Out." With the cardboard tube tucked under her arm, she climbed the gate that closed off a drive and dropped to the other side.

Fields of native buckeye and yarrow rambled to a two-story gabled farmhouse that looked as if it dated from the mid-nineteenth century. Beyond were two barns. Solar panels glittered on all the tin roofs. No one answered when Maud knocked on the front door. After she knocked again, Alice appeared from around the side of the porch, as Clark lumbered behind. At the sight of Maud, he moved in front of Alice.

"You don't have to take her out, Clarkie," Alice said, stroking his back. Barefoot despite the brisk weather, she wore a black T-shirt and loose overalls smudged with paint and grease. "You made it."

"You were right about the gate being low."

"It's symbolic. I have a gun," Alice said. "You mind waiting? I'm finishing a coat of paint."

"Sure," Maud said. Alice had already made her climb a gate that she could have left open. And now she was going to make her sit and wait. She followed her and Clark around to the side of the house. She'd thought that Alice had given up art, but apparently she now painted.

Porches, it turned out. A drop cloth covered the floorboards and a paintbrush balanced on a rusty coffee tin depicting a 1950s housewife with a tray of doughnuts. Inside was gooey white paint that looked homemade and let off the smell of linseed.

Alice pointed at an iron bench, indicating, Maud translated, that she was to sit down. Then Alice went back to painting the top of the deck railing, drawing the brush over the board, tucking the bristles into the corners, following the grain in the wood, squatting, crouching down to paint the underside. Clark settled next to the paint can. This side of the house looked out on more former pastures, recolonized by native grasses and flowers that rolled to the foot of a mountain.

"Done," Alice said finally. "Thanks for the patience."

Flashing her palm at Clark, she opened the door to the house. Maud followed her inside. The entire two stories had been knocked open and painted that same white. A fireplace rose up to the roof like a cobblestone road to a ceiling broken by two square skylights. Against one wall was the suggestion of a kitchen with a concrete counter, a stove, a refrigerator. Against another wall stood a bed with a white comforter. It was surprisingly vertiginous to walk into a house anticipating rooms, walls, division, and to find yourself floating in colorless space.

Alice plunged her hands into the sink and scrubbed a splotch of paint off her elbow. "Coffee or tea or water or nothing?"

"Coffee, please."

"It's not exactly coffee. It's chicory. Oat milk good?"

Maud nodded as if she drank chicory with oat milk all the time. What was this project Alice wanted her to do, and, more important, was she going to fund the restoration?

Studiously, Alice put a kettle on the stove and ground the chicory in a hand grinder. When the drink was ready, she handed Maud a full mug. "Give it a sip. What do you think?"

"It kind of tastes like soil," Maud said.

"I guess that's a good thing, coming from you." Alice started toward the door. "Shall we take this to the library, as you English ladies like to do? You can show me your design. I know you're dying to."

Clark traipsed behind them down the stairs. "Your place is beautiful," Maud said.

"Thanks. It was a dump when I bought it. Taken me years. And I'll never be done."

They passed a barn with a bolt on the door and, oddly, windows that had been whitewashed. They skirted a compost trench that shivered with worms, then Alice hauled back the sliding door of another barn.

"After you," she said.

The interior had been transformed into a library; every wall, up to the ceiling, supported books on metal shelves. A rolling ladder hung from a rail. As with the bench on the porch, the finish on the metal had been stripped away. The books, mostly used copies with tattered spines, were sorted by size and color: a block of leather-bound classics with gold lettering floated next to a square of paperbacks in Day-Glo tangerine and lime, a science fiction series, translations from German and French and Greek, poems by Audre Lorde and Emily Dickinson, *The Arabian Nights*, Baldwin's *Giovanni's Room* next to Marx's *The Communist Manifesto*. An overstuffed chair and a footrest sat in the middle of the room.

"You've read all these books?" Maud said.

"I read four hours a day. Adds up." Alice waved at a wall. "You'll find your girl Virginia scattered over there."

Normally Maud would now ask Alice about her favorite Woolf novel or tell an anecdote about Monk's House. But she was pretty sure that such an aside wouldn't be met with the expected engaged response. She didn't want to stand here holding another door open, only to have Alice blink at her and not budge.

"Ready to see the design?" she said.

"Do you mind taking the footrest?"

"I'll take the floor so I can spread it out."

On her knees, she unrolled the plan from the tube. Alice sat in the chair, feet on the footrest, a hand on Clark's head. This might be it, Maud thought, her only chance. She kept her eyes off Alice so her impassivity wouldn't throw her.

She stayed with the plants: trellised pumpkins winding up the adobe bricks, the yerba buena gushing past blackberry canes, the bed of native plants foraged by the people who had taught Juana Briones about herbology. As she talked, she almost forgot Alice was in the room.

"I won't use chemicals," she said. "I've learned about traditional methods of fertilizing. If something dies, it dies."

She looked up. Alice was picking a scab on her arm.

"This really doesn't interest you, does it?" Maud said, feeling drained.

"Sorry," Alice said. "I find gardening incredibly boring."

"Gardening is all I've got," Maud said. What was the point of this exercise? She should just leave now, climb the gate and head home. She rolled up the plan.

The chair creaked as Alice adjusted her legs. "I do realize that this is a sickening dynamic," she said. "Money does this. Every time."

"It'll be more than a garden," Maud said. "There'll be the house and cultural programs. Enrichment activities for kids. Summer camps."

"The problem," Alice said, "isn't the garden or the kids—though I do find kids boring." She crossed her feet on the footrest. "The problem is the Presidio. I don't like the idea of giving money to a shrine to the military industrial complex that doubles as a pretty park for dot-commers. I made a promise to myself when I found out my father had dumped this inheritance on me that I wouldn't do more harm with his money. Turns out that's harder than it sounds."

Did that mean no? It probably did. "Maria will make sure that the money goes where it's supposed to go," Maud said. "Only to this project."

Alice studied her. "Are you about to cry?"

Capping the tube, Maud shook her head. She wasn't going to cry, but she did feel dejected and ridiculous and also angry—a confusing combination. "If you don't fund the project, it's not going to happen," she said. "At least, not now."

"And you really want to make that garden, don't you?" Something had gelled in Alice's voice. She wasn't playing. She was asking.

"Yes," Maud said. "I really do."

"I could tell when I saw you planting that pomegranate tree."

They remained there, Maud on the floor, Alice in the chair, for what felt like an hour. Then Alice stood up. "Okay. I'll fund it."

"You will?" Maud almost jumped up and hugged her. It was going to happen.

"My father's family made their money from the slave trade," Alice said. "And it's been festering on the stock market for two hundred years, bankrolling who the hell knows what. There's no balancing the bad it's done. I just need to get rid of it as fast as I can."

"And you'll give Maria enough for the house and exhibits as well?" Maud said, as she followed Alice back outside. "The school programs? The summer camps with the subsidies? The ten-year budget?"

"You're a closeted romantic, aren't you?" Alice said with a chuckle. She gestured at Clark. "Yes. Whatever was on that proposal Maria showed me. Now, can we go figure out what to do about this goddamned plant?"

Clark accompanied them past an electric generator and a

smaller building that seemed to be an outhouse, to the edge of a field, where he settled at Alice's feet. Maud recognized fescue and oatgrass and purple needlegrass, the edges of sedge and round tips of rushes, all kept green by the coastal fog. Jutting throughout—the problem plant, she assumed—was a wiry weed that she didn't recognize.

"I think I see your issue," she said. "Has it always been here?"

"Nope," Alice said. "Most of this area was a flower garden when I bought the place. I pulled everything out."

She explained that she was trying to return the land to what it had been "before people fucked it over. I've been seeding native grasses. A few years ago, I got a bad mix." She kicked at a tuft of the grass. "This stuff keeps coming back. I dig it out every spring. I can't get rid of it."

"It looks like a variety of pampas."

"Whatever it is, it isn't native. And I want it gone."

"That'll be hard without spraying," Maud said. "Which neither of us wants."

She thought through the reading she'd done about natural landscaping methods.

"You could smother the field with plastic to cook the roots through this summer. You'll have to kill everything, the good grasses too, and then reseed the entire field next fall with a better mix. I could do it for you if you want." She pointed across the field. "I'd probably have to go all the way to that fence for it to work."

"How much would that cost and how long would it take?"

"Four mornings of work? Two hundred each time?"

Alice looked up at the sky, as if doing the math with the help of the clouds. From what Maria had told Maud, her inheritance amounted to almost sixty million dollars. Clearly she wasn't using the money on herself.

"Could you do it for one seventy-five a session?" she said. "And a hundred for today?"

"Deal," Maud said.

Alice took a hundred-dollar bill out of her back pocket.

"But please don't make me climb the gate next time," Maud said.

"Okay."

"And I really don't like chicory."

"I'll make you tea instead." Alice smiled, showing her square teeth.

Back in the car, Maud texted Maria. *She said yes!*

She did?! What did you tell her?

Nothing much. I agreed to do the project here. I almost lost my temper.

It's hard not to with her. Seriously? The whole thing?

Yes!

Hallelujah!

Driving back along Highway One, Maud thought about Alice's offhand comment: "You're a closeted romantic, aren't you?" She'd said those words with no intonation of a question. And she was right. That girl who used to bike along her street and see carriages pass by instead of cars, who used to peer through the gates of Lone Pines and escape to the moors of England, that girl was still inside her, looking back in time with a lantern that hid the shadows. Casually, not knowing her, Alice had called out her fatal flaw.

15

Now that the funding was confirmed, the goal was to restore the house and garden over the next four months for a public opening in mid-June. On top of designing the garden, Maud started to write copy for explanatory placards and educational materials. She met again with the naturalist who had trained her the year before, and he helped her expand the bed of medicinal plants that Juana Briones might have used as a healer: soaproot as a purgative, black cohosh as an abortifacient.

She returned to Esperanza on a Wednesday to start smothering the grasses. This time, not only did Alice not make her wait—the gate was open—but she came to the porch at the sound of the car.

"I'm off on my hike." She looped a canteen over her chest. "There's mint water in the house for you. I don't do ice. No freezer. Sorry."

"I usually forget to take a break when I start working," Maud said.

"That doesn't surprise me. The outhouse is that building over there. Good luck."

Alice left, and Maud unloaded the back of the car. Then she started to lay down plastic, first flattening the grasses with a wooden board, one square foot at a time. On a bathroom break, she walked to the barn with the white-washed windows and looked through a gap in the slats. She could make out a massive shape. That must be *Basket 4*, she decided, the last sculpture in Alice's series, the one that had never been sold. But why paint over the windows? She didn't think Maria was right about Alice being paranoid about the press. As she walked back to the field, it came to her. Alice doesn't want to see it, she thought. She's hiding it from herself.

She stopped at noon, just before Alice returned from the mountain.

"I can come back tomorrow," she said.

"Let's stick to Wednesdays," Alice said.

The following week, Maud worked faster and harder, trying to get the middle of the field done, rolling out the thick sheets of plastic.

"Spotted a whale," Alice said, passing by as Maud hammered in stakes.

"There's a view of the ocean?" Maud said.

"There's a hell of a view of the ocean. You want lunch when you're done?"

"Sure," Maud said. She had plenty of time before she needed to pick up Ella and Louise.

"I'm going to the library to read," Alice said. "The table will be set at twelve."

The table, it turned out, was metaphorical. As Maud

carried the leftover plastic sheeting to the car, she saw Alice come out on the porch with two bowls. "Lunch," she yelled.

The bowl Alice handed her was filled with grains Maud didn't recognize, crushed nuts, and dates, all swimming in a glumpy sauce. "Enjoy," Alice said. She tore a date in half and shared it with Clark. Maud sat down next to her on the bench. They seemed, already, to have entered a new phase. Alice no longer appeared interested in challenging Maud, as if some hesitation had been laid to rest. But as they ate, she didn't utter a single word.

"Is this cumin I taste?" Maud said, three-quarters of the way through her bowl. "I like it with the cashews. I'll tell my husband. He's been making Indian food lately."

"Correct." Alice glanced over. "Are you worried I want to sleep with you?"

"No," Maud said. "Why?"

"You seem nervous. And you just flashed the husband badge."

"I was just trying to make conversation."

"That's why people shouldn't try to make conversation," Alice said. "They can suggest a subtext they don't mean." She fed Clark another date. "For the record, when you walked into that conference room, I knew you couldn't be straighter."

"I'm sure I could be straighter," Maud said, feeling strangely hurt.

"Sorry." Alice ran her finger inside her bowl and licked off the sauce. "I didn't mean anything by that. Except that I'm not trying to sleep with you. I have a lover. And other lovers. I don't need to make a play for a straight woman who doesn't wear a wedding ring."

"I don't wear it when I work," Maud said.

"Uh-huh," Alice said.

They went back to eating in silence until Alice looked over at her contemplatively and said, "Have you ever slept with a woman?"

"Not completely."

"What, just waist-up? Wearing a blindfold?"

"A couple of make-out sessions," Maud said. "Liberal arts college experimentation." It was embarrassing to remember how liberated she'd felt at the time. She set her bowl on her lap. "How does it work? Having a lover and other lovers?"

Alice was picking a piece of kale from her teeth. "My partner and I sleep with other people."

"I mean emotionally."

"It works well." Alice looked at her as if she'd asked an unanswerable question. "It's not a problem when it's not a problem."

Back in the car, Maud looked at her phone and saw that Ella had texted: *Threw up in science. Have a fever. Throat hurts. Nurse says pick me up.* Below was a text from Peter. *Can you get Ella?* And another text, a half-hour later. *I'll do it.*

Sorry I missed your messages, she texted them both. *Working.*

Peter replied. *We're home. I was in a meeting. Have to leave ASAP. You coming?*

Driving back, Maud thought about Alice's romantic arrangement. A lover and other lovers. She'd never considered talking to Peter about an open marriage, even though each of them had opened the door on their own. An open marriage had worked well for Virginia and Leonard Woolf—she used to marvel at their partnership—but they hadn't had children. And Peter was nothing like Leonard.

When she arrived at the house, he came down the steps as she came up. "Hoping I'll make it," he said and yanked open his car door.

Inside, Ella sat in bed with a popsicle. Maud put her hand on her forehead, which didn't feel too hot.

"My throat's on fire and Dad's pissed," Ella said.

Ignoring the comment, Maud plumped the pillows.

"I thought I was going to sit in the nurse's office all day," Ella said.

"It was only an hour," Maud said. "It turned out okay, didn't it?"

Going back down the hall, she was annoyed with Peter, with both of them, really, for acting as if she'd done something wrong by being caught up in her work, as Peter always was. She measured out a capful of cold medicine and brought Ella a glass of orange juice. When Ella's fever rose again, she took her to the doctor's office for a strep test. The test positive, she ran to the pharmacy for antibiotics after dropping Louise at soccer practice. Standing in line for the bottle of pink medicine, she thought about Juana Briones losing three of her children in the same month, one after the other, from illnesses that Ella and Louise were vaccinated against. She let her ruminations about open marriage go. Gratitude, she thought, handing over the prescription slip, as if the word itself were a dose of medicine.

Ella stayed in bed during dinner. Two bites into her meat loaf, Louise asked if she could play sick with her sister, so the two of them cuddled up to watch a movie on Maud's laptop. Tie still on, flipped over his shoulder, Peter barely spoke as they ate, though he kept clinking his fork on the plate.

"What?" Maud said as they cleared the table.

"What what?"

"Why are you mad?"

"You know that I have a standing meeting on Wednesdays."

"Yes, I know. And I have a standing job. For my benefactor."

"You said you'd be done by noon."

"It took longer."

Why hadn't she said that she'd stayed an extra hour eating lunch with Alice? Then again, why did she have to account for her time?

Peter was scrubbing his plate as if trying to remove a layer of porcelain. "You know Ella's not out of the woods," he said.

"She has strep. Strep has nothing to do with the other issue. What are you talking about?"

"I'm not talking about anything," he said. "Good night."

She was too disconcerted to work, so she went to bed with a novel and turned off her light when she heard Peter coming down the hall from his study. Eyes closed, she listened to him brush his teeth in the bathroom. She thought about Alice's house and library, those bastions of light made out of dim, discarded buildings. Her cloud of a cover on the bed. Her ceramic mugs. Her diet, determined by her own desires and principles. Her lover and her other lovers. Alice didn't have to compromise with anyone. When you married, you did nothing but compromise. And you lost your ability to make a home exactly as you wanted, down to the last detail. And then she was back at Montgomery Place: cracking open the windows to let in the spring air, making a bouquet for the coffee table, changing into a dress before going outside to meet Gabriel.

———

Several weeks passed. She mixed mushroom compost and peat moss into the soil of the Briones garden and wrote a brochure about the numerous species of manzanita growing by the bay. She finished designing the garden. Wednesday mornings, she returned to Alice's to lay down plastic. Each time, they had lunch. They talked or they didn't, eating to the sound of Clark's munching; he now seemed less wary of Maud. She learned more about Alice's lover, Gloria, who had been in the army before becoming a veterinarian and played blues harmonica, but only at her own house, "because it gives me a headache," Alice said. Gloria slept at Esperanza two nights a week, and Alice slept at Gloria's house in town two nights a week. They weren't married, because they both thought it was a disastrous institution, but they were legal partners, "in case we have to pull the plug on each other."

"Sounds dreamy," Maud said. They were sitting on the porch with their lunch as Clark napped inside.

"Well, that part's sad, but what can you do? And we don't dwell on it. I take it your marriage sucks."

"Probably not more than the average marriage."

"Dreamy," Alice said.

Maud laughed. The power dynamics of their initial meetings had vanished, and it felt as if they were becoming friends. "You had me at my missing wedding ring."

"I thought you were into Juana Briones because of her gardening skills and her magical teas. But maybe it's because she had the guts to leave her husband."

"Juana Briones's husband beat her," Maud said. "Peter's a good father and a reasonably good husband, especially now. I just don't want to be married to him."

It felt good to say this out loud.

"Does he want to be married to you?" Alice said.

"I don't think so. But we have kids. And our eldest isn't doing well." She told Alice about Ella's self-harm.

"I used to do that," Alice said. "In my father's study with his scissors." She pointed at herself with her fork. "And look how well I turned out."

"Did you just stop?" Maud said. "Like you stopped making art?"

The ability to start over seemed one of Alice's greatest qualities.

"I found other ways to release tension," Alice said. "Heroin worked for a while. Et cetera, et cetera."

When their conversations moved to Alice's past, she usually rerouted them. But Maud was learning more about her with each visit, her questions peeling back the layers. It felt good to hear a closed-off person open up, to feel that you were privy to a hidden landscape. Alice was a lone wolf like Gabriel, but rather than roving the world, she'd created her own territory and barred nearly everyone else from it. Sitting next to her on the bench, Maud felt a magnetic pull similar to the pull she'd felt for Gabriel. Not sexual, really. Or at least not physical. A spiritual connection, she thought, as she watched Alice pet Clark, her hand meandering down her dog's back. And what those hands had made. What that mind had conjured. Maud looked at the painted-over barn, remembering that basket at the de Young. How could someone with that much talent and success simply decide one day to quit?

After eating, they walked to the finished field, which was now smooth as ice.

"I'll come back and check it again in the fall," Maud said. "No charge."

"Women shouldn't offer to do anything for nothing," Alice said.

"I'll come back in the fall for a hundred dollars. Better?"

"Yes." Alice handed her another envelope of cash.

"Or I'll come back before. For free," Maud said. "For leisure." She put the envelope in her pocket.

Alice eyed her. "Are you sure you don't want to sleep with me?"

Maud laughed. "I like you. Don't you like me?"

"Yes, you sap," Alice said. "I like you too. Do you hike? I'm away next week on a camping trip with Gloria. But come back the Wednesday after next? I think you'll dig the view."

St. Patrick's Day was a holiday that trumped all others for Maud's family. She and Louise made soda bread the night before, as Maud had once done with her grandmother, measuring the flour in an empty tin can, spoiling milk with lemon juice to make buttermilk. She added raisins to the dough, cut in a cross, and tucked the baked loaf into a dish towel with a penny on the top to bribe thieving leprechauns.

"Remember to wear green or Grandpa will pinch you," Louise yelled down the hall the next morning as Maud and Peter got dressed. Peter looked at Maud, aggrieved.

"Wear the socks from last year," Maud said and dug them out of his drawer.

A few blocks into Burlingame, down the street from Lone Pines, Maud's childhood home was a dingy split foyer clunked down on a quarter-block lot next to her father's old garage with its faded lettering: "Healy & Son Auto." That son, Maud's older brother, Kevin, had worked with her father for twenty years and now owned a car dealership in a strip mall on the edge of town. Although Maud's parents could have made millions by selling the property, they ignored the increasingly inflated offers that came their way, even for the lot with the garage. They had long said that they planned to die right here and have their wakes in the living room. As for the garage lot, they didn't want rich dot-commers in a McMansion as neighbors.

Inside the house, aunts and uncles, cousins, and family friends sat on the overstuffed furniture, drinking Guinness and Irish coffee. The air was raw with the bleach that Maud's mother used on virtually every surface, and the stale smoke from Maud's father's thrice-daily cigars. A piano, inherited from a grandmother and which no one had ever played, stood by, lid open, in the living room, adorned with a doily and a cut-glass bowl of ossified peppermint candies. Irish knicknacks—a Celtic cross, a framed map of the island, a dried bouquet of shamrocks—hung on the walls.

"Happy St. Patty's Day," Maud's father said from his recliner. "Give the old fella a smooch."

Eyes rheumy, toupee askew, he made as if to get up, then plopped back down. Dutifully, Ella leaned over to hug him. Louise kissed him on the cheek.

"Happy St. Patrick's Day, and can I feed the pigeons?" Louise said.

"Don't you always?" he said. "Go get the seeds from your grandma."

Maud's elderly twin aunts, who were tucked together in an armchair that swallowed their frail bodies, gave Maud their spotted, trembling hands. The family was divided, as Louise put it, into real Irish like the aunts—the generation that had immigrated—and the American Irish, like Maud's parents, the ones who wore shamrock pins and green Mardi Gras beads.

"Get you one, sir?" Maud's uncle held up his glass of whiskey to Peter.

"I might later," Peter said.

"'Might later' is British for yes," Maud's father said. "Get your poor man a drink."

"Don't bother," Peter said to Maud. "I'll get one myself in a bit."

"What's the point of being married, then?" Maud's father said.

"Very funny, Dad," Maud said.

While her mother mostly ignored Peter, her father had always gone so far out of his way to be friendly that his dislike was obvious.

Annette walked by with a tray of emerald deviled eggs. "Aunt Julia just asked me if I'm going through the Change yet," she said. "See you in five minutes, you know where."

"I'm already ready," Maud said. She brought the soda bread to the kitchen, which was flatulent from the cabbage leaves and turnips stewing on the stove. Dressed in green slacks, a green blouse, and a sparkling green top hat, her mother almost looked happy as she squeezed drops of green food coloring into a pitcher of lemonade for the children.

"Will you and Peter carry Dad's walker when we go to the parade?" she asked Maud. "He won't want to bring it, and he'll end up needing it."

"Especially after all that whiskey." Maud set down the bread.

"Be respectful," her mother retorted. "He's only had his usual."

"He's only had his usual" was always her reply when Maud

or Annette questioned their father's drinking, meaning five glasses of hard liquor a day. Maud's father believed that alcoholics couldn't walk up or down stairs, and the fact that he could was proof that he wasn't.

"I'll go check on the kids," Maud said.

"You mean smoke with your sister. I saw her go to the garage. Grab a can of mixed vegetables while you're there. The aunts need their fiber."

Under a monkey tree dripping with bird feeders, pigeons pecked at the seed Louise had sprinkled. She and a set of third cousins were drawing on the concrete walkway with a handful of the lava rocks that covered the yard. Ella was with the smaller children, pushing them on the creaking swing set. Aside from the tree, the only plant life was a ratty cypress shrub. How, Maud wondered, as she often did, had she developed a love for gardens in this wasteland?

Kevin pulled into the driveway in his minivan. Mandy, Maud's sister-in-law, waved from the passenger seat, hair budding in its perky bob. They had seven children and another on the way and lived in a rambling, vinyl-sided house in the hills outside of Burlingame. Devout Catholics, they didn't believe in the separation of church and state, abortion, birth control, gay rights, or homosexuality in general. Ever since Maud and Kevin had fought loudly about contraception ten years ago, the family had enacted a moratorium on discussing politics when together.

Maud waved back and quickly ducked into the garage. Since closing the business, their parents had used the building not only to store canned food for the parish pantry but also as a museum for her father's collection of vintage tools. Hammers, axes, and saws rusted everywhere on hooks. It was a creepy, postapocalyptic setting, frozen as it had been when the garage shut down, receipts still pinned to the bulletin board, the wall calendar turned to October 2000.

Annette was in the office, perched on the desk with a pack of cigarettes and a Playboy lighter abandoned by a mechanic.

"Kevin and company just got here," Maud said.

Annette flicked the lighter and sucked the flame through a cigarette. "We might need to upgrade to pot," she said in a whirl of smoke. "Although I already had some this morning to recover from last night."

She had texted Maud at midnight: *Did not go well*, a message that came as no surprise. Annette had planned to talk to her Match.com date about becoming more serious.

"He wants to go slow," she said now. "Any slower than this, and we'll be going backward."

"Do you even like him that much?"

Thus far, Maud had only heard about the man's habit of clicking his tongue when he and Annette had sex and the fact that he might be a Libertarian in Democrat clothing.

"I don't know." Annette sighed. "You think it's me, but the pickings are seriously slim out there." She funneled out another cloud of smoke, then handed the cigarette to Maud. "I should just give up. Get fat. Let my hair go gray. Stop pulverizing my poor face."

"You might meet nicer men if you stopped all that."

"No, I'd meet the same kind of men but twenty years older." Annette brushed ash from her blouse. "Maybe I should look forward to the Change," she said. "Maybe once I lose all my estrogen I won't give a shit about men anymore. I'll get a cat and commit to my vibrator. Speaking of which, I think you—"

"Don't," Maud said. "My finger works fine." It had been months, though, since she'd used it.

When they went back inside, they found that card tables now filled the living room, kitchen, and dining room, sprinkled with the shamrock confetti that Maud's mother would carefully scoop back into a plastic bag for next year. As Maud and Annette brought out the three platters of corned beef and cabbage, the Clancy Brothers sang from the stereo about the wild colonial boy and sweet Molly Malone, all the sufferings brought on by the English.

Mandy's five-month belly pressed against Maud when they hugged.

"How are you feeling?" Maud asked. Mandy's pregnancies were usually a safe topic.

"Enormous," Mandy said. Her T-shirt read "Leprechaun Inside."

"She's got me doing the freaking laundry," Kevin said.

"How awful for you," Maud said.

They passed around mustard, tartar sauce, and ketchup to perk up the bland, boiled food. Teetering at the head of the table, Maud's father made his usual toast about the road rising to meet them all.

"Tell the one about the man who painted his donkey green," someone shouted at Maud's maternal uncle, who stood on his chair to deliver the joke as the women cleared the table and brought out a porter cake that Maud's mother had made, along with Annette's chocolate-covered strawberries, which their mother eyed suspiciously. "Since when are strawberries Irish?" she asked.

"The stems are green," Annette said.

"I read about your Juana Briones," Maud's mother told

Maud when she finally sat down. "The first woman in California to get a divorce. What a claim to fame." She scooped up a bite of porter cake.

"She never got an actual divorce," Maud said. "And that's not her claim to fame." The buzz of nicotine was wearing off.

"It's fifty percent of marriages these days, Ma," Annette said.

"Tragic," Kevin said from down the table. "It should be illegal."

"Please tell me you didn't just say that, Kevin," Annette said with a groan.

"Where did you read about Juana Briones?" Maud asked her mother. To her knowledge, her mother had never stepped foot in a library.

"On the internet. Kev set it up for us so your father can look up football scores."

And then the table was off to a discussion of the 49ers, the aunts and Peter looking lost.

Maud ate her porter cake. She remembered being eleven and sitting in the kitchen at dinner with her family, sharing a thought that had come to her like a revelation during Sunday Mass: the Holy Mary had been a teenage mother. Her mother had reached across the table and smacked her face. "It was an Immaculate Conception," she'd said. "Don't you try to be clever." But Maud hadn't been trying to be clever—she'd been trying to understand what seemed to be a flagrant contradiction. After that, she kept those thoughts to herself.

Once the women had done the dishes, Maud and her mother helped Louise and her cousins get ready for the parade and then dropped them off to their dance troupe on Burlingame's main street. Soon after, the parade kicked off with the Shriners, who scooted by in their tiny cars, honking their horns, decorated fezzes on their heads.

"There they are," her mother said as Louise and her troupe high-stepped along the asphalt to the beat of a bodhrán. Maud lifted her phone to take a picture. A six-foot leprechaun tossed green Hershey's Kisses into the crowd. Kevin's dealership had sponsored a float that cruised down the street, this year's "Colleen" doing a queenly wave from atop a papier-mâché shamrock.

"You could compete for the title next year," Maud's mother said to Ella.

"Maybe," Ella said.

"Thanks for humoring her," Maud told Ella when her mother had walked away to join her father, whose walker fluttered with celadon streamers.

"Her friend from church over there asked me how I liked volunteering at Lone Pines. I guess she was visiting someone and saw me. She told Grandma, and that's what Grandma said."

"Going to Lone Pines is nothing to be ashamed of," Maud said.

"I know that," Ella said.

"Maybe Grandma was trying to protect your privacy."

"I don't think so."

"Yeah, I don't think so either," Maud said.

She stood next to Ella and watched the parade go by, as bagpipes—Scottish but apparently close enough—played. Proud Irish Americans celebrating a country most of them had never seen. Maud herself had been only twice, even though for years she'd lived across the sea. No matter what I do or what I think or what I learn, it's all in me, she thought. These people. These stories. These lies.

16

The work at Tennessee Hollow accelerated as the weather warmed. Contractors were making adobe bricks for the Briones house and the walled garden, pouring a mixture of straw and sand into molds spread out in the parking lot. Maud started to plant the tomato seedlings, corn kernels, and beans. Sharing this progress with Alice, however, was less than rewarding.

"Do you want to come closer?" she asked Alice the day of their hike. She'd unrolled the garden design on the porch as Alice laced up a boot, one foot on the railing.

"I can see fine from here," Alice said.

Maud held up the paper. "Lots of vegetables, a bunch of herbs, and a few fruits."

"Sounds great." Alice plunked her other foot on the railing. "Maria's a peach, and you're adorable, but I don't know why you two bug me with this stuff."

Maud rolled the design back into its tube. "We thought you'd want to know what you're paying for."

"I hear she found an aspiring actress to dress up as Juana Briones at the opening." Alice laced her other boot. "I hate that living-history shit. I told her, if you're going to pretend to be Juana Briones, you'd better have bruises from your abusive husband and a bunch of kids running around screaming and driving you up the wall."

"Living history gets children interested in history," Maud said.

"Living history gets children interested in schmaltz."

"Yes, well, it's not that easy. Should I tell my girls that life is brutal, people are cruel, and then you die and become worm food?"

"You don't really think that." Alice looked at her slyly. "You believe in heaven, don't you? A little bit? Come on, I know you do."

"Stop it. No. I don't." Maud followed Alice off the porch. "I mean, I don't believe in it, but I'll be glad if I find out I was wrong."

"Aha," Alice said. "Knew it."

The trail started in a grove of fir and oak, climbing over a ferny forest floor. They stopped talking as the earth tilted into a climb. Maud was already winded. Although her arms had strengthened with her work, her lungs struggled at this brisk pace. She wanted her body back, not to be thin but to be strong, to feel her muscles locking into place. They passed through a meadow, where the first wildflowers—freckled leopard lily, grape-like clusters of sky lupine—smeared color through the grasses. Beyond a pine grove, the trees fell away, and she found herself on a tooth-shaped cliff, faced with endless gray ocean that poured off the horizon. The wind shoved her body and slapped her cheeks. She felt as if she were floating; the clouds were suds in a great blue bath, the sun a bright plug in the drain. "Wow," she half-yelled to Alice as her hair roared around her face.

"Told you," Alice yelled back. "Who needs heaven?"

She pointed at a boulder sheltered from the wind by a torqued pine tree. For the next half-hour, they sat together on the hard surface, wedged close, legs touching, and watched the waves rise, curl, and vanish, as they passed Alice's canteen back and forth. A pelican circled, dove into the waves, and broke free with a fish flapping in its beak. Seaweed swayed in the tide pools.

"Thank you for bringing me here," Maud said when they got up to go.

"I thought you'd like it," Alice said.

Halfway down the trail, Maud recognized the smell of fennel, another invasive plant, brought to California from Italy. She thought of Alice's quest to return her land to what it was before humans fucked it over, a senseless boundary drawn around an impossible task. You couldn't return the land to what it had been. The soil wasn't the same soil. The wind wasn't the same wind or the sun the same sun. Was it the artist still in Alice? she wondered. That purity of intention, that obsessive blindness.

"Is your fourth basket in your barn?" she asked.

Ahead on the trail, Alice scoffed. "You and your curiosity," she said. "Yes. Does that brain ever slow down?"

"Why don't you sell it if you don't want to see it?" Maud said.

Alice didn't skip a beat. "Because it's accruing value in there," she said. "*Basket 1* bought me my place. *Baskets 2* and *3* still pay my bills. And that last basket will keep me here when I'm old until it's time for Gloria to clock me. The four of them got me out of being the asshole they turned me into." Arms swinging as the trail steepened, she glanced back. "I assume you read my interviews. Don't you think I was an asshole?"

"No. I think you were an artist."

"I was never an artist," Alice said. "I was being an artist. That's why I was an asshole."

They were passing through another meadow, sunlight illuminating the poppies like paper lamps, bees worrying Queen Anne's lace.

"I don't buy that," Maud said. "I've seen your basket at the de Young."

On her first visit to the museum, she'd stood in front of the sculpture and felt awe not unlike that she'd felt on the cliff. The basket had been so big, so unapologetic, so simple yet surprising. Those years at Monk's House, she'd worked in the presence of genius, and she had sensed it again that day.

"I only like the first one," Alice said. "When I didn't know what I was doing and didn't pretend to know." She waved her hand at Maud. "Like you when you garden. I saw it when you were digging the hole for the pomegranate tree. You were there, and you were somewhere else."

"Yes," Maud said, as redwoods towered over them. "That's how it feels."

But then, Alice said, she became someone. An outsider, feminist, queer artist. "Always talking. Always explaining. Blah, blah, blah. Smoking that pipe. I started to hate myself. I mean, really hate myself. And then, you know. More drinking. Harder drugs. Waking up on the floor in some apartment, not remembering where I was. I'm sure you've seen the movie. I was killing myself. Not like your previous girlfriend in a river with stones in my pockets. A slow, humiliating death."

It was as if walking loosened Alice's tongue, or maybe, Maud thought, the words had been driven out of her by the wind on the cliff. "And then one day, you saw the Pacific Ocean," she said, encouraging Alice on as the trail crossed a shallow stream and they hopscotched over the rocks.

"Well, not quite that simple," Alice said, "but close. I came out here for the opening at the de Young. I was on that stage, fried, ready to do my shtick. And then"—she leaped to another rock—"I didn't."

The artist declined any questions, the newspaper article had said. Alice sat in sunglasses on the stage, electing silence. She skipped the reception, she told Maud now, and walked out of Golden Gate Park, into the city, through the Presidio, over the Golden Gate Bridge, along Highway One. "I wasn't thinking," she said, "for the first time maybe ever, my head was empty. Eventually I saw the sign for this place. And I stopped walking."

"You walked all the way here from the de Young?"

"I keep a fast clip, if you haven't noticed."

She left everything in New York: clothes, books, friends. "Got clean. Started working on this place. Went into town one day and saw a notice about an abandoned Dalmatian. Met Clark. Fell in love. Met his vet. Fell in love."

"And lived quietly ever after," Maud said.

"Yeah, I guess. Until this bigmouthed garden historian came along."

Esperanza reappeared, its silver roofs glinting. Clark waited at the trailhead with his muzzle resting on his front paws. "You don't miss sculpting?" Maud said. "You don't miss that feeling?"

"It doesn't matter if I miss it," Alice said. Clark nosed her leg, and she scratched his ears.

You do, Maud thought, watching her still face. That's why those barn windows are whitewashed. But you don't know how to have it without all the rest.

"Want lunch?" Alice said.

"Yes, please," Maud said. "And I want to go on that hike with you again."

"Then I guess you're coming back next Wednesday."

Monday morning, while Maud was running irrigation lines at Tennessee Hollow, her phone rang. It was the nurse at Ella's school.

"There's been an incident," she said, and Maud's body seized.

"The cut isn't deep," the nurse added.

On her way out of the Presidio, Maud called Rita's office at Lone Pines. She left a message for Peter, who was at a conference. She called the mother of one of Louise's friends to ask if she'd take Louise home, and then called Annette to ask her to get Louise from the friend's house after work. Under all of this management, she shook and screamed.

In the nurse's office, Ella sat on a vinyl bed. She leaned into Maud's hug and didn't resist when Maud took her hand in the parking lot. Maud waited until they got to the car to ask, "Where?"

Ella lifted her T-shirt, then a bandage. A line—about an inch and a half, still eking blood—skirted the side of her belly button.

She'd never cut there before. Was that significant? Why had she done it again?

"What did you use?" Maud said, evening out her words.

Ella took the scissors out of her pencil case and handed them to Maud. "I self-reported, Mom."

"I'm glad you did, sweetie." Maud put the scissors in her purse. "But why did you do it in the first place?" She regretted asking the question. She had shown how upset she was.

"I want to talk about it with Rita first."

Maud let out the parking brake. "Your appointment isn't for three hours. Are you okay going to work with me? I left in the middle of something."

"Yeah, sure," Ella said.

Maud wanted to grab her and shout into her ear, Why? Instead, she started the car and drove onto the road.

At Tennessee Hollow, Ella sat under the pomegranate tree while Maud finished running irrigation lines. She checked her phone, but Peter still hadn't texted back. She felt horribly alone and afraid. She will never get better, she thought. This will never end.

"We still have an hour," she told Ella. "I want to show you something." She didn't want to go to Lone Pines early and sit in that office.

A half-mile toward the ocean, she parked on the side of the road, and they hiked through a eucalyptus grove to a clearing strewn with chunks of serpentine rock. The Raven's Manzanita, an evergreen shrub, hunkered in the shade. Its urn-shaped blossoms peeped from ragged leaves.

"There are clones in other parts of the Presidio, but this is the parent plant," Maud said. "It's the only one in existence."

"It looks dead," Ella said.

"All of these plants kind of look dead. They have to put up with a lot out here." The ashy, serpentine soil, she explained, was filled with poisons from the earth's mantle, such as chromium, nickel, and asbestos. Her words trailed off. Ella was staring at the plant, absorbing nothing that Maud was saying. And why should she? Maud thought. Who cared about a shrub? Why had she brought Ella to see it? She didn't know how to help her daughter.

"It's one of the nice things about having a specialty," she said, "knowing things other people don't know. You'll see." Her voice swallowed the sentence.

"I'm okay, Mom." Ella shoved her hands into the pockets of her windbreaker. "I know it doesn't help, and it didn't this time. It didn't make me feel better. I won't do it again. I promise."

Maud nodded. "I love you," she said.

On their way to the car, her body was leaden. Ella might believe in her promise, but Maud couldn't. How could Ella know what she'd do next month or six months from now? You found clarity, and you made resolutions, and you had epiphanies, and then you lost the clarity, and you broke the resolutions, and you watched the epiphanies turn to sand. The night Peter arrived at Montgomery Place, standing outside with him, she had been sure with every ounce of her certitude that leaving him was the right thing to do. A day later, she couldn't conceive of it. She had been sure she loved Gabriel. A day after that, she thought he might be a monster.

Peter met them at Lone Pines, car keys still in hand. He and Maud sat in tense silence until Rita opened the waiting room door. Eventually Ella returned and took a seat in the waiting room. "She's gonna talk to you alone," she muttered.

"I know this relapse is frightening," Rita said once they'd sat down in her office, "but Ella and I just had a very good session."

"Did she tell you why she did it?" Maud asked.

"She was triggered by a nightmare she had last night about being in the hospital in Rhinebeck."

In the nightmare, Rita continued, Ella was held down by men without faces. They told her to stay calm. "They said they needed to look at her. As the doctor did at the hospital in New York."

"I don't understand," Peter said.

"The genital exam," Maud told him.

"You said the doctor was gentle."

"He was. And he didn't touch her. Only the nurse did. And barely."

"It was a dream, not a memory," Rita said. "It's awkward to talk about this with her dad in the room. That's why Ella stepped out. We discussed the lack of control she felt when she was admitted to the hospital and during that exam. She lost her coping mechanism when her self-harm was discovered."

Maud remembered the animal cry that had poured from Ella when the doctor had first tried to look between her legs, and what she'd thought that must mean about Gabriel.

"So, what now?" Peter said. "We have to stop her from doing this to herself."

"We keep at it," Rita said. "I think Ella made a breakthrough today. She said that the cutting didn't give her relief. That's huge. I suggest that we increase the frequency of therapy for a while and also think about upping her antidepressant dose, as we've discussed doing before. She's onboard with all that."

Yes, they said. Yes. Whatever you think we should do. Whatever might help.

Driving home, Ella next to her in the passenger seat, Maud remembered something she'd learned about the people who'd first lived on the bay. They believed that a sick person had been taken over by an evil spirit, much like the Christian idea of possession. Along with administering herbs, the shaman would chase the evil spirit from the patient's body to help make them well. She'd known for a while that she was still possessed by that summer at Montgomery Place. She wondered now if Ella was too.

Annette met them at the door to the house. "Problem," she whispered to Maud after giving Ella a hug.

A herd of ants had swarmed Louise's sugar cube Sphinx. Louise had taken it to the sink to wash it off, and drowned ants and lumps of sugar now covered the basin. Sobbing, she lay facedown on her bed.

"We'll make another one together," Maud said.

"Why didn't I just wipe them off? I mess up everything."

I mess up everything—Ella used to say that sometimes. Maud sat down next to her. "No, you don't."

She almost told Louise that it didn't matter, that the next Sphinx would be better, that practice makes perfect. But this loss, she knew, was about more than sugar cubes. "We'll make a new one."

Louise kept her face buried. "I wanted you."

"I'm here now."

"Ella always gets you."

Maud heard a noise and looked at the doorway, where Ella stood. "I'm sorry, Lou," she said, starting to cry.

Maud opened her arms, and Ella came to the bed. She held the girls as they cried together, feeling hollowed out and helpless.

Later, after Annette went home and Ella and Louise were asleep, she and Peter sat on the living room couch. "We took her to the hospital because we were worried she'd been molested," he said, "and now she thinks the doctor molested her?"

"She doesn't think that."

"No, but she feels it."

It was the closest they'd come to mentioning Gabriel since Peter had asked her months ago whether anything more had happened with him. He looked spent. Maud felt a surge of resolve. She put her hand on his knee.

"Come to bed?" she said.

In their room, they stripped off each other's clothes, and she climbed on top of him. Peter didn't open his eyes, and eventually she closed her eyes too. Neither of them made a sound. Finally, Peter came with a sigh. With a quick kiss on her shoulder, he turned toward his nightstand. Maud lay next to him until he fell asleep, then got up and went to the kitchen. She took an ice cube from the freezer and held it to her cheek until it melted. The ice burned, but it felt good to withstand the pain.

17

O nce again, she and Peter went through the house, gathering scissors, knives, and razors and putting them sharp-side down in an empty oatmeal tin that they locked in Peter's desk drawer. The fidget basket returned to Ella's room, full of plastic tangles and tins of putty to keep her hands busy. Every day that week when Ella got in the car after school, Maud asked her if she'd self-harmed, and then she'd ask again every night before Ella went to sleep. Finally, Ella said the question was triggering. "It's like asking an alcoholic if they'd wanted a drink today. Just ask me in therapy instead."

Maud was back to watching for signs, inspecting Ella's exposed skin—arms, neck, ankles—worrying whenever she left the room. She tried to sleep next to Peter, then went down the hall to check on Ella several times during the night. Friday, she realized that she hadn't told Alice about not coming Wednesday to hike, but then how would she have told her when Alice didn't have a phone?

Two more appointments with Rita staggered by. Both times when Maud came into the office at the end, Ella's eyes were red and her voice stuffy.

"Anything you'd like to discuss?" Rita said to Maud.

"Did you do it again?" Maud asked Ella.

"No."

Louise was still thrown by the relapse. Maud caught her watching Ella with her lower lip sucked in. Maud bought two boxes of sugar cubes, and they spent an afternoon building a Taj Mahal because, Louise said, a new Sphinx would never be the same. That night, Annette dropped off CBD gummies meant to help Maud sleep, but they didn't work any better than the melatonin she'd tried. Lights off, the house creaked around her as she wandered from room to room, looked in on Ella, went outside to the deck, and, shivering, sought the glow of the city in the fog.

The following Wednesday, she drove to Esperanza. She was still sleeping poorly, bolting awake several times during the night, and she felt so fuzzy-headed and loose-limbed that she couldn't imagine going on a hike. But she missed Alice.

She was on the roof as Maud walked up the drive, and she dropped down the ladder, a hammer in her back pocket, a beaten-up raffia hat shading her face.

"I didn't know you were coming," she said, "I might have shot you."

Her face was back to the impassivity it wore when they first met. She pulled off the hat and fanned her face. "It's only nine," she said. "I don't hike until ten, if that's why you're here."

"Sorry I went AWOL," Maud said. "Something came up. And then I wasn't sure how to let you know."

"I have a mailbox," Alice said. "You drive by it every week." The hat moved back and forth, fanning her face. She was angry, Maud realized, and she was also being unfair. Someone without a phone or computer should accept a lack of messaging.

"I don't sit around here waiting for you to show up, you know," Alice added. "I have a schedule."

"Ella cut herself again," Maud said.

"Big mistake, having children."

"It's not funny." Maud felt as if she'd been slapped. And she wanted to slap Alice back. "It's not something to joke about."

"I'm serious," Alice said. "I think it's a mistake."

"Forget it," Maud said. "You can't understand. You have one serious relationship. With a dog."

"I have another serious relationship," Alice said. "It used to fascinate you." The hat stilled. "Why did you come here anyway?"

"To see you," Maud said. Her body wanted to leave, but her anger was ebbing. I hurt her feelings, she thought. I made her sit around and wait for me. I made her feel dependent on another person. "I'm sorry," she said and then, ridiculously, added, "I should have sent a letter."

Sighing, Alice put the hat back on her head. "Or even a postcard after the fact."

"Or a carrier pigeon," Maud said, and they both started laughing.

"Yeah, yeah, okay. I'm sorry too," Alice said. "That wasn't a nice thing to say about children, even though I think it's true." She walked toward the house. "Come on. You're taking a nap."

"No, I'm letting you work."

"You're taking a nap. You staggered the whole way down the drive. I thought you were drunk. You're gonna run your car off the road and into the Pacific. I'll be haunted for the rest of my life by a straight, Catholic ghost."

"I'm really not that tired," Maud said, but she followed her into the house.

"Your eyes are so bloodshot they look like they're bleeding. What time do you have to get those kids from school?"

Maud told her the pickup time for Louise. Alice took something out of a metal box next to the bed.

"Lie down. I'm heading back up there to finish. You'll need these. Turn your head. She squeezed an earplug and slipped it into Maud's ear. "Other side." The foam expanded, muffling Alice's voice. "I'll wake you up in two hours."

The bed was soft and the sheets musky. Alice flipped a switch on the wall as she left, and on the ceiling shutters crawled over the skylights. The room went black as the bottom of the sea, a drenching, exquisite nothingness. Who would have known that in the middle of the day this luminous space could be so transformed?

Earplugs by the bed and shutters on the skylights. She has insomnia, Maud thought, closing her eyes. Just as she had another life, so did Alice, a life with Gloria, her work on the land and the buildings, the walks she took with Clark before dinner, the hours reading in her study. Those other lovers. She listened to the rhythm of Alice's hammer on the roof, and it was as if she were kneeling next to Alice, the two of them pounding, or as if Alice were pounding for both of them, and it didn't matter whose hand held the hammer, and then the thudding started to fade, and she thought, She was right—I'm falling asleep.

She woke up not knowing where she was, and then remembered. She pulled out the earplugs and went outside. Alice was still on the roof, Clark flopped next to the chimney, licking his paws with his velvety tongue.

"You still have ten minutes," Alice said. Like a cutout, she was framed by the sky, the sun glancing off the roof.

"How does he get up there?" Maud said.

"He can't climb the mountain anymore, but he can climb a ladder."

"Thanks for the nap."

"I don't like surprises," Alice said. "And, all right, I missed seeing you. Even though you make me talk too much."

That night, lying next to Peter, Maud put her hand between her legs. The sensation came back so easily and without context, almost without trying. When Gabriel's face appeared, unrelenting, stubborn, she didn't fight it. It felt good to be back in the fog.

April bloomed into May with yarrow and poppies at El Polín and blue hound's tongue and popcorn flowers in the fields at Esperanza. The Briones house and walled garden stood again on their foundations, the house roofed in tile, the garden roofed by sky. Seedlings tiptoed from the soil: the golf clubs of bean seeds, the pronged tongues of squash. The yerba buena and strawberry plants gathered speed. Maud loved this infancy of a garden when you didn't yet know what plants would be hit by disease or eaten by slugs or toppled in a storm, when everything remained that pale green of possibility.

Now that the Tennessee Hollow project was ending, Maria had found Maud new work in the Presidio's victory garden, which had been planted by officers' wives during World War II. Three mornings a week, Maud crossed the bridge to cut a new walking path through the beds. On Wednesdays, she drove to Alice's for lunch and a hike.

One of those days, as they sat at the viewpoint, she asked about Alice's father.

"Around twelve, I realized that I didn't like him," Alice said. "He didn't like me much either. Why waste time with people you don't like just because you share DNA?"

"Because you love them even though you don't like them. Have you not heard me describe my brother?"

"You can dislike them so much that you can't love them." Alice and her father hadn't spoken for twenty years when he died.

"It's weird he left you all that money when you were estranged."

"He probably did it to punish me, because he knew I wouldn't want it. I was supposed to be his docile, pretty daughter who went with him to the symphony and laughed at the gross jokes of his awful friends. I wasn't supposed to have opinions, and I definitely wasn't supposed to like pussy. Or maybe he had a fight with wife number four and left me his fortune to spite her." She looked over at Maud. "Why are you making that face?"

"It's sad," Maud said.

"For him or for me?"

"For him. Losing his daughter."

"All kids leave their parents. Some of us slam the door on our way out."

"I can't see it that way," Maud said. "And it's hard for me to believe that he did."

"Because you're madly in love with your children," Alice said. Eyes on the ocean, she said it offhandedly. In the high sun, her hair was a skein of shadow and light. Yes, Maud thought. I'm madly in love with my children. But why can't I have more than one mad love?

18

At Ella's Lone Pines appointment two weeks later, Rita said that she thought Ella could move down to one session a week.

"Are you sure?" Maud said.

"I want the time for other things," Ella said. "Like tennis."

"We can always increase the frequency again if needed," Rita said.

Ella didn't talk all the way from the outpatient center to the parking lot.

"Are you upset?" Maud asked in the car.

"Having fewer sessions is a big deal. Aren't you happy about it?"

"I'm happy. It's just . . . things are good right now. I worry about how you'll manage when there's a new stressor."

"There are always new stressors. And some stressors don't go away."

Maud glanced at Ella as she started the car. What stressor wouldn't go away? Did Ella still think about Gabriel?

"I am happy," Maud said. "And proud of you. I know you're working hard, and I know it's exhausting. I can tell that you're feeling better these days."

It was the way Ella moved now—more surely, as if she weren't being tugged backward by a rope, a new carelessness in her simplest gestures like buttering a piece of toast. She was ending the school year with high grades. Her friendship circle had expanded. On her Instagram page, she beamed and laughed. With no help from Maud or Peter, she'd applied to be a counselor at the camp that she used to attend at Marin Headlands.

That weekend, she and two friends lay on the deck, sunning themselves in their bathing suits, as if they lived in Southern California, not Northern.

"I don't know whether to tell you guys to put on sunscreen or sweaters," Maud said from the sliding glass doors.

Ella looked over languidly. She was wearing a bikini, no trace of the cut on her stomach. "We're fine, Mom," she said.

Peter walked down the hall with the recycling bins stacked in his arms.

"She seems so good," Maud said, taking one of the bins. "It's hard to believe."

"I'm glad she has friends now. And nice ones."

She followed Peter down the front stairs. He knew that she herself had a new friend and that the two of them went hiking. He knew that Alice made Maud lunch and that she had a dog. But he had no idea what Alice was to her. Because I haven't told you, she thought, as they reached the street. And you haven't asked. Since that one awkward night, they hadn't tried to have sex. Now Peter took the lid off the recycling can. Does your loneliness feel like mine?

Maud wondered. An ache that rattled her body, loud as the bottles raining against the steel can.

When she showed up at Alice's that Wednesday, a pickup truck was pulling through the gate onto Highway One, driven by a woman in aviator glasses. As she passed Maud's car, she lifted her hand off the steering wheel and raised her middle finger.

"I think the person leaving here just flipped me off," Maud told Alice. She'd found her around back, looking for ticks in Clark's fur, a pair of tweezers in hand, reading glasses on her face.

"That was Gloria." Alice pinched the tweezers and yanked out a tick. "And she probably did flip you off." She dipped her finger in alcohol and pressed it to Clark's skin.

"Why?" Maud said.

Ignoring the question, Alice put the reading glasses in the pocket of her shirt and picked up her canteen. "You still want to check the grasses to see if they're dead?"

Maud nodded, and they headed toward the field. "She knows I'm not gay, right?" she said.

"That's part of the problem."

"If I were gay, she wouldn't care that we spend time together?"

"If you were gay and we were sleeping together, she wouldn't care. But you aren't gay and we aren't sleeping together."

Maud wondered what scene had taken place before she drove up to the house. An argument, clearly. She rolled back one of the plastic sheets, finding slimy, anemic grass. "Very dead." She jammed the stake that fastened the sheet back into the ground.

They headed toward the trail. With the work in the garden and her weekly hikes, Maud had lost most of the weight that she'd gained the year before and could keep up with Alice. "You said you weren't attracted to me," she said.

"Yes. Although it would be interesting if I were, since you're so repressed."

"I'm not repressed. I'm just not having sex right now."

"Thus spoke the woman who kissed two girls in college."

"Did you tell Gloria about that?"

"I told her when she asked. I have my flaws, but I don't lie, as I had to repeat to her five times this morning."

They crossed the stream, jumping from rock to rock. Maud couldn't remember what those two girls had looked like, only the surprise when she'd opened her mouth to their tongues. She hadn't gone further, mostly because she wasn't sure what to do next. She'd had a handful of male partners before she met Peter, short-lived boyfriends and one-night stands. And for years the sex with Peter was great. When he brought her home for the first time, they christened every room in the manor while his mother was on her daily walk: on the bear rug in his father's abandoned study under the glass eyes of a stag's head, against the flocked wallpaper of the second-floor hallway. Naked with her, Peter lost his reserve, and so did she.

Alice was walking fast, almost marching.

"Are you mad at me?" Maud asked.

"No. I'm mad at Gloria. I just had to spend two hours talking to her about my feelings. I had work to do." She shook her head. "I'll walk it off. I'll be in a good mood by the summit."

"You don't have to be in a good mood," Maud said. "You don't have to be anything with me but what you are."

Alice stopped on the trail. "When you say stuff like that, you don't help the situation."

"What situation?"

"Gloria has decided that we're having an emotional affair. She was very definitive about it. In a very annoying way. I said I don't see the point of an affair without sex."

"This isn't an affair," Maud said. "It's a friendship."

"Gloria doesn't buy that." Alice squinted at Maud. "What do you tell your husband about me?"

"Not much."

"That's what she thought." She walked on. "Apparently I'm doing the same thing about you. At first she said I was being evasive. But she knows I'm not a liar. So now she's decided that I'm not telling her something that even I don't know. Which has to be the most patronizing thing you can say to someone."

The truths about yourself that even you don't know, Maud thought. She'd wondered that about Gabriel. Ella's young face smiling at him, when she smiled so rarely. Her with a Coke on a couch. Him standing under a shower, naked, as she sat in the next room.

At the viewpoint, seagulls coasted over the distant cliffs. A pod of dolphins sawed its way across the steel sheet of water. Alice pulled the cap off the canteen and took a long drink. She looked miserable.

"Do you want me to stop coming here?" Maud said.

"No. I want Gloria to chill out."

Again, Maud felt the warmth of the lie she'd told Peter, only right now it felt more like heat, uncomfortable and menacing.

"I already had an affair," she said.

And the story spilled out. She described separating from

Peter for the summer and meeting Gabriel, falling in love, that day in the woods, the disastrous ending.

"I hadn't felt that way in forever. No, ever. It was never like that between Peter and me. I felt so real. So seen. But I was wrong about him. I thought I loved him, and he could have molested Ella."

"He didn't, though, did he?" Alice said. "It sounds like he was being a typical straight man. They all flirt with teenage girls."

"No, they don't. Peter doesn't."

"Right," Alice said. "Peter. The model husband who doesn't beat you. Anyway, how is it an affair if you were separated and had agreed you could sleep with other people?"

"It wasn't when I did it. I made it into one by not telling Peter."

Alice groaned. "That's a ridiculously Catholic thing to say."

"Maybe," Maud said.

Looking out at the ocean, she could feel Alice's gaze on her face.

"Why didn't you believe this Gabriel guy?" Alice said.

"Everything was chaos that night at the hospital. It seemed like Ella was hiding abuse. We didn't know about the cutting yet."

"I mean after," Alice said. "Why didn't you ever find out his side of the story?"

"He never contacted me."

"Why didn't you contact him?"

"What?" Maud looked over at her. "Fly to Nevada and ask him?"

Alice's gaze was steady and piercing. "That's what I'd do," she said, "but I don't like living in suspended animation."

She's right, Maud thought. I don't want to ask him,

because I don't want to know. I want to be able to believe that it was all a misunderstanding. I want to be able to go back. I still want that sweetness.

Alice was silent as they walked down the trail, and Maud knew this might be the last time she saw her—the drama with Gloria would continue, and Alice would get worn down.

When they came to the barn with its heavy lock and white-washed windows, she stopped by the doors.

"Can I see it?" she said.

She knew what she was doing. No one else had walked inside that barn, and the last time Alice had done so, she'd been queasy with withdrawal and trembling with self-disgust. It was too much to ask. She was asking.

"What is this?" Alice said. "You show me yours, I show you mine?" Her voice was unruffled, but at her sides, her hands trembled.

"Yes," Maud said.

Alice glanced at the doors. "Fine," she said. "I'll get the key. But don't say it's beautiful."

The lock clicked open, and the door creaked on its arthritic hinges, letting out the smell of long-gone livestock, damp hay, a metal tang. The sculpture stood in a swirling snowfall of dust. Maud walked toward it, and Alice followed. In the dim light, the basket was a solid shadow, impossibly huge, magisterially indifferent, heavy and light, purpose-fully sloppy, solid and shattered. Maud felt Alice standing behind her as if their bodies were joined.

"I can hear what you're thinking," Alice said.

"It's beautiful," Maud said.

19

Sunday evening, she was sorting laundry with Ella at the washing machine, separating wet bathing suits from T-shirts and shorts, when the doorbell rang twice and Peter called, "Maud? Someone here for you."

He said it like a question, and, walking down the hall, Maud wondered if Alice was at the door. On the deck, sunglasses on her head, stood Gloria. A bird-boned woman with a strong jaw, she looked as if the next gust of wind could carry her toward the ocean.

"Is Alice all right?" Maud said.

"Who is this?" Peter asked Maud.

"Alice is fine." Gloria's eyes narrowed. "Alice is great. She just fucking broke up with me, thanks to you."

"We're friends," Maud said. "That's all."

"Alice doesn't have friends."

Peter was looking back and forth from Maud to Gloria, seemingly ready to shut the door if needed. Ella had come up behind him. "Who is this?" Peter asked Maud again.

"I'm the partner of the woman your wife is playing gay with," Gloria said. "Going on hikes, taking naps in our bed, wooing our dog. Asking to see the sculpture that even I have never seen."

That had done it, Maud thought. That had been a step too far. She should have walked straight to her car that day and not stopped by the barn. But she'd had no idea this would happen. She'd thought that she and Alice were saying goodbye. Alice didn't ask her to lunch. She didn't say, I'll see you next week.

"I'm sorry," she said, coming up with nothing else.

"Stop fucking with her," Gloria said. "Stop fucking with me. Just stay the fuck away." As she walked to the stairs, her shoulders heaved.

"Wait." Maud followed her down the steps.

Gloria swung around. "You don't understand. Alice isn't like other people."

"I know that," Maud said. "I'm not trying to replace you."

"She doesn't have room for both of us. She's choosing you." Gloria's chin crumpled. "The minute you showed up, she shut me out. And now, it's goodbye." She sniffed hard, as if staving off tears. "Are you going to be there when she can't sleep? Or if she relapses? She was a disaster when she moved here. I wasn't sure she'd make it."

"I'll stay away," Maud said.

"It's too late. She doesn't go back on her decisions. If you know her, you know that. She just marches on."

Maud heard the grief in her voice. "Then catch up to her," she said.

Peter and Ella were still standing in the doorway when she walked back to the house.

"What the bloody hell was that?" Peter said.

But Maud barely heard the words. She'd noticed Ella beside him, hands in fists, body stiff, looking more furious than Gloria.

"You're doing it again," she said. "I can't believe you're doing it again."

"Sweetheart," Maud said, "what do you mean?"

"Gabriel." Ella looked at Peter.

"What about him?" Maud said.

Here it comes, she thought. No more lying. No more pretending. For either of us.

"You texted him when I was at his place. About meeting by the hedge." Ella took a shuddering breath. "I followed you that day. I was there."

Maud dug her fingernails into her closed hands to keep herself there, to not turn and run as fast as she could down the steps, get in her car, and flee Ella's agonized face, flee the images flashing through her head: her back against the tree, Gabriel thrusting into her, her hands clutching his back, her head rubbing against the bark.

"Oh, Ella," she said.

Peter put his arm around Ella's shoulders. "Love?" he said. "What are you talking about?"

"Daddy," Ella said, hanging her head. "I'm so sorry. I didn't want you to know."

She started to cry, and Maud knew from the seizing of Peter's face that he understood.

"It's all right," he said to Ella. "Everything will be all right."

"All this time, you kept this to yourself?" Maud said.

Weeping, Ella nodded. "I only told Rita. I wasn't even going to tell her. It came out after I had that nightmare about the hospital. She wanted me to say something to you. But I didn't want to. I didn't want Dad to know." She peered up at Peter. "Daddy," she wailed, "I didn't want you to know."

Peter tucked her head into his chest, hiding her face from Maud.

"You don't need to take care of me, love," he said. "I take care of you." When Maud moved toward them, he held up his hand. "Go."

"Ella," Maud said, "I'm so, so sorry. Please let me hold you."

"I want you to go too," Ella said, sobbing. "Please go away."

One arm still around Ella, Peter grabbed Maud's purse from the entryway table, threw it at her feet, and slammed the door.

When she was down the stairs, in her car, Maud's phone started buzzing with a voice mail from Alice. "I'm calling from a pay phone. Gloria just went nuts. She might show up there."

She drove down the hill without attaching her seat belt, into the dusk, barely seeing the road, onto the freeway, into the bare, sun-baked hills strung with utility lines. Her head spun. She thought about going to Annette's, but then she'd have to confess to her sister that she'd lied about sleeping with Gabriel, and the thought of hurting someone else she loved was too much. She pulled into a motel off the freeway with a glowing vacancy sign. For hours, she sat on the bed in a room with a popcorn ceiling, smelling old cigarettes and old sex. She walked the dingy carpet from the bathroom to the door. The numbness in her head soared into searing pain. Eventually, she fell asleep.

At five o'clock, she bolted awake and emailed Rita. An

hour later, she left a voice mail asking Rita to call as soon as she could. The air conditioner rattled and wheezed. She left another message.

At seven-thirty, Rita called back. "Are you safe, Maud?" she asked. "Do you need help? I just talked to Ella and Peter."

"Why didn't you tell me?" Maud said, starting to cry again.

"It was Ella's decision. I'm her therapist. And there was nothing in what she revealed to me that required disclosure."

"Please, please don't talk to me like I might sue you," Maud said. "Please. She's my daughter."

Rita's voice softened. "She told me what she saw after she had that dream about the hospital and self-harmed again. She's wanted to tell you for a while. We've been working on this. She was terrified about how Peter would take it."

We were separated, Maud thought. I wasn't cheating on him. He cheated on me. But Ella knew none of this, so what did that matter now? The truth didn't always matter. Facts didn't always count.

"Is this why she ran away that night at Montgomery Place?" she said. "Because she saw us?"

"I can't talk about it, Maud. I'm sorry."

"Did he do anything to her?"

"There's not much more to know about the situation with him," Rita said. "I understand that this must be awful, Maud. I do. I'll help you find someone."

"I only want Ella," Maud cried.

She lay on the bed for the next hour as outside the freeway hummed. She prayed for the first time since Ella had disappeared that night. Please, whatever you are, fix this somehow.

She texted Ella. *I love you. I'm so sorry.*

She texted Peter. *Is she OK?*

The dots of a reply appeared. *She's fine.*

Can we talk?

Not here. I'll meet you.

He sent a link to a café in Sausalito, some foreign territory where they'd never been. Waiting for him two hours later, Maud looked up child custody laws on her phone, becoming increasingly frantic. At fifteen, Ella was old enough to be an emancipated minor. She could decide to never speak to Maud again. Maud would have no legal rights in court. And what about Louise? What would Peter and Ella tell her? Her mouth was dry and her vision blurred. When Peter walked up to the table, she said, "Will you try to take the girls from me?"

"It's always about you, isn't it?" he said, sitting down. "Two years Ella's been holding this in, trying to protect me. She keeps apologizing, Maud. *She's* apologizing to *me.*"

"I'm so sorry," Maud said.

His mouth twitched. "Are you shagging Alice Lincoln too?"

"No. Of course not."

"What's the point in my asking? Why believe a word you say? You sat next to me in those bloody counseling sessions and lied over and over. I knew something had happened with him. I decided to trust you when you said nothing did. You've done this our entire marriage. Obfuscated. Managed me." The vein pulsed in his temple.

She needed him to answer her question. "Will you try to take them from me, Peter?"

His smile was cruel. "Even if I wanted to, I doubt it would work."

"Please say you won't."

"Don't tell me what to say." He stood up. "Ella has an appointment with Rita tomorrow afternoon. I asked your mother to take Louise. I said you had something for work."

"I'll take Louise." She was still terrified by his answer.

"Don't you think it would be better for her to be with your mother right now?"

"Let me pick her up from her sleepover today, at least," she said. "I'll drop her to you at the house. I won't come inside."

"Fine. But drop her at the Sausalito diner. I'll be there with Ella at ten. Then you can get what you need from the house for a few days."

A few days? He was kicking her out, but how could she protest? He was right that she'd lied to him. He was right that she'd met his honesty with deception. He was right that she'd been doing so for most of their marriage.

"What do I tell Louise?" she said.

"Tell her that you and Ella are working through a problem. That's what I'm planning to say."

An hour later, she sat in the car in front of the house where Louise had slept, willing her eyes to be less puffy. The girls had camped in a tent in the backyard and were still outside, her friend's father said when Maud came to the door. She followed him through a kitchen with flour and milk and butter still on the island, the smell of pancakes in the air, an older daughter typing on her phone at the table. This life is over, she thought. All of this is over. My family is over.

Outside, in a tent under an oak tree strung with fairy lights, the girls were talking and laughing. Maud blinked back tears as she helped Louise locate a missing sock.

"What's wrong with your face?" Louise said in the car.

"Nothing." Maud turned on the ignition. "I'm going to drop you to your dad and Ella for breakfast out. Ella and I are having a little fight."

"About what?"

"It will all be okay. I'm just going to sleep away for a few nights while she and I work it out."

"That's weird." Louise's brow scrunched as she studied Maud. "Were you crying?"

"I just didn't sleep well."

Peter came out of the diner alone when Maud texted from the parking lot that they'd arrived.

"Was the sleepover fun?" he asked Louise, studiously not looking at Maud.

"Why isn't Mom coming in?" Louise said. "Why was she crying?"

"She and Ella are working through something."

"I told her," Maud said. She hugged Louise. "I'll leave your sleeping bag and backpack in your room."

"Where's Ella?" Louise said. "I want to see her."

Peter took Louise's hand, and they walked into the diner. Maud drove to the house. She took her suitcase out of the closet, where it had sat since the return from the Hudson Valley. She packed pajamas, a toothbrush, a couple of shirts and pants, underwear, only enough for the few days that Peter had mentioned, since more than that was unthinkable. Then she left, locking the door behind her.

20

She sat in her sister's living room, cross-legged on the floor. Next to her, Annette was pressing her thumbs into Maud's palm, having said something about acupressure points. Sage burned in a ceramic dish next to a geode. Annette kept telling her to breathe.

"We need to calm you down," she said.

"I can't calm down."

For the last two nights that she had been at her sister's condo, Maud had been texting Ella every few hours—*I'm so sorry. I love you*—the messages piling on top of each other. She called Peter again, leaving voice mails that became increasingly frantic. Finally, last night, he'd called her back and agreed that she could pick up Louise from school today, in an hour.

"I don't think this is working," she told Annette, starting to cry again.

"Do you want some pot?"

"I have to drive."

"Let's try something else, then." Annette stood up. "You can't pick up Louise like this. Come on."

In the bathroom mirror, Maud's eyes were so swollen, she could barely make out the pupils. Her nose was raw and chapped. I'm falling apart, she thought. I can't handle this. Annette opened the makeup drawer. Closing her eyes, Maud surrendered her face to her sister, whose fingertips glided over her skin, reminding her that she wasn't alone.

Two days ago, when she had arrived at Annette's door with her suitcase, she rang the doorbell and burst into tears. Annette took one look at her and pulled her inside. Maud blurted everything between sobs. "I never told you I slept with him because I thought you were right about him. And I messed everything up. I messed Ella up. She'll never get over this. She'll never forgive me. Peter's so mad, he might do something crazy. Try to take custody. You know how he can be when he's angry."

Annette had put her hands on Maud's cheeks and held her face. "Listen to your big sister. You are not going to lose your girls. We are going to figure this out. I am here. Hold on to me."

Now Annette told her to look up. "You'll need a lot of this," she said, as she patted concealer under Maud's eyes.

Maud remembered that night with the policeman at Montgomery Place, how he'd said Ella was hyperventilating. Peter had stood right there with them, and Ella thought he'd been betrayed.

"There," Annette said. "You look less like a corpse. I'm going to say something again until you hear it. You didn't cheat on Peter. Peter cheated on you."

"I can't tell Ella that. The girls can't know that about him."

"Well, he can't make you into the villain. Don't give him all the power." After walking Maud to the door, she took down a horseshoe that hung on the wall. "Go get Louise," she said. "Bring this with you. It can't hurt."

"Where do I put it?"

"Keep it in the car. Are you sure you're okay to drive?"

Maud nodded. She felt as if she were five years old again, walking to kindergarten the first day, Annette carrying her backpack, giving her instructions about how to answer the nuns' questions, which bathrooms to use that didn't stink so much, what not to eat for lunch in the cafeteria.

"Go on," Annette said. "You look great."

When Maud pulled up to the school, Louise was already on the sidewalk, not chatting with her friends as she usually did.

"It'll be okay, Mom." She leaned over for a hug.

"Of course it will." Maud pointed at her face. "Look, Annette wanted to do my makeup. She's such a nut. Tell me about your day."

She drove to an ice-cream shop in Mill Valley and told Louise to get as many scoops as she wanted, like one of those divorced fathers she used to pity.

"Did your dad say anything more about what's going on?" she asked.

"Not really."

Peter wouldn't, she thought. As angry as he was with her, he wouldn't do that to Louise, just as she wouldn't tell the girls what he'd done. When the server came to their table, Louise ordered a banana split and then let the ice cream melt as she pushed it around with her spoon. Watching her, Maud was pounded again by grief.

"I know this is weird and hard," she said. "Ella's angry at me for a good reason. You and I will talk it all over one day when you're older. But for now I just want you to know that I love you and your sister and that I will make things right."

"Okay," Louise said.

When she dropped Louise at the foot of the stairs, Louise didn't ask her to come up, as if she understood the new rules. By the time Maud got back to Annette's, the mascara had zebraed her cheeks. She hung the horseshoe on the wall and called Peter. He didn't pick up, so she called him again.

"What?" he said.

"I need to see Ella, Peter. You need to get her to agree."

"I don't need to do anything. Give her a few more days. Give me a few more days, Maud. It won't go well if you don't. Do you understand that?"

"I'll wait a little longer. But I want Louise for a night."

They agreed on Thursday for the exchange. For the next two days, Maud worked at the Presidio, because, as she told Annette, the last thing she needed at the moment was to lose her job. She texted Ella every morning that she loved her and was sorry. She lived on coffee and water and the protein bars and scrambled eggs that Annette made her eat. She slept in a thin layer of unconsciousness with no depth for dreams. She picked up Louise from school, bought her to the ice-cream shop, and dropped her back at the foot of the steps to the house. She cleaned Annette's floors, went grocery shopping, made dinner.

"I think it's time for the six-o'clock rule," Annette said on Wednesday when she came home from work and found Maud sobbing in the bathroom. This had been Maud's idea after Dale died: try to save up all your crying for six o'clock, then let yourself go as hard and long as you liked.

Annette had a bag of food from their sister-in-law, Mandy. "She dropped this off to me today at the office," she said, putting the bag on the kitchen counter.

"Do they all know I'm staying here?"

"Louise told Mom. Mom called me. I told Kevin. But they only know that you and Ella had a fight and that now you and Peter are fighting. I told them you're too upset to talk about it." She looked in the bag. "Oh my God," she said.

"What?"

"There's enough food in here for twenty people."

"That's what she's used to cooking for."

Mandy had made lasagna, cookies, brownies, and Cobb salad. They ate the leftovers the next night with Louise. The feeling of her daughter next to her on the couch, toes pressed against her leg as they watched a movie, soothed Maud. But as she started to drift off beside Louise on the pull-out couch, Louise said, "When are you coming home?"

"I'll stay here a little longer, and then your dad and I will figure out the next steps."

"Are you guys getting divorced?"

"I don't know," Maud said. "But you'll always have both of us."

"He's taking us to Disneyland," Louise said softly. "He got all the tickets today. It's gonna be so fun."

Maud waited for her to go to sleep, trying not to panic. Why would Peter take the girls away without telling her? And why would he take them to Disneyland, a place they both found trite and saccharine and that they agreed was a waste of money? When Louise started to snore, she woke up Annette.

"I think I might need to talk to a lawyer," she said. "Peter's taking the girls to Disneyland."

Annette raised her sleep mask. "I don't think taking your children to Disneyland is grounds for legal action."

"He didn't say anything to me about it. I've texted him twice today. He didn't answer. If he wants full custody, he'll probably get it. What judge is going to give custody to a mother who did what I did in front of my daughter?"

"Whoa," Annette said. "This isn't the eighteenth century. You're not going to lose custody. Tell Peter you need to talk to him. Tell him to his face that you need to see Ella. And fucking remind him to get off his high horse, or I will."

Peter didn't reply when Maud texted. The next afternoon, she dropped Louise at the foot of the steps and texted him again.

I'm here, she wrote. *Will wait.*

Eventually he came down the steps, a dishcloth slung over his shoulder.

"How's Ella?" she said.

"She's fine. She sees Rita every other day. It seems to be helping."

"Louise told me you're planning to go to Disneyland."

"I think the girls could use a change of scenery. Going to the Happiest Place on Earth suddenly seems like a good idea." Although Peter was standing only a few steps away, he seemed all the way up on the deck.

"What about school?" Maud said.

"They have two days off. It's on the calendar."

"I'm losing my mind, Peter," she said. "I need to see Ella."

And then she saw that he was blinking fast, holding in his tears, as she'd seen him do once or twice at Lone Pines.

"I'm losing my mind too," he said. "I have the knives

locked up again. I follow her around the house wherever she goes. I can barely think at work. I'm doing what I can here."

Up those stairs, behind his anguished, angry face, Ella was in the house, maybe looking through a window, trying to see them on the street. And Maud knew that she too was afraid, knew it the way she used to know Ella was hungry as a baby before she'd even cried from her crib. They could lose each other now. She couldn't let that happen.

"She needs to see me," she said. "She needs to tell me everything. I need you to convince her."

"I don't need to do anything," Peter said.

"Yes, you do," Maud said. "Whatever you think of me, I'm her mother."

"We have an appointment with Rita again next Thursday," Peter said, already walking away. "I'll talk to Ella about you coming."

All day, Maud kept checking her phone for a text. Finally, one appeared.

Be there for the first half of the session.

The weekend dragged by, followed by two more days of picking Louise up from school, taking her to ice cream, and dropping her at the house. Maud kept texting Ella the same phrases every morning and night. Knowing that she would see her soon alleviated some of the terror.

"I think you'd better call Mom," Annette told her as they ate microwaved chicken pot pie out of paper trays. "I've been holding her off, but if you don't, she's going to show up here tomorrow."

Later, Maud dialed her parents' number and asked her mother to get her father on the line as well.

"I know Annette told you that I'm staying with her for a while," she said.

"She told me you aren't eating," her mother said.

"I'm eating. It's been rough."

"Well, make sure that you do," her mother said. "Low blood sugar runs on your father's side of the family."

"Hang in there, kid," her father said. "You and Peter will work it out."

"I don't know that we will, Dad."

"I guess the world won't end if you don't," her mother said.

After hanging up, Maud sat on the couch with the phone in her hand. She was going to disappoint her parents even more than she already had. She was going to be their divorced daughter. And how strange, how humiliating even, that she cared—some old root system like the prayers that came to her mouth in moments of crisis to a God she didn't believe existed.

Thursday morning, she drank three cups of coffee to clear her head and ate the bowl of instant oatmeal that Annette made her force down. In the waiting room at Lone Pines, her heart palpitated whenever the door opened. Finally, Peter and Ella arrived. Ella barely looked over when Maud stood up.

"Rita said to go right in," Peter said. "I'll wait here."

Maud followed Ella, wanting to touch the back of her arm, smooth the strand of hair that had come loose from her ponytail, grab on to her and not let her go.

Sitting across from Rita's desk, she knotted her hands and waited.

"Ella's written things down to make it easier for her," Rita said.

Ella took a folded piece of paper from the pocket of her sweatshirt. "I thought Gabriel was my friend," she read aloud. "But then I started to think that you were telling him stuff about me behind my back. You acted strange with him. All jokey and smiley. And I woke up one night to go to the bathroom and you two were sitting outside. I knew you were probably doing that all the time. Then one day when I was at his place, he was in the shower, and he got a text and I read it. It was from you. About meeting by the hedge."

She paused and glanced up at Maud. The room grew close.

"That afternoon, after you dropped me off from camp and left, I went down there and hid behind a tree, where I could see. I was going to tell you and Gabriel that I knew you were meeting each other in secret. I was mad at him too. I saw him waiting then you got there and I was going to do it. But you went into the forest and I didn't understand why. So I went too." Her face blanched. "And I saw."

"Do you want to take a minute?" Rita asked.

Ella shook her head. She turned back to the paper.

"After, I ran to the house. I just wanted to stop it. I didn't want Dad to know. And he was coming that night. I hated Gabriel." Ella's mouth trembled. "Then when Dad came, you two said that you were staying and Louise and I were going back with him. I knew you and Gabriel would do that again. You'd fuck each other again." Her voice rose. "That's why you wanted Louise and me gone. So I thought, I'll run away. It was dark, though, and I got scared, so I went to Gabriel's because I knew he wasn't there. I was going to wait until there was more light and go back on the road. I don't know where. But I fell asleep. And then it all went so fast. I didn't think all those things would happen. I didn't think I'd have to go to the hospital and that they'd give me those drugs. And do that exam. And that they'd think I was doing something awful with Gabriel." She folded the paper, eyes on the floor. "Something like what you did. That whole summer."

It wasn't the whole summer, Maud thought. But this wasn't a moment to protest. And she wanted the answer to another question. "Is there anything else you haven't told me?" she asked, her body growing hot.

Ella nodded. "It was my idea to use Gabriel's Wi-Fi. I went over there to ask, and he let me. I told him not to tell you. He wanted to. He said he was going to if I didn't. And it was only three times."

"So it wasn't every day?" Maud said. "It wasn't like you said at the hospital?" Dizzying relief swept through her body. She tried not to show it on her face.

Ella shook her head. "I said that so you wouldn't go back with him."

"Why don't you tell your mom how you'd like to proceed from here ?" Rita said. "And then we'll see what she thinks."

Ella took a long breath. "Every time I see you, I see you and him. I can't see you and not see that."

"What Ella would like," Rita said, "is to keep things as they are for now but to schedule another session in a week."

"And you don't want to talk until then?" Maud asked Ella.

"I want to be just with Dad for a while." She looked at Rita, then back at Maud. "He says you're fine at Annette's."

"Yes," Maud said, "I'm fine at Annette's. I miss you so much. But I'm fine."

Walking down the hall to the waiting room, she felt a

physical force as strong as the power she'd needed to push Ella into the world fifteen years ago, alone despite the doctor, nurse, and Peter in the delivery room.

"Can we talk outside?" she told Peter.

"There's no one here."

She sat down next to him, lowering her voice so the receptionist wouldn't hear behind her glass partition.

"Thank you for encouraging her to talk to me."

"It was the right thing to do. It's not what I wanted." He took his suit jacket off the back of the chair. "I want her to never speak to you again. I want both girls to hate you. I want you to be miserable for the rest of your life." He stood up. "But I know that would be bad for them. So I'm not telling them what I think of you. And just so you know, it's taking all my self-restraint."

"And I'm not telling them either," Maud said, as Peter put on the jacket and tugged down the sleeves. "About how you cheated on me. I don't want to make things worse for Ella. But she needs to know that we were separated that summer. You can tell her, or I will. Even better, we should tell her together."

Peter looked incredulous. "You shagged your perverse boyfriend right in front of her. You lied to me about him for two years."

"Yes," she said, standing up with him. "I did. And I'm sorry. But I want Ella to know that I wasn't cheating on you." She cleared her throat, and then added, "And Gabriel wasn't perverse. He was naive."

She believed this now. She believed it fully. She understood why he'd opened the cottage door to Ella and why he'd let her come back when she knocked again. Three times, not every afternoon. He'd wanted to tell her, and told Ella he would. She hadn't been wrong about him.

Peter stared at Maud for a moment before picking up his briefcase.

"I want a divorce," he said.

21

For the next few days, Maud reeled in the ivy that had grown through the open door of the garden at Tennessee Hollow, uncoiling it from around the staked beans and the wispy cornstalks. She trimmed the mat of yerba buena, which seasoned the air with its minty smell. Moving her body helped to keep her mind from whirring with the fear that Ella would never forgive her.

"My head's a mess," she told Annette. "And the future is a black hole."

They were walking through Annette's neighborhood as the sunset painted the city in watercolor hues.

"Remember how I was the summer after," Annette said.

And Maud did remember: Annette hollow in her bed, sapped by grief, weeping with the curtains shut as Maud cleaned tissues off the floor, cracked open the window, murmured to her, I love you. You are going to be okay. This life her sister had made on the other side of that wall of misery wasn't perfect. But it was a life, and it was hers, and, Maud reminded herself, as she'd told Annette back then, sometimes living was simply about getting out of bed.

On Friday, Louise spent the night. On Saturday, Maud helped her with her homework at Annette's kitchen table. On Sunday, the three of them went to Golden Gate Park to take out a paddleboat on Stowe Lake. Knees moving up and down, tossing popcorn to the ducks, Maud eyed Louise's face for signs of distress.

The next session with Rita at the end of the following week was less revealing than the first. This time Ella said little. Mostly they sat in excruciating silence.

"I love you," Maud said. No answer.

"I miss you so much." No answer.

Then, as Maud had negotiated via text, Peter joined them from the waiting room.

"Your dad and I were separated that summer," Maud told Ella. "I know that doesn't change what you saw or how it made you feel. But I wasn't being unfaithful."

She saw Ella take in the information and process it. All that suffering for nothing. Protecting Peter, keeping their marriage intact, when it was already over.

"So you dumped Dad and then fucked someone else right away," she said.

"I didn't dump your dad," Maud said. She raised her eyebrows at Peter, who glanced at the ceiling.

"It was more complicated than that," he said. "Your mom and I had agreed to take a break."

"You'd sensed that things weren't good between us, hadn't you?" Maud asked Ella.

"I don't know," Ella said. "Maybe." She started to cry. "And you guys never told Louise and me. You just let us go to New York not knowing."

"We weren't sure," Peter said.

"I was sure," Maud said. "And I see now that we should have told you."

Ella glared at them both. "You guys suck."

"I'm sorry, our time is up," Rita said. "Shall we schedule another session? Maybe next week?" Ella replied with a shrug.

Maud went back to Annette's condo, waited until six o'clock, then let herself weep.

She and Peter met the next morning at the same café, he in his suit, she in her gardening clothes.

"I hope we can do mediation," he said. "It's cheaper. I want fifty-fifty custody."

"What about I take four days to your three?"

"No. I want fifty-fifty. I'll come home early. I'll figure it out with work."

There was a scab on his throat; he must have cut himself shaving. Yesterday, when he picked up Louise, he'd had a five-o'clock shadow. She needed to remember that he was suffering too, and with him suffering churned into anger.

"I could get the girls after school for you," she said.

"Your days will be your days. Mine will be mine. I'd like to see you as little as possible. And as you've said, you'll be working full-time." He took a sip of the coffee he'd bought at the counter.

She felt gutted. A week not seeing the girls at all. How could she bear it?

They discussed the house—there was a year left on their lease. She told him he could have it. "And I won't ask for alimony." She knew it was a mistake to say this, even in an unofficial conversation. But she didn't want Peter's money.

Whatever happened now, she had to support herself on her own.

"We'll work out the details in mediation." Peter pushed back his chair.

"Wait," Maud said. She told him that for now she wanted to get Louise from school every day and keep her until dinner. "And I want Ella to start coming to my place too in a couple weeks. Then we'll add in weekends."

"You don't have a place."

"Like I said, I'll find one."

She watched Peter walk out the door. They were *you* and *I*, no longer *we*. Mixed into the dread and despair and guilt, she felt relief.

But how to find this place she had referred to, given her salary and the Bay Area's extortionate real estate market? That night, laptops side by side, she and Annette searched for a reasonable rental not too far from Sausalito. Finally, Annette shut her laptop. "New idea. I'll give up the condo and move over the bridge. We can even buy something together. Mom and Dad have said they'll help."

"They can't afford that," Maud said.

"They might sell the lot with the garage."

"They don't want to."

"They might anyway. Give the three of us our inheritance early, Mom says."

"I see there was a family meeting," Maud said.

"There was a family phone call."

"I'm not making them do that. Or you." She was touched, though; for all their faults, her family always came through. "Does this mean you told Mom and Dad that I'm definitely getting divorced?"

"I thought it would be better for you if I broke the news."

Maud knew what her parents' silence meant. They had nothing good to say, so they weren't saying anything. The world hadn't ended, as her mother had commented, but divorce was a failure. Maud's marriage had failed. You could comfort yourself with statistics, tell yourself that a twenty-year relationship was a good run. After all, when marriage was invented, no one lived this long. But it was still a jagged gash through your life, even if it was what you wanted.

The girls left a few days later for Disneyland. Louise texted Maud pictures from Peter's phone of the Matterhorn, a parade of princesses, the boat for "it's a small world." Finally, Peter seemed to get the hint, and he took videos of Louise strapped into rides, beaming and squealing. Ella stayed out of view. Maud wondered if her attitude toward Peter had changed since the last session, if she was glowering at him as they waited in line. There was some relief in not being the sole target of her anger.

But Ella would probably forgive Peter soon enough, Maud thought as she stood in the shower at Annette's condo. She herself had made the more inexpiable mistake. A mother wasn't supposed to leave her marriage. A mother was certainly not supposed to have sex in the woods while her daughter watched. And even more complicated than this, Ella had been jealous. How in the world, Maud wondered, water pounding her face, would Ella untangle all those emotions?

She was getting ready for the opening at Tennessee Hollow, which started in an hour. Annette would meet her after work to celebrate. She got out of the shower and toweled off. She put on a pantsuit and stepped into a pair of flats. She was now a single mother whose children were gone to the other half of their lives.

She rallied when she saw the garden with its sateen ribbon over the entryway, matching the one on the door of the house. A crowd milled past the dry bed of El Polín, children chasing monarch butterflies, parents balancing plates of crackers and cheese and paper cups of wine. At the microphone set up by the pomegranate tree, she followed Maria's speech with her own, reading directly from index cards, trying not to sound nervous. She described how Juana Briones and her sisters would have watered the plants with buckets of water drawn from the stream, and about the problems they might have encountered, "pests and disease like the one that you can see on the pumpkin plant now."

It had started two days ago. The leaves had turned a sickly urine-yellow with spots like cigarette burns. She'd sprayed the vines with milk and cut away the withered leaves, but she knew the plant would soon be dead.

"We did something good here," Maria said after the ribbon-cutting. She looked euphoric. "And I can't believe Alice showed up."

"She did?" Maud hadn't seen her in the crowd.

"Over there," Maria said.

Down the dry run of El Polín, Alice sat on the empty well. Clark was sniffing the adobe bricks. He licked Maud's hand when she walked over.

"Nice speech," Alice said.

"Thanks." Maud scratched behind Clark's ears. She wished she had more index cards for what to say now. "Did you and Gloria work things out?"

"We're working on working things out," Alice said. "She's calmed down. I'm trying not to blow my stack."

"She was wrong about us," Maud said. "But she was a little bit right."

For the first time since they'd met, Alice looked sad. "She said you told her not to give up on me. I came here to tell you to take that same advice about your own situation. And to say a proper goodbye."

Maud opened her arms, and Alice stepped into them. Maud felt her body resist and then give. Alice let go first. "You're such a tease," Alice said. She tapped Clark on the head. "Goodbye, sweetheart."

"Goodbye," Maud said. "Make sure you leave the plastic on through the fall. It only takes one seed."

She watched them walk away, Clark lumbering at Alice's side, back to the road, back to the bus, back to Esperanza, out of her life.

The next morning, she called the University of Nevada and asked about the summer institute that Gabriel ran near Death Valley. There were daily sessions in the classroom from ten to noon, the receptionist said, and fieldwork in the afternoon. Professor Crews held office hours before his classes.

22

D riving a rental car out of Las Vegas on Thursday afternoon, Maud felt as if she'd landed on another planet. The land was flatter, balder, more elemental than anything she'd seen, as if all the vegetation had been removed with a blowtorch. Sunlight shot through the windshield. On the straight, uncomplicated road, she veered between fear and excitement. She had no idea how this conversation would go, and she wasn't sure how she wanted it to end.

As the road shucked off the city, it collected smaller towns. The mountains rose taller; tumbleweed tripped over sand. A ghost town slumped by, followed by the skeleton of an abandoned uranium mine. She turned in to Beatty, a town of strung-out, rickety buildings, brightened only by a bubblegum-pink billboard for Heaven's Ladies Brothel. She passed a sign for Yucca Mountain and an RV camp touting natural hot springs.

The University of Nevada's Death Valley Summer Institute had once been a cattle ranch, its barns converted into classrooms. Around a modern cafeteria that gleamed like a spaceship, students sat against the walls, talking in the shade. Maud blasted her face with the air-conditioning and ran her fingers through her hair, then she stepped out into the heat.

Gabriel's office stood at the end of the complex behind a warped and peeling door. When Maud knocked, she heard him say, "Come on in."

He must have been expecting a student. He winced when he saw her on the threshold. They stood in a silence that she knew she should break but couldn't. Gabriel looked heavier that she remembered, his jaw shadowed by jowls, more of a weary handsome now.

"This is my office hour," he said finally. "Students come by. If you're staying, could you shut the door, please?"

Once, this would have been a joke to tease her about how she was standing there with her hand still on the knob. But she couldn't imagine that mouth smiling, and his voice was a mallet.

She closed the door and walked to the middle of the room, which was empty save for the desk, a couple of chairs, and a water cooler.

"I know Ella lied about how often she went to your place," she said.

Gabriel stared at her, then he let out a laugh she'd never heard him make, dry and quick, like a broom whisking.

"And that's why you're here?" he said. "To make that announcement?"

The water cooler gurgled. Out the window lay baked grasslands, barbed wire, hard sky.

"I needed to talk to you," Maud said.

"Then I guess you might as well sit down." Gabriel nodded

at one of the chairs in front of his desk, and she took her place across from him. Who was the judge and who was the accused? If he couldn't see his part in all this, she would get up and leave.

"Why didn't you tell me back then that she was coming over?" she said. "Why did you lie to me?"

Gabriel shook his head. "I didn't lie."

"Lying by omission is lying."

Gabriel closed his eyes, then opened them again. "I thought I was helping. Building trust with her. You two were having a hard time." He let out a long breath. "I was going to tell you. I told her I would. Then it was too late."

"But why did you let her come over in the first place?"

"It was stupid of me," he said. His face tightened. "But it wasn't molestation."

He was leaning back in his chair, not in the way he used to at the table—relaxed, lulled—but as if a fire burned in a pit between them. Something had scarred him too, Maud thought. She was taking it all in now: the bare office, the bleak terrain outside, not Turkey, not that place he'd loved.

"Ella was hurting herself," she said. "Cutting her skin. Did she tell you that?"

"No," Gabriel said. "Of course not. I would have told you. I barely talked to her when she was in the cottage. I worked in the other room. Just those three times. And I was so clear with her that I'd tell you if she didn't. Why did she say something different? I don't understand."

"She saw us together," Maud said. "That day at the hedge."

She watched Gabriel put the story together, his side, her side, Ella's side, the complicated geometry.

"She thought I was cheating on Peter," Maud said. "I

should have told both of the girls about the separation at the start of the summer. I know that now."

Gabriel took a moment to reply. "I should have told you Ella came to my place," he said. "Actually, I should never have let her in. I've known that for a long time." He looked out the window. "Is she all right?"

"She's getting there," Maud said.

"I'm glad."

She wanted to weep at the waste of it all, at the sight of his hands on the desk. Instead, she said, "What happened to you?" And, looking away when they caught glances, Gabriel told her.

The night Ella ran away, while Maud was at the hospital with her, he sat in an interrogation room at the police station for hours. The detective kept asking over and over again, "Did you expose yourself to her? Do you watch porn? What kind of porn?" Gabriel grimaced. "They confiscated my laptop. I tried to explain. But I could tell from their questions that Ella was saying something different. Then you called." He stopped and gathered himself. "I can still hear it, you know," he said.

As he watched her with those same dusky-blue eyes, Maud remembered the glare of the bathroom tiles. She remembered gripping the phone to her ear. She tasted again the malice in her words: *I'll kill you if you did.*

When he came back from the police station, Gabriel continued, there was a note from Harriet on the door of the cottage. She asked him to leave Montgomery Place by the end of the day.

"I would have left anyway," he said. "I couldn't have stayed after what happened. But she didn't stop there."

Back in Ithaca, he was called to a meeting with his depart-ment chair and the college dean. Both had received emails from Harriet. Gabriel explained to them that he'd been cleared by the police. "And legally, there was nothing the university could do, because legally, I hadn't done anything. Only it turns out that didn't matter." He shrugged. "You can't prove an intention. You can't prove a thought. I'd lis-ten to myself and think, Why would anyone believe this guy? We all know it happens all the time."

The next thing he knew, he'd been taken off the dig in Turkey. "Funding, they said. Bullshit." Swallowing, he cracked his knuckles. "I couldn't take it. People thinking that of me. I quit. Which in hindsight was also stupid. You know what it's like to not have your work. I fell into a hole for a year. I'm just getting out of it. Sort of." He gestured at the room. "This isn't exactly a dream job. I may never work on a major dig again."

"You will," Maud said.

"Maybe," he said. "Probably." He smiled weakly. "We'll see."

His body hadn't moved. He was keeping his distance. "I really can hear it," he said. "Like you're saying it again in my ear. I thought you knew me better than anyone."

"She was my daughter," Maud said. "I thought you'd hurt her. That's all I knew at the time."

He sighed. "I still feel like a fool."

"You're not a fool," Maud said. "Neither of us were. We were in love."

Then Gabriel's face relaxed, and the walls disappeared. Night descended, and they were back at their table with the stars coming out and the candle burning, and the sweet, moldering smell of the orchard.

"It was great for a while, wasn't it?" Gabriel said.

"Yes," Maud said. "It really was."

She watched him for another moment over a distance she knew now was impassable. Then she got up and left.

Outside, the noon sun pulsed, and the handle of the car door burned. Her flight from Las Vegas left at eight, but she didn't want to drive back to the city yet. She headed down the main road toward Death Valley, reentering California, stopping at the ranger station for a map. She asked for a hike to a summit, and the ranger suggested Dante's View from the Black Mountains, which overlooked the badlands. He told her that she should take the short trail in this heat. There were warnings all over the wall; a barometer read 110 degrees. She bought a bottle of water and went back outside.

In the parking lot below Coffin Peak, she slathered her face and arms with sunscreen and put on a hat. She found the trail, which cut through sand and rock. The sky and the sand and the mountains and sun melted together. The rocks glimmered around her like water, the heat blasted the back of her neck. As she pulled her body up a rock scramble, lizards skittered away. She stopped to drink, then forced herself onward. The rocks parted, and the trail flattened, rising again to a false summit. She kept moving, alone, the only person on earth, watching her feet move over the uneven ground, carrying her to the viewpoint.

Hands on her knees, she caught her breath. Looking up, she was no longer in Death Valley. The ocean floor bucked as tectonic plates crashed into each other. The water carved those fragile bluffs that cradled Baker Beach. Egrets flew over freshwater marshes. Redwoods grew. Rivers wove underground. Seaweed danced, and grasses pushed their roots. Maud stood on the summit and took in the power, the endurance, the mystery of rock, water, seed, air.

ALCATRAZ

2014–2015

23

For centuries, the island sat unoccupied in San Francisco Bay, a moody coin on the bright surface of water, streaked with seagull guano, inhabited only by sunning sea lions. People gathered eggs from its shores after paddling across the bay in their canoes. When Juan Manuel de Ayala and his men docked on its banks, he named it Isla de Alcatraces, island of the pelicans, thc word "alcatraz" in Spanish originating in the Arabic word for sea eagle.

Years later, Alcatraz was turned into a fortress and then into a military prison. The U.S. Army sculpted cliffs with dynamite blasts and hauled soil from Angel Island to hold their cannons in place. The families stationed on the island used that soil to plant a formal Victorian garden of agave, mirror plant, fuchsia, and roses. In front of their houses, sweet peas, lilies, and poppies grew.

During the 1930s, the secretary to the warden began a gardening program for prisoners. Elliott Michener, a counterfeiter, was allowed to retrieve handballs that had flown over the recreation yard walls. One day, after finding and returning a key to a guard, he was rewarded with a position as a gardener. Having no botanical background, he taught himself the ways of plants through reading and experimentation. He spent every moment of freedom in the greenhouse and gardens. Guards brought him the seeds and bulbs he requested from San Francisco. He left bouquets on the dock for families visiting prisoners.

After twenty-nine years, Alcatraz shut down. In 1969, it was occupied by Indians of All Tribes, who offered the U.S. government $24 for the land, based on the selling price of Manhattan Island. After the occupation, the island joined the National Park System. And for decades, the gardens disappeared in a thicket of weeds.

Two months after her trip to Nevada, Maud joined the restoration effort. She worked five days a week, all day, on the slope below the cellblock, trimming and planting, a break from the constant worry about money, the relentlessness of Ella's resentment, the concern for Louise, and the emptiness of her weeks without the girls. She'd hoped to stay at the Presidio, but there had been no full-time position available, and she needed health insurance. On Alcatraz, she wasn't in charge, and she didn't care. She'd have to earn her stripes again with a new group of people.

She clung to the rock, to the ferry, to the salary that came every two weeks. She tended the seedlings, cleared blackberry canes from the rose garden, and spent long afternoons in the archives, looking for clues to plants long dead. At five o'clock, she returned to the apartment that she rented in Corte Madera, with a view of a parking lot and carpeting that smelled of dog. Her life was no longer full of crises and secrets, but it was lonely. Whenever the girls were with Peter, she was so haunted by their vacant beds in their vacant room that she kept the door closed. A homework paper left behind by Louise on the kitchen table could send her spirits plummeting.

The girls shifted between Peter's house and her apartment according to the custody agreement of one week on and one week off. This wasn't what Maud had wanted. She and Peter had gone around and around in mediation. She'd proposed splitting the week, two days then five days, but Peter found that too convoluted and disruptive. When Maud broke into sobs during one of those sessions, he said she could visit the girls when he had them. So, on Wednesday nights during his weeks, she rang the doorbell for a good-night hug on the deck.

Ella's anger retreated, regathered, and rose. Just when it seemed she had worked through the trauma of keeping her secret for so long and her anger over being kept in the dark about the separation, she started to resent her parents for what had come before: "I was depressed for months. You and Dad didn't notice."

We did notice, Maud thought. What do you mean? We were worried about you. She bit the inside of her lip to keep herself from talking, the pressure of her teeth a reminder to let Ella get it all out. She had decided that she wouldn't be defensive in these sessions. She'd find her own therapist when she could afford it. The silver lining was that Ella blamed Peter too, which made her feel less alone.

"She can be so tenacious," Peter said one night in front of his house when Maud picked up the girls. "Does she still do that to you?" He'd grown a beard and had taken up jogging, which meant, Annette said, that he was starting to date. It was the week before Christmas and half of their old ornaments hung on a blinking tree in the living room behind him. The other half hung on the tree Maud and the girls had maneuvered up the steps of her apartment building.

"Yes," Maud said. "But it's getting better." The holidays seemed to be softening Ella. Then, because Peter looked disappointed, she hastily added, "She had two extra years of being mad at me."

Other than this, her conversations with Peter were short and civil and over text: about pickup times or ensuring that the right shoes and schoolbooks were packed in the large duffel bag that moved between their homes.

As spring arrived, Ella seemed to be letting go of her anger. She hugged Maud goodbye when she left for Peter's. She described her father's failed attempt to buy her menstrual products with beleaguered affection. ("Super-plus tampons. Next time I'm going with him.") She had little to lament when she and Maud sat in the family therapist's office together. They moved to a monthly session, then a bimonthly session, and in May they all graduated from family therapy. Maud bought herself a carrot cake on her week alone to celebrate; every night she mined a piece straight from the box with a fork.

That summer, Peter was officially seeing a real estate agent who drove a BMW and made pasta from scratch. Maud kept herself from asking the girls about his girlfriend too much, but the two of them dropped information now and again.

"I mean, she's okay, I guess," Ella said, "but she never stops talking."

"She's probably nervous," Maud said. "You two can be toughies."

"We're perfectly nice to her," Louise protested.

"Typical that he finds someone in five minutes," Annette said. She unspooled a stretch of packing tape. "Men have it so easy."

They were helping Maud's mother box dishes in her parents' kitchen. Seemingly out of the blue, their parents had decided to sell the house and garage and move to a retirement community.

"Do you think you might start seeing someone too?" her mother asked, studiously matching Tupperware lids with their containers.

"I'm not ready yet," Maud said. "And it's not that easy to find a someone."

"For what it's worth, I think you'll have an easier time than your sister," her mother said. "You'll keep your best interests in mind."

Maud uncapped a pen to label a box as she and Annette rolled their eyes at each other.

On the drive home from her grandparents' house, Ella was quiet. Later, she came into Maud's room and sat on the bed. Maud put down her book. "What's wrong?" she said, seeing Ella's expression.

"Do you think you'd be with Gabriel now if I hadn't said what I did?" The trouble on Ella's face seeped into her voice.

"I don't know," Maud said truthfully, "but I promise you that it doesn't matter." She pulled back the covers. "Want to sleep here tonight?" Ella nodded and climbed into the bed.

They left it at that. What Maud couldn't say to Ella was this: Thank you for being brave. Thank you for saying something.

Thank you for giving us a chance. And thank you for finally freeing me from that marriage.

Several weeks later, on a gloomy afternoon of pressing fog and shrieking seagulls, she was in the Victorian garden on Alcatraz, pruning the roses, when an idea made her stop and set down the shears. It came with a jolt, followed by a shimmer, and she thought about it for the rest of the day as she gardened.

The history of the world existed in every plant that grew on the island. Not only the history of the Western World. The entire world. The history of the very cosmos. Mineral and vegetal and animal and human. From this one chunk of rock, you could travel everywhere and whenever.

After dinner, she sat at the kitchen table with Ella and Louise as they did homework, and she plotted out her idea on a piece of drafting paper.

"It would be a website with clickable photos and links," she told the girls. "With descriptions of every plant on Alcatraz. You'd click on a sentence or a word in the description, and it would lead you to other information about history, botany, literature, geology. You might start with a tulip and end up in Stone Age Africa. I'll have to learn the technical stuff."

"Go for it, Mom," Louise said.

"Sounds cool," Ella said.

Maud stayed up late for weeks, thinking and taking notes, before pitching the project to the Alcatraz Foundation. Besides the website, they loved her idea of an interactive tour that could be downloaded to visitors' phones. Maud helped the development office write a grant proposal, and amazingly the funding came through a week later. The donor wanted to remain anonymous, Maud's boss told her, "though they say you'll know who they are. They're a serious piece of work." Alice, Maud thought, the name soaring through her body. That night, as she wrote a thank-you note, she remembered standing together in the barn, looking at the basket. Something all your own. Something you saw in nothing and brought into the world. She was still learning from that friendship, even though it had ended. And, she thought, as she dropped the envelope in a mailbox, maybe one day she would learn that it hadn't.

The first entry that she completed was on the iris, which grew on Muslim graves and in the wild on the African continent. Which figured on the woodblock prints of the Japanese artist Hiroshige. Which was the fleur-de-lis on the French flag. Which was named in the *Homeric Hymns*, picked by Persephone before her abduction by Hades.

In August, with her portion of the money from the sale of her parents' property, Maud bought a condominium on the edge of the Presidio. The building had bad plumbing and warped facia, but it backed onto a eucalyptus grove and was a thirty-minute walk to Tennessee Hollow. Maud lined the balcony with planters of scarlet runner beans that curtained the rusted railings, and filled a blank spot in the living room with a Victorian loveseat to accompany her cheap Scandinavian furniture. Mornings, before leaving for work, she laced her hiking boots and looped through the park to Inspiration Point, sometimes joined by Maria. Below, in the misty crux of the valley, the vibrant jumble of the garden waited for another day of children.

One hot weekend, she and the girls painted the condo, each room another bright color: blue, yellow, pink. Done, they were speckled from their hair to their ankles.

"This place looks like a rainbow vomited," Ella said, and they laughed.

"I guess neither of you will be interior decorators," Maud said. She wondered whether white primer could erase this mess.

"If we do, it won't be thanks to your genes," Louise said.

The girls were flopped on the floor against the tarped loveseat. Ella was picking paint off her knee as, next to her, Louise swigged lemonade straight from the bottle. Maud wanted to press the moment in the pages of time. She wasn't sure of much, but she knew one thing: from now on, they were moving forward.

ACKNOWLEDGMENTS

Thank you to Zibby Owens, Kathleen Harris, Anne Messitte, and the rest of the wonderful Zibby Books team for giving *Hedge* a warm and innovative home. Thank you to Samantha Shea, agent extraordinaire, for her input on early drafts and for her generosity and constancy. Thank you to Leigh Newman for acquiring *Hedge* and for her excellent editing.

Thank you to my Baltimore crew who read this novel in its many stages and kept me afloat through the writing: Jessica Anya Blau, Betsy Boyd, Elisabeth Dahl, Kathy Flann, Christine Grillo, Elizabeth Hazen, James Magruder, and Marion Winik. Thank you to my fellow Zibby Books authors for creating a nurturing community. Thank you to Julie Chavez, Sandra Miller, Alisha Fernandez Miranda, and Michelle Wildgen for the midnight phone calls and last-minute reads. Thank you to Alexis Washam and Madison Smartt Bell for their editorial insights.

Thank you to the experts who taught me about gardening, garden restoration, archeology, and the people and places described in this novel: Gabriele Rausse, Frazer Nieman, Christa Dierksheide, Kari Jones, Amy Herman, Claire Lieberman, Michael Pappalardo, Helene Tieger, Christopher Lindner, and Amy Parrella.

Thank you to the scholars whose work I consulted, in particular Jeanne Farr McDonnell's *Juana Briones of 19th-Century California*, Malcolm Margolin's *The Ohlone Way*, Clint Smith's *How The Word is Passed*, Barbara L. Voss's *The Archaeology of Ethnogenesis, Race and Sexuality in Colonial San Francisco*, and Caroline Zoob's *Virginia Woolf's Garden*.

ACKNOWLEDGMENTS

Thank you to Bard College, Historic Hudson Valley, and Monticello. Thank you to the University of Baltimore and the Virginia Center for the Creative Arts.

Thank you to my family, especially Cecilia Delury, who read my every draft, and my daughters, who are more important than any book and also the reason that this one was written.

Thank you to Don Lee for his nonstop contributions to *Hedge* and for being the best partner on the planet.

ABOUT THE AUTHOR

Jane Delury is the author of *The Balcony* (Little, Brown) which won the Sue Kaufman Prize for First Fiction from the American Academy of Arts and Letters. Her short stories have appeared in *Granta, The Sewanee Review, The Southern Review, The PEN/O.Henry Prize Stories,* and other publications. A professor at the University of Baltimore, she teaches in the MFA in Creative Writing & Publishing Arts program and directs the bachelor of arts in English. Originally from Sacramento, California, she now lives in Baltimore with her family.

 @jane.delury

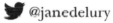 @janedelury

www.janedelury.com